THE MAGNIFICENT
Mary Ann

PHILIP KRASKE

encompass
EDITIONS

THE MAGNIFICENT
Mary Ann

PHILIP KRASKE

encompass
EDITIONS

Published by Encompass Edition, Kingston, Ontario, Canada. No part of this books may be reproduced, copied or used in any form or manner whatsoever without written permission, except for the purposes of brief quotations in reviews and critical articles. For reader comments, orders, press and media inquiries:

SECOND EDITION 2016
first edition 2010

www.encompasseditions.com
or
www.philipkraske.com
640 Sand Bay Road,
Lansdowne, Ontario, Canada K0E 1L0
tel: (613) 659-3666   -   mob: (613) 572-3666

the
OCEAN COOPERATIVE
group
ISBN: 978-1-927664-06-3
Cataloguing in Publication Program (CIP)
information available from Library and Archives Canada
at www.collectionscanada.gc.ca

interior design by Jean Shepherd (jean.shepherd@videotron.ca)
cover design by Robert Buckland (words@encompasseditions)

Love, though in a sense it may be admitted to be stronger than death, is by no means so universal and so sure. In fact, love is rare—the love of men, of things, of ideas, the love of perfected skill. For love is the enemy of haste; it takes count of passing days, of men who pass away, of a fine art matured slowly in the course of years and doomed in a short time to pass away too, and be no more. Love and regret go hand in hand in this world of changes swifter than the shifting of the clouds reflected in the mirror of the sea.

Joseph Conrad,
The Mirror of the Sea

To Steve and Lisa

1 "Hal!—yeah, blond, curly hair. It's gotta be you. I've been looking for you for years!"

Not the kind of thing you expect from a veteran flight attendant in the middle of the night—though it was 6 A.M. back in Chicago—high over the Pacific, the West turning into the East far below my Business Class recliner. I was awake, having already slept several hours, and was reading Patrick O'Brian's thoughtful, articulate biography of Picasso.

"Years. Imagine that," I said guardedly.

"Well, actually, it's not me, actually, that's looking for you, I mean. It's someone else—someone I know." She lowered her voice, though the fellow on the window seat had slept like wet cement since an hour out of Seattle, and signs of life were faint indeed among the three other passengers in Business. "Can I talk to you privately for a sec'? I'm Ruth," she added, on the sound idea that private chats ought to start out with both people knowing each other's names, and walked off towards the galley at the head of Tourist. I marked my place in *Picasso* and got up, ready for anything.

Anything, that is, except what happened. Events in life rarely have sharp beginnings and endings, but this one did. The beginning was sharp and comically unlikely, the ending sharp and darkly foretold. The in-between, however, is my story, or rather our story, those blazing months a few years ago when Mary Ann refocused my eyes. She was her own Picasso.

I followed Ruth the flight attendant past the snoring and slack-of-jaw, aboard an American carrier wafting us all to Taiwan. There I wished to ask some detailed questions of The Taiwan Power Company

7

about redesigning their nuclear plant's control panel. I was—and am—a nuclear engineer, and if you notice me cautious in my upcoming conversation with Ruth, it's because I had started my career in the nuclear field a decade before, M.I.T. diploma in hand, working for the Department of Energy, which employed me for three years to keep our nuclear arsenal in tip-top condition. I know all seven steps in making a nuclear bomb, and if some joker wanted to make a firecracker, something that would really wake up the neighborhood, he might give me a nudge—like aboard an airliner in the middle of the night—and ask if I'm in the market for an extra paycheck. Not to worry, though. Nowadays I design nuclear power plants. I'm happy just keeping the lights on.

In the kitchen, Ruth asked me what I'd like to drink, cracked open a tiny bottle of orange juice, dumped noisy ice into it, poured out, put the cup on a napkin, and handed the lot to me in one veined and experienced hand. "Okay!" she huffed. "Now—where to begin?"

Ruth was in her mid-forties, face melting southwards off a Barbara Streisand nose, and as with most long-time flight attendants, she had the weak skin and tired eyes that her mask of makeup only accentuated. Her hair was supposed to curl under her jaw, but it was too long, needed cutting, and caught and snagged and dragged in clumps over her shoulders like fallen party streamers. Beside her, a female Chinese flight attendant sat, elbows on splayed knees, reading *The China Post*. They must have served Tourist, because I had seen neither one before.

"My god," she said with a chuckle. "My god, my god, my god. I just can't believe it. You really are Hal. I knew it was you this time."

"Well, I'm glad to be of service," I said, just to be polite. "And you've been on the lookout for me for years?"

"Yeah. Actually, gosh, it would have be-e-en, going on-n-n, six—no—seven years ago now."

"So you're going to return that wallet I lost, right?"

Either the humor was lost on her or she didn't hear, for she was taking a clipboard from a shelf beside the breakfast trays; on it was a computer printout: the passenger list. "Yeah, every flight I look for you, checking passenger lists for a Hal. See? Seat 12B—Hal Dormund. All over the world. You can't imagine how many times Hals have chewed me out for bugging them. Well, actually, it hasn't been that many."

"Well, I sure hope you have the right Hal this time," I said, mustering a chuckle for her.

"Oh, I do—you're just the way she described you. Blond curls, square jaw, real hunky."

"She. She have a last name for me?"

"No, just Hal."

"And you're Ruth."

"Ruth Lazerno. Okay, let's, um, let's do this right." She put the clipboard back and set her feet. "Okay, I know this seems pretty weird...."

"Horsefeathers. Happens every day."

Ruth laughed. "Yeah, you're the guy, all right. You're Hal."

I took an important sip of juice.

"Okay, best thing to do then, is, is, okay! I'll just tell you the story."

Which proved to be more an epic than a story. She zigzagged all over, adding dense wads of irrelevance, and said, in effect, that on a flight seven years earlier, I had had a heartfelt conversation with a fellow passenger and given her life-changing advice. About halfway through Ruth's saga, the Chinese attendant harrumphed, folded up the *Post* with a mighty crunch, and went for a walk through Tourist.

"Mary Ann Jaalkov, whom I talked to on a flight to Chicago—departing Newark, which I almost never use." I shrugged. "Well, I *am* from Chicago. That much connects, but... Doesn't ring a bell, Ruth, doesn't do a thing for me."

"You fly a lot?"

I nodded over my juice. "About thirty times a year." I had concluded during the story that Ruth, whatever she was after, was sincere about it, and that I could be honest with her on basic matters. "I run a small engineering company with two partners."

"*Really?* That's great! What kind of engineering?"

"Oh, we make a better mousetrap," I said carelessly. "So what is this Mary Ann Jaalkov to *you?*"

Ruth brushed away some hair hanging near her lips, for which I was grateful. "Well, Mary Ann met you on this trip to Las Vegas, right? I used to—"

"Chicago," I corrected her.

"Oh yeah. You got off the flight in Chicago, and she stayed on for continuing service to Las Vegas."

"Right."

"I used to be based there, see, and—you know Vegas? Go there to gamble, but don't, under any circumstances, live there. It's hot and the weather's always the same, and well, anyways, Mary Ann was my live-in caretaker for my mother. I couldn't afford a decent place for her, and Mom had this kind of slow-acting pancreatic problem—not cancer, exactly, but just about. The doctors were always saying...."

You understand why I shorten my conversation with Ruth.

"...Then, about a year ago, Mom finally passed away, and I put the house up for sale, but Mary Ann was still living there six more months because, I mean, who in their right mind wants to live in Vegas, right? Like I say, hot, hot, hot. Well, I eventually did sell it—like for a song—but by then Mary Ann had got a new job and left, and that was the last contact I had with her."

"Must've been tough on Mary Ann, your mother dying on her," I said, nothing else occurring to me.

"No, I told her what to expect. Mom just went downhill, which is where she wanted to go, to tell you the truth. But I gotta hand it to Mary Ann. She stuck it out for six years!"

"Stuck it out?"

"Mom was not the sweetest soul."

"Ah."

"She taught Mary Ann to cook, though, that's for sure. Soups, especially. At the end, Mom only wanted soup, and Mary Ann had to make a new one every day." A breath. "To be honest, Mom was kind of a bitch towards the end. She ran a furniture factory all her life. Didn't go too well—kind of ruined her retirement. You know the type?"

"Sure do. Sounds like me."

Ruth laughed and patted my arm. "You're the right Hal, all right. Mary Ann said you have the quickest sense of humor, and you speak really, really, um, clearly—she was right there, too."

I chuckled more for her, all the while rummaging in my soul for a fresh jar of *Patience* and scooping deeply. "So, cutting to the chase then, Ruth...."

"Oh! Right!" She grabbed a napkin and wrote out Mary Ann's name and a phone number, complete with area code, which she explained was for Las Vegas. "Now y'see, you gotta call her. I promised her I'd look for you on flights and tell you to call. Okay? Please? Even if you're married."

Ruth waited for me to say if I was married, but I said, "You know her phone number without looking it up?"

"It used to be Mom's phone number in Las Vegas. When Mary Ann left, she wanted to keep the number in case anybody called. So I had the line transferred to her name. She pays for it, though."

"For the last six months," I said.

"Roughly. Listen, you, you just can't imagine the impression you made on her. She was always asking me if I was still looking for you on flights."

"And the conversation I had with her was seven years ago."

"It would have been in August—or September, maybe," Ruth said, apparently hoping to jog my memory. "Do you often talk to people on planes?"

"Sure. Passes the time." It really did more than that. People on airplanes speak far more freely. It's the most temporary of relationships, and it's usually difficult for anyone else to hear you. Women had told me their problems with children, men had cried about their lost glorious youths, a plumber heading for a Florida vacation had talked me through my divorce. Airplane conversations are snapshots. Especially since my lousy marriage years earlier, I only wanted snapshots of people; I found that by going any further, I quickly hit the common crud: baseball bombast and the shocking ignorance that makes up most political opinion.

"So you'll call her?" Ruth said, pushing the napkin at me along the counter.

I took a breath. "With all respect to you and Mary Ann," I began. I use this phrase in contract negotiations whenever I want to insult someone politely. With the Orientals, the Latin Americans, or the Russians, the translation never lets me down. "With all respect, Ruth, this is the kind of talk that I associate with a rather homely, desperate woman."

"Oh no, not at all. Mary Ann is attractive. In fact, I'd say she could be downright beautiful—if she dolled up a little. Her skin problems were clearing up at the end." Off my look: "I mean, I only saw her at home, taking care of my mother, and she just wore, you know, a track suit or something. Oh! Wait! One thing: she has a great smile. You can see it a mile away. That's her best feature, actually." A hesitation. "Maybe she's a little shy."

I longed for *Picasso*.

"Ruth, *why* is this so important to you?" I moaned. "She was just your mother's caretaker, you haven't seen her in six months, she hasn't seen me in seven years. C'mon: she's moved on."

Ruth's eyes moved sideways: the glance of guilt. "It's because I owe her, okay? I owe her one big favor."

"Because she did you one?"

"No. Because, well, she did a lot for my mother, she was a, a fountain of sunshine—even though my mother treated her pretty much like shit." Ruth sighed. "Okay, *I* treated her pretty much like shit, too, actually, if you really wanna know, okay?"

Ah, the selfish motive: the need to remove a guilt. Now we were getting down to basics. "How so?" And if that indiscretion bothered her, too bad.

"Because, y'see, I could have done more for her, Mary Ann, like, when she needed the help. I was too busy, though, and working and... Look, she was a great caretaker, and I didn't want to lose her and have to look for another, okay? That's the truth."

I nodded. And waited for more.

"I mean, I still feel bad about it. That's just the kind of person she is—she stays with you. That's why I've been checking passenger lists all these years: the last thing I told her was that I'd keep looking. That's why she wanted to keep the telephone line, get it?"

"Yeah." I sighed again. I was trapped.

"Okay? Please? Promising me you'll call her will take a load off my mind. Really."

I shrugged. "Well, I admire your sense of duty."

"Look, if you're in a relationship and worried about having to put her off, don't—it's not that kind of, of thing. I mean, like you say, she's moved on. You were a sort of a...you helped her get her life straightened out at a critical moment, and I think she'd just like to thank you."

"On a two-hour flight from Newark to Chicago seven years ago—Jesus!" I laughed. It was unbelievable.

"That's right."

Well, there was nothing to do but bite the phone number. I picked up the napkin. "All right. All right, I guess you deserve that much—after all this time of asking Hals if they're *the* Hal. Okay, Ruth, you're on. I just hope you got the right guy."

"Oh, I do. And tell her it was me that contacted you, okay?" Ruth insisted. "Just so she knows."

I tucked the scrap into my wallet, glad to have a divider between my Taiwanese cash and my Brazilian. "You'll get full credit—promise."

"Oh, bless you! Thanks so much!"

End of conversation. I never saw Ruth again, though it's worth mentioning that she kissed my cheek, teary-eyed, when I got off the plane in Taipei. But I wondered and wondered—through Taipei, Bangkok, Moldova, Sao Paulo and Santiago, for AllPoint Engineering, most often in the person of one of its founding partners, Hal Dormund, answers the call wherever—wondered and wondered over the following weeks, What kind of person was Mary Ann Jaalkov to inspire that kind of guilt? *That's just the kind of person she is—she stays with you.* I thought about that sentence a lot. Certainly Picasso stayed with a lot of people. As O'Brian put it, just about everyone who personally knew him wound up writing a book about him—including O'Brian.

I didn't call her, though, till I had returned to Chicago. For the longer I thought about her, the more I figured that some homework was necessary. In my office, I fiddled with my computer and, after giving all manner of access codes, tapped into AllPoint's accounting files. I called up my old travel records and looked for a Newark-Chicago flight.

It was true. On September 8, seven years earlier, I had arrived in JFK at 2:36 p.m. from Frankfurt. I'd taken a cab to a client's office in Manhattan, and afterwards taxied over to Newark, this according to the scanned-in cabbies' bills. There I'd caught the 7:48 for Chicago. It was my only Newark–Chicago flight for at least ten months on either side of that date, so there was virtually no question.

But the flight itself? A woman? A heartfelt conversation seven years earlier? Two weeks' digging in the mines of memory had come up empty: a Japanese-American woman, too beautiful to be true and too married to accommodate me, had written down two rice recipes for me to try; a fashion model who "wanted to be taken seriously" had discussed her move into television news anchoring for an interested New Orleans station; a pathetic mother with two or three small children had described her marital separation to me before we had cleared the runway, and cried the rest of the way. That was all I had in the category of Heartfelt Conversations/Women/Unbedded.

The scanned-in ticket stub had me in Seat 20C—AllPoint puts up for Business Class only on international flights, and this goes for everybody, partner or not—and the airplane was a Boeing 737, which has four seats per row. Hence I must have been looking at her towards the window seat, which naturally was D. Maybe, possibly, I was looking at her most of the way against a low sunlight. This could explain, at least in part, why I had no memory of her face.

So much for sleuthing. I worked up a few talking points for the call: we had met on a flight years ago, your former employer Ruth had begged me to call, not easy convincing me. I squared my shoulders to the desk phone and punched the number with my thumb.

As it turned out, however, my talking points had to be turned into a single speech. For rather than an answered telephone, I got an answering service, and it had the following message, delivered by a young woman with a Southern accent, call it Louisiana or Texas:

"Hi, this is Mary Ann. I've left this old phone number open for anyone who has to leave a message, and then, like, y'know, I just, like, check back with it just every once in a while. So please, please, please, leave your message and a phone number, and I'll get back to you, okay? Especially if it's you, Hal."

2 The conversation with Ruth, I forgot to mention, had been in January; I left my message for Mary Ann Jaalkov the first week of February. By March, I had received no reply. Or at least my office hadn't. The address and phone number I had given in my message were AllPoint's. I could trust Telma Tzu, who answered our mail and phones, and had a mouth as perfectly shaped as it was discreet. Now and then I tested its sensual excellence with my own. She told me that I was no good for "a full-throttle whack," but perfect for "soft, philosophical sex." She added that this was a compliment, as sex of this latter type was hard to come by. I took her word for it.

My sexual tastes varied less, though my stable of lovers probably equaled hers. These were widely spaced across the planet and usually paid for in anonymous cash, mainly fine hookers in fine hotels all over the world. My favorite was a sinuous lass in Sao Paulo whom I liked to call "my mermaid." And there was Sonia, who was as close to a girl-friend as I had, a bouncy Mexican woman with an incipient roll of fat around her stomach, a husband in jail in San Antonio for armed robbery, and a seven-year-old son who loved me to read to him. I was a temp, as she was for me, and little Tom would be well into video games by the time I was eased out of the picture.

Years before, when I was finishing up with the military and starting AllPoint Engineering, I had had a wife, too: a chic, intelligent, cultured woman who had betrayed me. Not that she had done something with another man: she had misrepresented herself to me. For no sooner were we married than she opened her dark side. She began to mention how I had "conquered" her, and I think that her feeling of being conquered—because I was better educated and as moneyed—was the start of it. She had a wistful nostalgia for being the Desired One, and for toying daily with many potential boyfriends. In time this nostalgia became a humiliation to her; and this, stirred together with a latent, and nearly pathological, hatred of men, brought out a streak of cruelty in her. She manipulated me with sex and good will, granting and withholding them to suit her. A timely public snubbing of me was another of her weapons.

After two horrible, bewildering years, I left her, and I think the sweetest moment in all that time was when I announced to her

15

shocked face that I had taken an apartment out of town and was moving that weekend.

But to be honest, once the euphoria of freedom was over, I found myself more angry with myself than with her. Dana had deep problems; as I write, they are strangling her, and now she has two children. But I could have—should have—seen them. Plenty obvious, they stuck through the interstices of events and utterances: like the time when she prodded me to raise hell in a good restaurant when a waiter forgot to serve me my steak, then brought it lukewarm; like her need, whenever she'd had a bad day, to go shopping or eat at a top-notch restaurant—anything to spend a bundle; like the angry grip of her pencil-thin fingers on her purse.

There had been signs to read, if I'd cared to, and at some level I had: I still remember a night months before the wedding when I lay in bed alone, sweating and anxious, and all I could think about was the sideways grind of Dana's jaws over a pre-dinner cocktail when a good friend phoned her to say that she and her boyfriend—some Internet mogul Dana was dying to meet—had completely misjudged the traffic and wouldn't be able to make it to dinner at the restaurant; at best we could get together somewhere for a nightcap.

Well, enough of that. Fortunately, it was all over before children came along.

After that period of my life, romantic love fell from my list of fine human institutions. Looking around my office, for example, I could see Ralph Keefaver, one of my two partners, standing with his arms piled like thick cobra coils on an office divide, looking at someone's computer and making his usual adroit observations. He's as brilliant a man as I've ever personally known. In fact, Ralph's specialty is a sideline of AllPoint's normal activity. Ralph calculates the life of a nuclear plant's vessel—the heart of the whole system, where water is turned into steam to turn the generators. It requires a deep knowledge of nuclear physics, the chemistry of metals, and a full understanding of the actual, real-life use of a power plant. Ralph's staff plunks eight inches of data down on his desk—Ralph prefers to do final calculations on paper—and a week later, triumphant Ralph plunks down on mine a single sheet with a few numbers on it: the months of life remaining to the vessel with heavy use, medium use, and light use.

"Tell the damn Brazilians you can take that data to God Almighty, and He'll tell 'em the same thing." I suspect that God Almighty checks His calculations with Ralph.

But more to the point: what on earth did his wife Tammy see in big, bovine, bald, boxy Ralph? I often laugh, watching him chew on the end of his Bic pen while looking at his computer screen. He has no ability with words, has an assistant write his reports for clients, and couldn't put together an outfit to save his life. Tammy dresses him every morning.

Or my other partner, Jean-Jacques Zonik. He's a forty-year-old Frenchman who'd already been through two marriages and at that time was grinding down number three. She was 24, a monumentally spoiled brat and a former Miss Chicago who'd thought it was cool to marry the Dashing Frenchman. But I had often lied to her—and the other two—for Jean-Jacques, timed his trips to Grenoble to see our biggest European clients and spend an extra day and night there before flying back.

"What can I say you, Hal?" he told me with a Gallic grin. "How can I deny a woman zee greatest screw of her life? Ooh, la! To be a great lovair is an obligation very heavy." I asked him once what he thought marriage was for—Jean-Jacque's virtue is that he has no illusions about himself—and his answer was this: "To have someone to push you, Hal. To push her back and argue about stupid sings and realize how stupid everysing is." And if *she* has affairs? "Bettair—zen she will know what she has married. No, dear friend. If she is careful making me a good quiche from time to time, and calls me a fool when it is necessary, zat is all what I ask."

As to your correspondent, at the age of thirty-seven, I was, according to my sister Beth, "not swimsuit-model material, but definitely business-suit." With my good hair and fine shoes and fresh Porsche, I had enjoyed the more vivid part of what womanhood has to offer, and free of the drearier matters like commitment, fidelity, and folding her undies after a load of wash. Okay, once or twice a year, I gathered myself for a full-blown, new-shirt date; by dessert all I wanted was to be home with a beer, a bowl of popcorn, and the Durants' *Story of Civilization*.

In short, I felt that I had walked through the one-way mirror of love and stood in another room watching my luckless dates try to work up some sort of chemistry with me. Love I defined as little more than sexual attraction plus whatever fiction one wished to see in the person—as I had seen in chic Dana and her 38-inch bust.

On a mid-March morning, just back from another business trip and deep into 246 pending e-mails—what on earth did people do before e-mail?—I looked up to see Telma sailing through AllPoint's staff of thirty-eight still-deodorized engineers to my corner office. She is, by the way, half Colombian and half Taiwanese, soaked in a Philadelphia childhood, herself the victim of a no-good New York ex-boyfriend who had brought her to Chicago, where he had lined up a great job and a deal on a house. But the job didn't last long—because he was caught swiping computer components from his employer—and he left her for a Florida babe with enough silicone in her chest to caulk the Sears Tower. Telma had staggered alone under the mortgage for more than a year; I gave her hand, and not only because of that perfect mouth. When she finally sold the place—at a loss—she treated me to ribs at Michael Jordan's restaurant and then dessert at her new studio apartment.

"Hal, guy who cwalled last week for ya's out in duh lobby," she said in her Philly thump, leaning through the doorframe and swinging her shiny black hair for me. She lowered her voice. "Says it's poisonal."

"Personal," I said blankly.

"Yeah, says he's here fuh someone cwalled Mary Ann. Hey, and he's built like a damn bull walrus. Smells like last-week's hamburguh, though."

Blanker still: "Mary Ann."

"You wanna handle dis outsoide?" Telma whispered.

Then I remembered who Mary Ann was. My first impulse was to say yes, I wanted to handle it outside. I checked this. If the guy was Mary Ann's husband, I wanted friendly witnesses to warm my back. "No, show him in."

"Hey, you didn't do sump'm stupit, did ya? I mean, like, you're the all-time king o' safe sex."

"Jeez. Does he look pregnant?"

"I'll ask," Telma giggled and dashed away again to the reception.

The bull walrus who came across the office was about my age, empty-faced, fat, pale, with a haystack of hair as bright as a pumpkin. His arms did not swing; they bobbed out from his body with each too-long stride; his belly wiggled with each jolt. A long key-chain nipped and leapt at his side like a tiny dog; it swatted a paper off Tim Althorp's desk, but the man either didn't notice or didn't care. He wore a dirty-yellow jacket—too light for a Chicago March—open over a gnarled, brown shirt. He was the type of man who rarely shaved, but he was indeed shaven, which told me he had prepared for the occasion. I was on my guard.

"Frank Jaalkov," he introduced himself. "Hey." He squeezed my hand hard enough to show that he was stronger than me.

I closed the door—everyone in the office had stared at him—and we sat down at my small, square meeting table, which I had hastily cleared of some sensitive documents. Jaalkov sat with his hands in his lap while his stink of tobacco came out to the attack. It swiped at me from across the corner of the table. "Big place," he muttered vaguely, tiny eyes sweeping the room and office outside.

"I was expecting a call, not a visit," I said.

"Yeah, swung up here on my way to Cincinnati—it's a favor for her," he explained in a Southern or Western accent, still looking around. "Don't get up this far, usually. Rockford once. That's why it took me some time to get around to you." With a hopeless tiny frown, he consigned me to the class who plays office instead of working for a living. "She been in touch with you lately?"

"Not at all."

"Well, she's kinda shy, goes slow. We're a purty tight family, y'know, even though we're kinda thrown across the country these days, her in Las Vegas and all." He had the same accent as Mary Ann: the buzzing Rs, the uh-sounds thick as if rising from a punch in the stomach, the tight that was pronounced tot.

"I thought that she had left Las Vegas."

"Well, yeah, she did, but…."

"You're not Mary Ann's husband, are you?" I said.

"No, no, hell! Brother." He jerked a thumb over his shoulder at the office. "Didn't that Chink babe tell ya?"

"Must have slipped her mind."

Another jerk of the thumb. "Hey—she give?" This in an inquiring whisper.

"Telma? She's terrific. We couldn't do business without her. So I've met Mary Ann's friend Ruth, and now I've met her brother," I went on. "Maybe her parents will come next."

"No, her dad lives in Oklahoma, though we're from Ark'nsas—that'd be a helluva trip for him, y'know. Mother's dead."

Yes: Arkansas. That was where the accent was from.

"And by the way, Ruth wasn't exactly no friend, accordin' to Mary Ann. Ruth was her goddamn boss."

I was distracted by laughter out in the office—five techies were standing around Jane Hagdorn's computer screen. Whenever the techies had a problem, they all stood in chorus and kibitzed and argued and joked till the problem was solved. AllPoint is a happy ship, I tell job applicants; multi-taskers, self-starters, achievers, strivers and can-do types need not apply—just good workers, and if they can bring a decent casserole to the monthly pot luck, their advancement in the company is assured.

"Been working here long?" he asked, though I couldn't understand why.

"Built it from the business license up starting eight years ago—with two partners."

"Ah. Right." Frank's little eyes roved around. "So you're doing purty well, then, huh?"

I was getting tired of this. "No complaints. Frank, are you here to see if I'm solvent enough for your sister to marry? Because I don't intend to. I don't even know her." I gave a brief explanation of my encounter with Ruth. "If you're here, it's because she listened to the message I left."

Frank performed an oily smile. "Yeah, ya got me, didn't ya? I was just worried about who Mary Ann might be thinkin' about havin' relationships with. I mean, after she told me about ya. Like I say, we're real tight."

"Well, I hope I've made the grade, but you can tell Mary Ann--"

"Hey, you married?"

"Should I be?"

"I mean, it's not like I'm going to let some two-timer go runnin' around with my li'l sister!"

"Nothing to worry about, then. I have five wives."

"Yeah—right," Frank said with an I'm-not-that-dumb grin. Then he pulled out a new tray of conversation: sincerity. He leaned forward and put his hands flat on the table. This stimulated his smell, which slashed another hunk out of me. "Look,—y'know, my comin' here today? It ain't like Mary Ann exactly asked me to come here, got that?"

"I got it."

"It's more like, y'know, like I just like to keep tabs on what she's doin' and who she's doin' it with. I mean, hey, she can do what she likes—I'm not sayin' that."

"No, you sure aren't," I said, and Frank couldn't decide if I was making fun of him, which I was.

"But it's like, see, her dad 'specially worries about her, and her bein' young and, like, sexu'lly desir'ble and all."

I swiveled, reached over to my desk, took a glass of water off and drank, all because I was still too polite to laugh my head off. "Well, Frank, you and her father may rest assured that you have nothing whatever to worry about as far as I'm concerned," I said grandly. "I met Mary Ann on a flight some years ago, had a chat--"

"Yeah, yeah, she told me all that. You made a big impression on her."

"Why? I'm curious."

Now Frank floundered. "Well, just your conversation and all. Made an impression."

"Yeah, but what exactly? Me, I can't even remember the conversation."

"Well..." Frank rubbed his now-sweaty hands. "Just kind of in general. She said it was kinda personal."

That was spur-of-the-moment bullshit. But what the hell was he covering up? And how could it possibly be worth hiding? Before I could ask, though, he wrenched the conversation back his way:

"Look, what I was sayin' here is: I don't want Mary Ann to know I'm checkin' up on her and all. So like when she calls, you mind not tellin' her? I mean, like, I am her brother, y'know."

I now regretted having put down my Picasso biography on the plane, spoken with Ruth, called Mary Ann, or agreed to see Frank. I decided to get rid of him and lose myself on the amoral and stupendous steppes of business. "You bet," I said. "Will do."

"Hey, great!" Frank said, as if he had expected much more of a fight. He got up, to my delight, and so did I. "An' one other thing: I need to know if she calls you."

"Fine."

"But without sayin' that you're gonna, right? I have to stay, like, the invisible man—you know, like the movie?"

"No problemo."

He pulled a grimy Post-it out of his pocket and handed it to me. "That's my cell phone number. I'm in my truck jus' about twenty-four hours a day."

"Right."

"Got 'er down at a truck stop suckin' up rates right now, so, y'know, I better get goin'." He glanced one more time out my window, as many of my visitors do, then stopped—shocked, as though Spiderman had just swung past. "He-e-e-ey, you know somethin'?" he said, smiling; he had very good, long teeth, though yellowed with tobacco. He started looking around, swinging his head from side to side in broad gusts.

"What's wrong?" I asked.

"Nothin', nothin'. Just that—" He stepped close to the window, which looked west at other skyscrapers and, between them, bits of Congress Parkway and Kennedy Expressway. "It's just that... Now that way's gotta be west, right?" He edged sideways till he reached the very corner of the office and pressed his face to the window there. He grinned. "Yeah, yeah, yeah. Yeah, that's it! Along behind that building, 'bout five miles down. There's the ramp that leads to the truck stop. That's where my old Bessie is!"

"You're right—there is a truck depot there." It was an odd feat, but an amazing one.

A moment later, Frank was weaving through the desks again, his chain swinging and twitching along his thigh. When the reception door swung shut behind him, I sighed with relief. Then I weighted my papers with rocks, opened two windows, walked out, closed the door, and went to make a new pot of coffee while the Lake Michigan wind blasted my office clean.

3 I traveled and returned and traveled again. Then, in late March, back from a trip to Sao Paulo, where Marisa, perfect in her ruby-studded thong, had given me four memorable evenings, I found a personal letter waiting for me at my office. The white envelope contained a sheet of paper and a ticket to a performance of a dance troupe—"The Sergio Adán Dance Company, featuring Sheena Biggs"—on April 3. "Please come," said the laser-printed words. "I'll meet you there." There was a scribbled signature that could have been President Kennedy's or Mickey Mantle's or yours, with "Mary Ann Jaalkov" printed out below it. The plain envelope, also laser-printed, had no return address.

I moaned. The ticket was at a Chicago theater in the center of the second row and had cost her 114 dollars. I snatched my agenda hopefully. No luck. It was Easter Week, when nothing moves because half of the adult workforce is home taking care of kids. I had nothing going for three days either side of that date.

"If I don't want to meet this babe, why the hell do I have to go?" I whined to the buildings across South State Street.

Because Mary Ann Jaalkov had blown 114 bucks on my ticket—and, no doubt another 114 for her own—that was why.

Well, it could be worse, I figured. The third was a Thursday, and this was just a theater date: see the show, a Drambuie afterwards, and the kiss-off: *Hey, this has been great! Good luck to you.* With luck, I would still have time for Sonia.

And so, some days later, I looped a conspicuously dull tie around my neck and went to the theater, arriving just moments before the starting time so that I would see her immediately outside. But only three people were standing around: two beggars and a cop who was coaxing them down the sidewalk. The usher whisked me to my seat just as the curtain was rising. All the better.

The woman to my right was a chunky dowager who breathed through her open mouth. I had passed both her and her husband in edging to my seat. To my left sat a thirtyish woman with long, frizzy hair who presented better prospects, but she did not acknowledge me in the least when I sat down, and actually turned to her own left and whispered something to another woman, who was taking notes on the show with an annoying pen that had a light on the end of it.

Is this some kind of practical joke? I thought. I decided to let her make her move as she saw fit. Both Ruth and Frank had called her shy.

At least the show was good. It had seven or eight dancers who performed a series of choreographies. The music was provided by two guitarists and a flautist, but the style of the choreographies ranged from classical to ballroom to passionate staccato-heel flamenco. Dance generally bores me, but this program was fun. The dancers swooped in and out, always changing costume, changing dance styles, all at a breakneck pace. Their stamina was incredible.

The star of the show, Sheena Biggs, was a striking blond woman with big, puckery lips. I swore I had seen her on television or something. After a while, I remembered from where: fashion-magazine covers and "People" columns in the newspapers. Sheena Biggs did cosmetics and fashion endorsements. And there was some kind of furor around her: she had dumped a boyfriend, the playboy mayor of Washington; dumped him for a football—baseball? basketball?—player. And the two men had had a dust-up of some kind in a restaurant. I could see why: Sheena had curves and knew how to use them, and her rich blond mane nearly reached her waist.

It was a good thing she had a second income: she couldn't hold a candle to the rest of the dancers. We nuclear engineers don't have much of an eye for modern dance, but even I could see that she was having—to be charitable—an off night: behind the music, less flexible, hurried, now and then decidedly ragged. And she took herself too seriously: she came charging out to "fill" center stage, and I could almost feel the audience deflate around me.

As the intermission applause died, someone behind me yelled, "Hey, Sheena, where's Rick?" Everyone laughed. Yes: Rick Pitcairn, the Jets' quarterback—he had taken a poke from the mayor and returned three of his own far more vigorously.

I remained seated, but received less attention than a bent paper clip. The woman with the lit pen was still jotting notes and shaking her head. Clearly, she was a journalist. She said, "You were so totally right, Clare. Sheena Biggs needs to dry out and shape up. She looks like hell."

"It's a one-night stand, and tomorrow she'll be in Minneapolis. She doesn't give a damn," said Clare—who was no Mary Ann, either.

I have too much respect for a 114-dollar ticket to give up easily. I tried the lobby. Maybe she'd arrived late, maybe there'd been a mix-up with the tickets, maybe she'd forgotten my seat number.

There I drifted through the well-heeled, stood close to the "sexu'lly desir'ble," and eavesdropped far and wide for a Southern accent. I climbed to the fourth step of the stairway up to the second floor and scanned the lobby, but neither Frank's little eyes, nor red hair, nor good teeth emerged from the crowd.

What the hell is going on here? I wondered tiredly. *Do you want to get together, or don't you?*

I went to the bar and got a glass of wine to stimulate my thoughts. Had she missed a flight? Should I skip the second act? I opened a soggy program on the bar, hoping to get an idea of what the second act held. Then, flipping the pages, my eye caught her name: Mary Ann Jaalkov. I slashed back the pages and came upon short biographies of the dancers: there she was.

"Of course, you fool!" I snarled at myself. "She's a dancer!"

The guy beside me burst out laughing—probably one of those shit-heads that posted unpunctuated messages on right-wing blogs.

"This Arkansas native," ran the blurb beside her name, "is the latest addition to our company. She trained under Miles Sipsky in Las Vegas, where she got her start in shows on the Strip. Her credits include engagements at the Western Star and the Thousand Diamonds."

There was no picture; I checked the front cover. The top half of Sheena Biggs's face occupied the bottom half of the page. Eight dancers stood in various poses above her glorious pate. But their actual faces got less space than Truman on his dime, and I saw nothing terribly Jaalkovian among any of the women—not even red hair, since the picture was in black-and-white.

So she's a dancer, I thought. *But this means I have to sit through the rest and meet her afterwards because if I don't, she'll be hurt.*

I made a few phone calls—Sonia was still available if I could get there before ten-thirty, Telma was busy—and returned to my seat. I caught glimpses of red hair among the female performers, though I could hardly settle on any single one, since they were prancing under multi-colored lights. Afterwards, I collected my coat and my thoughts: interesting show, washout Thursday night. The journalist with the lighted pen thought so, too: she was going to flay Sheena Biggs in the morning *Chicago Tribune.* I calculated the distance to the nearest café, calculated the minimally polite time I had to spend with Mary Ann Jaalkov, calculated the driving time to Sonia's—and took out my cell phone.

"Sonia, it's going to be no-go, I'm afraid. My doubles match ran too late," I told her. "And on top of that, we lost both sets."

The last bits of the audience trickled out irregularly like the last cereal from a box, and I stood in the lobby with my coat hung over my arm. The ushers were closing the auditorium doors, and I had no inclination to run around to the proverbial "backstage door" in the back alley, where I figured that humorless crushers would wad up anyone dumb enough to ask for one of the women. Finally, a chubby college-aged kid whose ushering jacket stayed closed by virtue of one valiant button, shuffled over and slurred, "Um, sir? Guess'mgonnahaf taskyout'leave."

"Look, this might sound a little incredible, but one the dancers is a sort of friend of mine—she gave me the ticket, see—and she asked me to—"

"Idon'domessages, sir," said the kid, who would someday be a bureaucrat in the Department of Energy. Out I went.

The Chicago wind blows its worst in March but reserves plenty of oomph for April. In coat and scarf I huddled within the marquee entrance, which made the hurricane bearable. I began counting slowly to a hundred. It was a practice I had started long, long ago when, as a kid, I had had bad trouble with my adult teeth, which had come in either crooked or not at all. Some of the sessions were terrible. One day, the dentist's nurse told me that if I just concentrated on counting slowly to one hundred, it would all be over before I finished. After that, the dentist was easier to bear.

I counted on and on, timing myself with the pendular shifts of my body from side to side. In front of me, taxis carried people away across the city. Between 72 and 79, a beggar came by and got a whole five bucks off the man swaying minutely under the theater marquis. There seemed to be a lot of hubbub for a Thursday night.

Then:

"Bet yer countin' to a hundred, right?"

I turned around—too fast. The woman before me was wrapped up in a down coat with the hood pulled into a tight little circle around her open face. I could see flecks of red hair over her forehead and little else.

"I'm on 94," I said, amazed.

She toddled three fond steps forward and swung up her hands which, out of the corner of my eye, seemed overly large. She took my right hand in both of hers and shook it gravely, as if I'd come back from a war with medals covering my chest. "Hello—again."

"Yes. Good to see you." I nearly added that I had no recollection whatever of her face.

"Sorry, guess I took a while. There was no hot water in the showers. Finally, I managed to shower with cold. Oh, that was awful, but what with you waitin' and—What's the matter?"

For the last hour, I had been working so hard trying to remember her face that I had completely missed the obvious. "Wait a minute." I stared, rudely. "Wait a goddamn minute. How old are you?"

She blushed deeply. "Um, twenty."

"So on the plane you were... what, *thirteen?*"

Mary Ann smiled thinly. "Yeah, thirteen. That was a terrible time. I was just—"

"You've been looking for me for seven years?" I shouted. "And what did you intend to do if you found me? Challenge me to a game of chinese checkers? Huh? Sign your yearbook, ask me to the damn prom? Jesus!"

She gasped. She brought a hand to her eyes, pinching their corners against the flow of tears. "I don't know. It was a stupid thing. I thought

27

I'd be more grown up for you if you saw me dance first." She was sobbing now. "I, I thought you'd remember."

I did remember her now, perfectly: that sniveling girl on the evening flight. (Had it really been seven years? I would have said three.) She hadn't been sitting beside me, but across the aisle, a skinny, pimply shard of pubescence crying into the tissues I kept passing to her. And it was one of my drifting flights, when I've been on the move for two or three days without a hotel bed, so besotted with scheduling and numbers and contract details that I can't think straight anymore. It happens to me maybe once a year and I simply start rambling to whoever has the misfortune to be seated beside me. One idea swings to the next, ironies and humors and coincidences blossom, and I just can't stop—not till my victim harrumphs or flatly tells me to shut up. Yes, this was the girl—red, bushy hair pulled back in a fat raccoon's tail. I remembered the wide-open, liquid eyes, honest as chestnuts, peering at me over the worn collar of a dirty-white polo shirt.

And now this: a temperamental 20-year-old on a roaring Chicago night. Why the hell hadn't Ruth simply told me about the anecdote and left it at that? Told me, including, of course, the pertinent fact that my listener on the flight had been on her training bra at the time. For that matter, why had an adult helped an adolescent search for a middle-aged man she'd met once on a plane?

Well. What was done was done, and Sonia had already been written off for the night. I remembered my manners and handed Mary Ann a handkerchief, as if comforting a kid whose team had lost the state basketball championship.

"All right, I'm sorry, too. I really had no right to expect you.... I mean, Ruth never told me you were a kid—that is, back then, on the plane. Thank you for the show, by the way. It was terrific."

She brightened. "Did you like it? Really?"

"A lot."

"Oh, good. Good, good. See, that's what I thought. I thought you'd better see me dancin' first. And grown up. 'Cause you told me I oughta do what I like most. And I wanted you to see me. 'Cause I took your advice."

"Well, you sure did. It was a great show. Thanks."

"I, y'know, please don't go. Please. I know I'm... and I'm sorry that this isn't... Gosh, can we go get something to eat? I'll pay—I brought my Visa card. I just wanted to, to...." She searched for words, her brow wrinkling furiously. "I just wanted to *express* to you my most sincere gratitude."

A gust of wind swatted us, but I hardly felt it. "You wanted to *express to me your most sincere gratitude?*" I repeated, testing each word in case any had changed its meaning.

"That wasn't right, the way I said that, was it? But I'll... I'm tryin' to...." The liquid eyes in the hooded face appealed. "Please, just a quick bite, just to, you know, kind of touch you a little, even if it's just lookin' at you across a table. Like, just, *to get back,* y'see, to where we were and see what everything is, see? I mean, c'mon, Hal, it's been so long!"

What can you say to that?

I suppressed a sigh. I straightened my shoulders. I pressed cheer into my words: "Yes, sure. That would be great. Heck, it's the least I can do for the free show. I know a place just up the street."

4

For Mary Ann, our conversation on the airplane had never ended. "See what I mean, Hal? All I had to do was follow what you said—'Do what you like most and do it well'— and ever'thing would be all right. And all that time in Vegas, 'specially when I was gettin', y'know, all that trouble with the other girls, I just remembered what you said about how if ya want somethin', ya gotta go after it. And you hit it right on the bull's eye: like what you said about how it ain't—it isn't—the effort or the sweat or the hard work that gets ya. No, no, no: it's the other stuff, like interruptions and obblegations, or when you're workin' away and happy as can be, and then the electricity cuts or a bulb burns out."

"Or the ADSL lines get saturated," I added drily.

"And sometimes, those girls in the studio they just did ever'thing to hurt me, 'cause they knew I didn't know a lotta things, but like you said, you just gotta, y'know, like, get over 'em; or I mean, ya gotta just, just, just go *wham!* and get 'em behind you. But that was horr'ble sometimes, that was. An' one time I just went and changed dance schools. That helped a little. But a lotta times, boy oh boy, I just hadda stand there and close my eyes and count to a hundred, and sure enough, by then, they'd all just disappeared 'cause it wasn't no good no more botherin' me and teasin' me if I wasn't gonna listen."

There had been no formalities, no introductions, no background, no explanations. To Mary Ann, we had walked off the airliner and into this café. She mentioned someone in the dance company called Alba, and I had to stop her and ask who that was.

"Oh. Yeah. We share an apartment, see. That's right, I didn't actually, like, tell you about her yet, did I?"

But she had told me elsewhere. I was not only her guiding star, I was her diary, like Anne Frank's Kitty, and since our conversation seven years earlier, she had written to me every night.

We were talking in Stubb's, a quiet café two blocks—downwind, thank goodness—from the theater, where I occasionally take AllPoint engineers to lunch, either to smooth feathers, jerk chains, or, most often, dump unwanted tasks on the unsuspecting. Company legend has it that the more expensive my lunch, the dirtier the deed I am about to perform; a hamburger means praise, but a well-done steak, doom. The booths have soft cushions and high backs, the glasses are spotless and pleasantly bulbous, the views limited, the music distant. Faces can redden in private, gratitude can pour forth freely, and especially towards the back of the place a middle-aged divorcé can sit placidly with a twenty-year-old dancer and know that the gossip will go no further than the bar, where Artie Sandinsky, the evening bartender and co-owner with his brother Jens, will swallow it into the capacious depths of his Polish belly.

Which was a good thing that evening, because the twenty-year-old dancer, once she had shucked her down-feather cocoon and rumpled her hair into position, was something to see.

Her head, rising on a perfect neck out of her cashmere sweater— "Ya really like it? Alba helped me pick it out."—could have been a marble bust: a forehead as sheer as a cliff, cheekbones stout and angular. She had Frank's blade of a nose, though more rounded at the tip. And Ruth had been right about the smile. When Mary Ann finally had reason to make one, she flashed a smile of long, brilliant teeth—no sign of tobacco stains there—this from between a thin upper lip and a chubby lower one. Frank had gotten the pumpkin hair, but Mary Ann had gotten a better deal: dark-red and wavy, which she wore short with feathery bangs. She also had better color. Frank's was the usual pale of the redhead, but Mary Ann's was deep and healthy, a point or two off copper, within shouting distance of American Indian. In summer, she would tan deeply.

"That's how I got into dance, see," she was saying. "You told me on the plane, 'What you need isn't a lot of money or background, what you need is a dream. If you have a dream, everything else will take care of itself.' And you were right. Soon's I got to Vegas, I enrolled in dance school, and I worked and worked and worked and worked. It was like I was tryin' to just, just, like...." She paused and I braced myself against the cushions. "You know when you step in a big ol' mud puddle and your shoes are all dirty?" she burst out.

"Yeah."

"Well, that's what I was tryin' to do, Hal: just get all the yucky stuff off me and be strong and flexible. And in the school you're safe—I mean, most o' the time, 'cept when some o' those girls come around—and, and, and, and... balanced, y'know, like. See what I mean?"

"Well...."

"I mean, like, your whole life is just, just like this:" With her hands, she formed a triangle balanced on its point, the thumbs touching above it.

"You mean 'focused'."

"Yeah! You're just *focused* on what you want to do, on where you want to go."

I took a long sip of a '98 Riesling that Artie had had the kindness to open for me, though I had asked for just a glass. Mary Ann drank water. "So our conversation sort of set your course," I said.

"Yeah—just that, it did! Up till then, I was just, y'know, pretty much scrapin' around and, y'know, like, like..."

Her dark eyes roved the table top for words, and again I tensed. She expressed herself in wild strings of metaphors. She seemed to own half the vocabulary of anyone else.

"Well, did y'ever see one o' those kids in a park with a kite? And sometimes that kite just takes a big ol' loopin' dive, and whoops! She goes down almost to the ground, and the guy pulls it, and it swoops up to the sky again."

It took me a moment to realize this was a question. "Yeah, I've seen that."

"Well, that was me till I met you. I just kept looping up and down, and scuffin' the ground sometimes, and I didn't even know that people could actually, y'know, do dancin' and get paid for it like a real job."

"A job."

"Yeah, like a job. You told me, 'Sure, there are people who dance for a living. It's extremely difficult to get into, of course—you have to be the best. But if you train hard, and you come to rehearsal ready to work every day, you'll make it. The pay isn't all that great, but you'll get along.'"

Could that possibly be a quote? I wondered. She had my cadences, almost my voice.

"And you made it—good for you," I said. Through her blizzard of words, this aspect hadn't really hit home to me. Mary Ann was a *professional* dancer in a *New York* dance company. And while New Yorkers will give you the time of day for your pretty smile, they will not give you a job on their stages. "You got the job with Sergio Adán through an audition, I suppose?" I asked.

"Yeah, and ever'body in the lobby was all nervous and sayin' how ya just get thirty seconds ta show your stuff, and they don't care about you or nothin'. But it wasn't like that at all. Sergio was so nice. When I finished he came over and we went up to his studio and he gave me a Coke, and he looked at my résumé, and he asked me about the show I was in Vegas, and he was just as nice as could be."

Because you had what he was looking for. "Great. Congratulations. When was that?"

"I guess, in October—when I left Ruth, remember? But I have to thank *you,* Hal, 'cause you straightened me up. You said it didn't matter one little bit if I didn't know a lot of things. You said, 'The real question, Mary Ann, is your attitude in life. It's having an open mind. Some things you do well and some things you just don't. You probably won't believe it, but I know a brilliant engineer, Ralph, who can do all kinds of mathematical formulas in his head but who can't put clothes together in an outfit. Or understand why one shirt goes properly with a pair of pants. Everything looks the same to him. Know what? His wife Tammy lays out his clothes for him every morning.'"

"She, ah, she still does."

Mary Ann giggled. *"Wow!"*

Word for word: sentences pronounced once during a two-hour monologue seven years earlier. She knew them like a kid who's listened a thousand times to the same pop tune.

I signaled the waiter to bring menus; this was turning out to be better than the show, maybe better than Sonia. He passed them out, and I, who knew the menu by heart, gave my order while Mary Ann fumbled in a purse for a tiny pair of glasses—the lenses no bigger than quarters. She put them on and squinted at the menu. Finally, she took them off, hung them from a corner of her mouth and said, "Dahling, what do you have that's really *good?*"

I stifled a laugh. The waiter told her, and Mary Ann ordered a Stubb's steak.

But the joke was on me.

The waiter left, and Mary Ann frowned. "I did that a little, y'know, like, too *hard,* didn't I?"

"Maybe a little over the top, yeah."

Mary Ann nodded in minute jerks to the table, brow wrinkled again, fat lower lip chewed, gravely tucking away this tidbit. "'Over the top,'" she murmured.

I sipped more wine. *Who is this?*

"Mary Ann, how did you come to take that flight from Newark to Las Vegas? I mean, if that's not too personal."

"Well, I told you on the plane—a little."

"My memory isn't as good as yours."

"Ever'body tells me that. Someone told me—it was this one girl in Vegas—that stupid people have a good memory. You think that's true?"

"I wish *I* had a memory like yours."

"Well, sometimes I wish I didn't remember anything at all—like Arkansas and all that...." She looked at the table, liquid eyes wide, and whatever she was seeing was another life and not a good one. "Yeah, okay... I mean, if I can't tell ol' Hal, who can I tell?" she murmured.

"Mary Ann, if you'd rather not…."

"No, it's all right. 'Cause I know you're gonna listen, like with both ears, not the way most people listen to ya like they left their sink runnin' or somethin'. But this is kinda like, you know, embarrassin' in a way. I mean like, now, now... now I'm *not* stupid, but maybe I coulda done some things better."

"Yeah, well…. Who couldn't?" I drank down the rest of my Riesling, caught Artie's eye and waved my glass. I wanted a full tank for the trip.

H er earliest memory was of clutching wet sheets to her chest and climbing a stepladder to hang them out to dry on a clothesline. At five she was already a working member of the Jaalkov family farm. Nearest town: Blue Ball, *Ark'nsawww*. She had no real memory of her mother; she had died when Mary Ann was three or four. That was what her brothers said, and she had three of them, all adults even then. Her father, whom everyone called "the Reverent," was always away "doin' his ministry."

He was some kind of Evangelical minister who wanted to get into television preaching. Mary Ann didn't know if he ever had. She still remembered kneeling at the Reverend's side at the coffee table, praying with the man on TV. If Mary Ann's mind wandered, the Reverend swatted her. Now and then, the Reverend jumped up and bellowed at the TV, "No, ya doggone quack! You think you're gonna convince the Lord Almighty with a prayer like that? My little pinkie's got more sincerity 'n you got! Come the Day o' Judgment, ol' Jesus is gonna hand you straight over to the Devil and tell 'im, 'Why don't you keep this one?' Doggone quacks!" Mary Ann yelled at the TV too: someday the Reverent would be preachin' on it, and then ever'body'd better watch out if they knew what was good for 'em.

She worked all the time when not in school, cooking and cleaning and washing. Nobody helped her. Nobody, in fact, seemed to think that unstinting manual labor was anything but an excellent upbringing for a child. And when this idea occurred to Mary Ann, the punishment for "shirkin'" was a dinnerless night in the barn, cuddled against Bolts, their donkey, for warmth.

"What about relatives or—whatever—teachers at school, Mary Ann?" I asked gently. "Didn't they—I don't know—take an interest in you or stick up for you?"

"Oh, Hal," Mary Ann sighed, "you're the first person I've ever told this to in my whole life. 'Cept Sergio a little. I just wanted you to know, y'see, 'cause I know I'm, I mean I *know* I'm not, y'know, all, all right, like a reg'lar adult woman. But I'm gettin' better, I think. Alba, she's been helpin' me a lot. She says I'm just makin' up for a lot o' lost time. And I've had some trouble with Sheena, too. That's why—"

"Sheena Biggs—in the show?"

"Yeah, she's principal dancer, see. She's, y'know, kinda—" she ground her knuckles together—"she's always sayin' rotten stuff to me. That is, till Santiago—he's another dancer and just as nice a guy as you'd ever wanna meet—he got into a big argument with Sheena for pickin' on me. That was like, like, before the Florida tour. Anyway, see, that's why I didn't call you up right away and I sent you that ticket instead: I was too, um, like, *not* ready. I wanted more, more growin' with her—with Alba, I mean."

She had no other relatives, as far as she knew, except the Reverend's sister, who considered Mary Ann's upbringing far too lenient. She once beat Mary Ann with a cane when a burp escaped her during a Thanksgiving dinner. She spent the night and the next week with Bolts.

Frank, youngest of the three brothers, seems to have taken charge of her. The Reverend being on the road so much, Frank took Mary Ann to the doctor—more often than not riding a horse into Blue Ball—and kept her clothed and fed. Reluctantly. Grudgingly. Truculently. How the hell was he supposed to buy a truck if "ol' Stupe-face"—only the Reverend called her by her name—kept gobbling up his savings? So Mary Ann kept her requests to a minimum, and if her pants were too short for her, she cut the cuff seams and let them down an extra inch. The other two brothers, Ted and Ham, were drunk when they weren't working the farm, and had little to do with her.

In the spring of her eleventh year, she ran away from home. She had committed some sin like breaking a plate or putting still-hard potatoes on the dinner table, and was sent to the barn for the night. The next morning was Sunday, and Mary Ann knew that all three of her brothers would be sleeping off their hangovers. She went up to the hay loft, opened the door there, shoved out a mountain of hay, and jumped into it from two stories up. She stole a handful of money from the jar Frank kept for his truck, and in the early-morning hours, ran all the way to Blue Ball. Through a couple of buses, she made her way to Little Rock. On the way, she got lucky. On one of the buses, she talked with the woman beside her, who said that she could arrange a job for her. During a rest stop at a cafeteria, the woman called her cousin, and at the Little Rock bus stop, Lillian was there to meet Mary Ann. A deal was quickly arranged: Mary Ann would take care of her baby while Lillian worked, apparently in a convenience store. In exchange, she would receive room and board and maintenance.

"What about school?" I asked at that point.

"Oh, Lillian, she worked at night, see. I just hadda be around in case the baby woke up. Gosh. She was cutest little black baby you ever saw."

"Wait a minute. You just walked in and registered for school?" I nearly added that a black woman registering a white daughter would arouse suspicion, especially in a southern state like Arkansas.

Mary Ann shrugged. "Yeah, I guess. I don't really remember that part."

It seemed strange, but then again, Mary Ann's deep complexion just might have saved her on that point.

It was in those eighteen months, give or take, in Little Rock that Mary Ann discovered dance. Between Lillian's house and the supermarket, to and from which Mary Ann hauled groceries in a red wagon, was a small, squat, cinder-block building which at that time was rented out for a ballet studio. After months of looking in through the window at the girls in their leotards and running home to try steps by herself, Mary Ann got Lillian to shell out for a weekly lesson.

The girls of her own age had started years before her, and at first she was embarrassed to be stuck in a class with kids who barely reached her shoulder. But the school allowed paying students to practice at the balance bar as much as they liked, a privilege rarely exploited. Mary

Ann went to the school as often as she could. A kindly teacher helped her along, and soon she startled her peers by entering their class and showing them up. It was her first success. School was torture; she could never understand the teacher, and other children laughed at her. This memory was particularly painful to Mary Ann, so I didn't ask for details. Teachers just seemed to pass her along from grade to grade.

This period in Mary Ann's life also ended with an escape, which was how we met.

Lillian had a weekend job as well. On a free-lance basis, it consisted of her letting men come and get an hour's "rest" in her bed. Mary Ann herself often showed the men in and watched the baby while Lillian was busy helping the men get their rest. (It's an even bet that Lillian planned eventually to enlist Mary Ann's help in her labors.) Then one day Mary Ann opened up the door to brother Ham. He was as surprised as she was, and just as well, for Mary Ann jumped away just in time; otherwise her story—our story—might have ended right there. She ran screaming to Lillian's bedroom, disturbing Lillian's guest, who was not yet fully rested. He was a big, no-nonsense type, apparently, and Ham figured that fetching reinforcements—his brothers were in town with him—was the better part of valor.

Ham dashed off, shouting that he would be right back. Lillian got rid of her guest, drove Mary Ann to the airport while talking nonstop on her cell phone, and put her on a plane to Newark, where her "sister" would take care of her. Mary Ann had no objection, that was for sure. Anything was better than a return to the farm and a month of sleeping beside Bolts.

When she got to Newark, however, the sister, who never bothered to take off her sunglasses, told Mary Ann that she couldn't take her in, after all. She would have to fly to Las Vegas, where "my sweet Aunt Georgia" would meet her at the airport gate. She treated the hungry girl to a pizza, put enough money in her pocket to ward off a child-abuse charge, and sent her on her way down the airport concourse with a flight attendant. Mary Ann got on the plane—what else could she do?—sensing that Aunt Georgia held no greater promise than Lillian's sister.

And she was right. Aunt Georgia, another gifted woman who could see perfectly at night without taking off her sunglasses, took Mary Ann off the flight attendant's hands in Las Vegas, listened to her new-found determination to work as a dancer, drove her to a dance studio at a local shopping center, and proposed to wait outside in the car while Mary Ann went in to ask for information.

"I took my time inside, y'know," Mary Ann said, looking down into her glass. "'Cause one thing I didn't want to see was Aunt Georgia's car drivin' outta the parkin' lot."

But that was Mary Ann post-Hal.

On the plane, she looked backwards down the airplane aisle and saw a nice man wearing a red-and-gold necktie "with little green shields all over it in little rows"—she had that right, too. He was walking up from the back of the plane to his seat. A seated passenger dropped something; he bent down, picked it up, and handed it back—"just like it was part o' your nature, just like scratchin' your neck or somethin'." The seat across the aisle from him was empty.

She went and sat down beside him and said she was in terrible trouble. What kind of trouble? Mary Ann explained that she didn't know what to do with the rest of her life. Hal told her of the good life that awaited her if she worked hard enough. You like dancing? Then do that: "Don't stop for anything, and never lie to yourself that you're doing something well when you're not. If you're honest with yourself, you'll make it." Another pearl amidst the avalanche that poured out of him during the two-hour flight.

With her remaining bit of Frank's truck money, which she had hoarded away, and the Newark sister's money, she enrolled for afternoon classes at Jack Powell's School of Dance there at the mall. Here, too, the school policy allowed paying students to work out as much as they liked. In the loading area behind the mall, she slept in the hollow of a loading dock, exhausted from all-day workouts in the studio. This went on for a short time, hardly two weeks.

The night janitor at the school, a UNLV college kid, had a good heart and good sense. He saw that Mary Ann continued to practice because she had no place to go at night, and invited her to sleep on the sofa of the apartment that he rented with three other college students. One of these was a young woman whose cranky grandmother went through caretakers like Kleenex. She called her Aunt Ruth. Soon Mary Ann was settled in Grandma Emily's home. Happy to have a decent caretaker—*and* one who didn't change every month—Ruth overlooked the sticky matter of school. This, I realized as Mary Ann talked, explained Ruth's sense of guilt.

Mary Ann certainly didn't complain. The job paid just enough for dance school, and she had food and a roof over her head. Whatever took place under it couldn't be any worse than sleeping with Bolts. Thus she began the long years of "showin' a good face" to the old bitch and her thorough criticism of whatever Mary Ann did, said, wore, cooked or cleaned. No human warmth was ever wasted on young Mary Ann Jaalkov.

Which was probably why she clung so tightly to her own world of beauty and purpose in the dance studio. Her morning housework done, she put on her jogging clothes and, to improve her resistance, ran for a half-hour across the city to Jack Powell's studio—and that city was Las Vegas, remember, where air-conditioning is practically a human right. Having no distractions, no school, no family, no real friends, no cell phone, little TV (Emily frowned on it), no computer, no video games, no toys, and almost no money after paying for her lessons each month, Mary Ann lived for the perfect turn, the crisp leap, the supple sweep of arms that had to look, as Powell put it, "like willows waving in a breeze." Here was beauty; here was the way to a better life—Hal had said so.

And Hal—to his own amazement—was right. Years later, in an open audition contested by hundreds, she got the one female open job in Sergio Adán's company.

5 It was midnight now, and the lonely were clinched to the bar near Artie, who poured drinks and spread Polish humor out of his immense supply. I had sat there myself at this hour, sometimes in despair, more often on returning from business trips that had kinked my sleeping patterns, and needed alcohol and a chat to be put to rights. As boys, Artie and his brother had escaped Communist

Poland by stowing away on a ship bound for Canada. They got as far as the coast of Sweden before being detected by a low-level officer. He offered them thirty days in the brig till they returned to Poland, or an ancient rowboat that had sat down in the hold for years—this for 560 bucks, which was all the money the brothers had. The brothers chose the boat. The next morning, when everyone except the pilot was sleeping off a vodka binge, the officer pointed out Ireland through the mist, handed them a coffee can for bailing, and said good luck. After a miserable two days, the brothers crashed against the cliffs of Stranraer, Scotland, much the worse for wear, but free.

I mention this because what went through my mind, as I watched Artie and listened to Mary Ann Jaalkov's story, was how all my life I had longed to be like them. I had gone to expensive private schools, been a Rhodes Scholar, had talked my way into Engineering at MIT after taking undergrad degrees in Statistics and Comparative English Lit—an education as round as a pie plate, as my parents had wisely insisted. My late father had been director of biological research at a big pharmaceutical company, my mother a concert harpist for six years with the Chicago Symphony Orchestra. One of my fondest memories is of my family sitting around the after-dinner table for a half-hour every night acting out a play—Gilbert and Sullivan, Tennessee Williams, O'Neill, Miller—each of us, including sister Beth and brother Henry, taking a role.

But how distant—how formal—my experience from Artie's or Mary Ann's! And maybe my train-track trajectory in life is why stories like theirs have always fascinated me: deep down, I've always silently envied vagabonds and hustlers.

"And the best part, you know, Hal," she said. "As soon as the last audition was done, Sergio called all the dancers into the studio and introduced me, and they all applauded, and ever' single one of 'em—'cept Sheena, she wasn't there; she always skipped practice—ever' single one of them stepped up and introduced himself, and, and, and…." Mary Ann began to wipe her eyes, then remembered herself and pulled my handkerchief out of her purse and dried them. "And Alba, she put her arms 'round me and said I was gonna live with her, and really, Hal, I never, ever, ever, *ever* been so happy." Her fingers bunched together, then burst apart. "Like findin' a, a, a *rainbow* in your salad. Only other thing like that was maybe when I heard your call on the answerin' service.

"And every day I go to the studio, and ever'body's happy to see me, and I'm learnin' Spanish, and Mrs. Thuy gives me recipes, and even when somebody plays a joke on ya—like this one Spanish guy, Antonio; he put a bug in an ice cube and put it in my water one time. Well, it doesn't matter one little bit: ever'body just laughs and has a good time, not like I'm stupid or nothin'."

Who ain't a sucker for a success story? My eyes misting over, I grabbed my glass and lifted it. "Well, here's to hard work."

"Yeah, that's a toast. I do that with Alba sometimes in our apartment."

We drank.

"Mary Ann, something that I don't quite get. You studied classical ballet, didn't you? In Little Rock and Las Vegas? I mean that's how it sounded."

"Yeah, pretty much. 'Cept at the end in Vegas. Then I did jazz. But that was easy. Flamenco's tougher."

"But you didn't dance classical tonight. Nobody did. There was a little of everything, but not that."

"Oh! No, heck, everybody studies classical. That's the base of all dance."

"Even—what—the flamenco stuff?"

"Well, yeah, sure. Especially flamenco. All your big flamenco stars— you know, like Joaquín Cortés?—they all studied classical."

"Is that so? Well, you learn something new every day."

"'Cept Sergio, he don't want nobody dancin' *en pointe* 'cause—"
"En pointe?"

"Um, like, right on your tippy-toes?"

"Ah."

"'Cause it's really easy to get an injury that way. And he's always tellin' us we gotta stay healthy, on account of he can't afford more dancers. Just eight regulars and two understudies and Sheena. 'Cause that's all the apartments he's got."

"Apartments?"

"Yeah, he got 'em from his great-aunt when she died—and the studio, too—and that's how he made the company. He pays us some money, and we get free apartments. And if you got a problem with the plumbin' or somethin', Santiago comes and fixes it. He's one of the dancers. He was a plumber in Spain. Oh, and he's really good-lookin', too. And he can really dance—wow, can he dance!" And she drew her hand through a swirling S.

I haven't mentioned that. Her hands were the adjectives and punctuation of her speech, and often more coherent than she was. They often leapt up from the table and dipped and dived or swerved or chopped. To hold an idea longer, they hovered at her forehead like an orchestra conductor holding a note. When she wasn't sure of something, they joined at thumbs and forefingers in an O.

We were on our dessert by now. Mary Ann had put down a whole sirloin steak, a potato, and a salad, and was having no trouble with the blueberry pie, either—cutting her food the European way, incidentally, not switching her knife to her good hand and with her middle finger on top of the knife handle. Strange, that. I also realized who she had been in the show, for Mary Ann did not have the usual reedy body of the dancer. She was broad in the shoulders and thick in the torso, with—essential information for the guys here—healthy breasts, wide though not deep. It was the type of constitution that would quickly run to fat if it weren't for her profession.

"Mary Ann, a question about Frank," I suggested. "How long has it been since you saw him?"

"Since I ran away? Never. Just Ham that one time." She shivered at the memory.

"Think he'd want to get in touch with you?"

Mary Ann's face wrinkled up. "Yeah—to drag me back to the farm and make me do his doggone wash, the big ol' creep!"

I said nothing, but I wondered what was going on. They certainly weren't the "real close" family Frank had described. Then what were they?

The waiter arrived with the check. Mary Ann sternly warned me against paying it while she pulled out her granny glasses again, looked it over, dropped her credit card on it, and told the waiter to put on twenty percent for the tip. New York had evidently taught her how to behave in a restaurant.

Meanwhile, I had mulled over another aspect: how had Frank traced me? "Your telephone number in Las Vegas. It's listed in your name in the phone book, I suppose," I asked.

"Yeah, sure—just in case Ruth couldn't remember the number when she sold the house."

"How do you get your messages on it from New York?"

She pulled out her cell phone. "I just call up the number, and when there's a little beep, I press the 1 button four times."

"Ah—1111. Your PIN number. Maybe kind of easy to guess, don't you think?"

A sheepish smile. "Yeah, I s'pose. 'Cept who'd wanna guess it?"

Only Frank. He could easily have looked up Mary Ann's phone number on a nation-wide search, heard her message, guessed the PIN number, and listened to her messages.

Again: why? If he or "the Reverent" had troubled to notify the police when Mary Ann ran away, a search would surely have dug her up. How hard could it be to find one 12-year-old girl with red hair who had shown up for school with a black mother? Clearly Frank and his family had done nothing about her disappearance. Yet now, almost a decade later, Frank was pulling out all the stops to get in touch with her.

Funny world.

*W*e took a cab to her hotel across downtown. In the lobby, she pulled off the hood of her coat, took off the coat, laid it over the back of a lobby chair and fluffed her hair into place again. There was a certain purposefulness to all of this, and I was amazed—staggered—to think she was going to ask me up to her room.

But with Mary Ann, the unexpected was the norm.

The fingers and thumbs of both hands joined: doubt. "Hal, could I ask you a favor? I mean, now that we've met again. Like, um, can I give you my cell phone number? And you give me yours?"

"That's a favor?" I said.

"No, I'm, look, it's not that part. Look, I, it's just because sometimes—lots of times—I forget my glasses, okay? But, like, I gotta read something? And just like now and then I have some trouble, see? That's the favor."

I waited. "What, exactly?"

"Um, what I mean is, okay, it's like this," she said with a determined huff. She was awkward, like a boy asking a girl out on his first date. "I was thinking that sometimes, when I really need to read something and I can't, maybe what I can do is take a picture of it—with my phone, you know?—and I can send it to you, and you can read it for me. You could, like, call me or leave me a message on my phone—you know, a voice message?"

"Yeah, I get it."

"'Cause, it's not like everyday or anything like that, but I, my glasses like, it always just seems that whenever something happens I don't have my doggone ol' glasses with me." She gave a queer wooden laugh, and I wondered if it covered embarrassment or mendacity.

"Well, sure. No problem."

We exchanged cell phone numbers. Then she huffed. "Okay! That's done."

And we moved on to the next task.

"Well, I guess that's, y'know, all...." She reached out and took my right hand in both of hers, as in front of the theater, brow wrinkled gravely over them. "I know that, like, you're up there and I'm... I mean, there's, you've got...." She sucked in her lips.

I took up the slack. I gave her a cursory hug and peck on the cheek, and finished off with a trite little speech about how I was glad to see her again and glad that my advice had meant so much to her. Mary Ann hardly noticed any of this. She stumbled on, chasing her butterfly ideas across the meadows.

"I know that, like, you must think I'm a little stupid," she began yet again, and I objected noisily. "Yeah, I know, Hal, but y'see, it's just that, see, I'm not...." Her hands gripped invisible jail bars. "I'm not like, *complete,* not yet. I'm not like, well, like people oughta be, or like, mostly they are. I mean, it's just that, y'see, there's a lot o' things I don't know, at least not yet. Do you see what I'm sayin'?"

"In a general kind of way," I said in a general kind of way. But I was thinking, *If this is a bed proposition, it's one for the record books.*

"But, y'know, I'm gettin' better. I really am, Hal. I've really learned a lot livin' in New York with Alba, and, and Sergio too. I mean, I'm gettin' lots of ideas about, about, about, like, how to *live*." Her right hand swooshed down a toboggan run.

"Sergio Adán—the head of your dance company."

She wet her lips again and went on, now very softly; I leaned close in order not to lose her words amidst the wind's mauling the big windowpanes.

"But y'know, Hal, I just think that, y'know, now and then maybe we could, y'know, talk about somethin'. I mean, it's not like I'm... I mean, nobody likes it in rehearsal if there's one guy who doesn't know his steps and he's messin' ever'body up. It's not like, I'm not, well, I mean, like, nobody's gotta *carry* me. Like if you want, I mean. Like I was thinkin' like maybe if you're ever in New York, we could, we could like, like, eat dinner again or just take a walk. There's lotsa nice places to walk in New York, y'know. Alba and I, we practically—"

I interrupted her because I finally realized where she was going with all of this: she wanted to see me again. And I cannot—at all, not even with the cheapest hooker in Hong Kong—abide the spectacle of a woman begging. (And what was this happy spark somewhere in my stomach? I see it more clearly in memory than at that moment.)

"Sure, Mary Ann, I'd love to. I go through New York practically every month. Next time I do, I'll call you, and we can—whatever—take a walk or something. You can never be bored in New York."

Her face lit up. "Really? You wanna do that? You had a good time with me?"

I gave that one covering fire: "Yeah, sure. Why? Haven't you?"

"Are you kiddin'? This has been the best thing that's happened to me! I've been so nervous about seein' you again that—"

At that moment, an argument spilled out of the elevators on the other side of the lobby and tumbled past us towards the reception desk. Mary Ann stepped around the other side of me. She was trying to hide.

"Leggo o' my suitcase, you motherfucking piece o' shit!" squawked a woman. "Guard! Guard! I mean, is there like *any* fucking security in this place?"

"Yeah, but it's hidin' from you, swee'hear'," said the man, rolling a suitcase the size of a washing machine across the floor to the reception, where the Iranian or Indian night manager braced herself as for the dentist's drill.

"I said gimme my FUCKING CASE!" the woman screeched.

The man had a New York Latino accent: "Keep yuh shirt on, swee'hear'. Just leavin' it in rece'tion for ya. Don' wancha ta lose it."

The woman I recognized immediately: Sheena Biggs. The man, a thin monkey with gray-flecked hair, mustache, and goatee, took me a few seconds: the choreographer who headed the company, Sergio Adán.

Adán said to the receptionist, "Don' worry, swee'hear'. She's just soh-fferin' her period."

"I mean, like, you really know what the hell you're doing, right? Do you like *know* what I am to your show? Do you have even like the slightest fucking idea?" She tried to jerk the suitcase away. Adán raised a buttock and sat on it.

"Can you get my deposit bohx outta the safe, please? Sergio Adán, Room 512."

"*I'm* the show, Serg'. Like it or not, it's me, me and me! Nobody goes to Hollywood to meet the extras. Have you given like the slightest thought to what'll happen if I'm not there?" She had a whining, nasal squeal, like a car without fluid in the power steering.

"People won't boo?" Adán guessed.

"You're a pig-bastard, know that? A five-star cocksucking fruitcake. Think a little about your dancers, why don't ya? Whaddaya think'll happen to them if I'm not around to bring home the bacon?"

"Cheer. Start a party." To the manager, who brought back a small deposit box: "Can I get a pen, too, please, ma'am?"

Sheena Biggs scanned the lobby—on the fear, probably, that her tantrum had reached the ears of some gossip writer—and saw Mary Ann and me. She smiled and came sashaying over, one step in front of the other like every corporate runway model you ever saw. She had corporate lips and corporate breasts, too, all suited up in Latex with heavy fur lapels—the fashion that year.

"Well, Little Miss Arkansas, and with a man! You must be the mysterious Hal! Hey, Arkansas, want me to explain to you what a man has between his legs? But that wouldn't interest *you,* would it?"

"I told ever'body that you were my boyfriend," Mary Ann murmured apologetically behind me. She came around front, and her face was pale. Her lips worked, kneading themselves. She might have been a little kid in front of the playground bully. "Hey, Sheena."

"Wow! Very nice, Arkansas! A looker. Mind if I give him a try?" Not breaking stride, she came right up to me, jerked me to her by the neck, and kissed me on the mouth, grinding her rubber lips into mine. I was too shocked to react. Finally, she pulled away with a loud *pop.* "Mmmmm—nice."

"Oh, Sheena, you shouldn't 'a' done that," Mary Ann murmured.

"Nice to meet you, too," I said brightly. I stuck out my hand. "Hal Dormund, AllPoint Engineering."

Sheen laughed wildly. " 'Hal Dormund, AllPoint Engineering,'" she imitated. "What's that, your alma mater?"

"No, it's actually a cutting-edge—"

But the rich and famous have the right to interrupt us peasants. Sheena grabbed my upper arm. "Hey—the truth now. Arkansas told you how she's getting better, huh? Didn't she?"

I couldn't get the surprise out of my face, which pissed me off. "Matter of fact, she did."

"Well, it's too, too *true!* She knows how to paint her nails now, and that babies don't come out your bellybutton."

Mary Ann face crinkled. "Sheena! Whaddaya gotta go and say that for? That ain't fair."

This made Sheena laugh wildly.

"Why don't you crawl back under your rock?" I snapped.

"Oh, I am like *soooo* intimidated." To Mary Ann: "Hey, nice sweater, Arkansas! You didn't stick any snot on the inside of it, did you?" To me: "She's always picking her nose and sticking it on the inside of her leotard."

"Not no more," Mary Ann muttered.

"At least she's not stickin' coke up her nose," Adán snapped from the reception desk. "Now get your ass ovuh here and sign this."

"She can dish it back if she wants," Sheena replied, lifting her head

47

slightly to him over her shoulder. "Go, ahead, Arkansas—not made o' glass. Or are you gonna call me a *big ol' rat?*"

"Well, y'are."

Sheena laughed wildly. "I love it!"

"Sheena, you wan' yuh severance pay?" Adán called across the lobby. "Last call."

"Kiss my butt, dearie." To us: "Like he can really blow me off."

Adán laughed. "Mary Ann, hohney, you wanna tell Sheena she's fired? She don' unnuhstand when I say it."

Mary Ann's eyes burst wide. "You're fired? Gosh!"

Sheena let fly another rivetting, echoing laugh, clapping ecstatically. "'Gosh.' Isn't that just too much? How long's it been since you heard good old country 'gosh'?"

"Don't mattuh," said Adán. "She can dance."

"So can my german shepherd! Like I'm sure she's gonna turn on a crowd."

"At least nobody will boo."

This hit home. Sheena swiveled and charged to the counter, where Adán had taken out some papers. The receptionist remembered something urgent to do in the back office and went to do it. "Fuck you! I gave the best show of my life. I can't help it if this is a Midwest dump-town where nobody understands art."

"Everybody unnuhstands a dancer walkin' through her show, swee'hear'. Fuckin' janituh could see it."

"So could the engineers," I called.

"Kiss my ass," she retorted. "Hey, Hal, did you know Arkansas can't tell the difference between the *Bea*-tles and *Bee* Gees? Says she's got bad eyes."

"Yeah, but aren't they beautiful?" I said—before Mary Ann could say anything.

"Now take the pen, hohney," said Adán as if to a first-grader, pulling her around to the desk and forcing the pen into her hand.

"And I'm dancing injured, too, remember," Sheena told him. "My right—"

"Yeah, yeah—yuh right fuckin' instep. Inflamed. Always inflamed. You work out fuh two hours—if you come—and you're injured."

"That's right. 'Cause half the time I'm away doing publicity and raising awareness for your fucking company!"

"'Raising awareness,'" Adán repeated. "You raise awareness fuh nothin' but yuh goddamn face. Now sign this and this, and yuh done. This one's a receipt for your severance pay, that one's—"

Sheen laid the pen down. "No. I'll give you this one last chance. Just out of professional respect. We forget it right now, okay? I'm the only person separating *your* fucking ass from bankruptcy, baby. I walk out that door: *you* are finished."

Still sitting on the suitcase, Adán propped an elbow on the reception desk, smoothed his 'stache and goatee, and waited. He was wearing a loose-fitting blue shirt and jeans. With his round-lens glasses and loose salt-and-pepper hair, he had a sort of retro-hippy, John Lennon look. "Y'know, swee'hear', I can't believe you. You've made a fortune turning your dancing into a national modeling career. You of all people oughta know how to read the writin' on the wall. And what's it say? 'Mary Ann Jaalkov.'"

Sheena laughed. *"She's* going in my place? Oh, you've *really* gone—"

"No. I'm putting *the cohmpany* in your place. Remember I told you I needed eight top-flight dancers for my big show? She's numbuh eight." He waggled his fingers at her. "Bye-bye, hohney."

"Little Miss Arkansas? Who doesn't know which ocean it is?"

"Sheena—c'mon!" Mary Ann cried in anguish. She turned to me: "Hal, there's just a few things I don't know, honest."

I said something consoling, but I could see it didn't do much for her morale; she'd had her heart set on making a good impression on me.

"Yeah, Little Miss Arkansas," said Adán. "Now sign."

Sheena looked back and forth between Adán and Mary Ann, back and forth, wildly. "Fuck this. *Fuck* this. And fuck you." She bent over the papers and started signing. "I'm going to Raymond Radow's company. He's been after me for years. I never went to him—out of loyalty to you. We'll bury you. My name fills seats. In two months, when you can't pay your people, you're gonna *beg* me to come back."

"My new show'll kick Radow's ass up and down Broadway."

"Your new show, your new show. When do we get to *see* this new show?"

"Soon as we get back to the Apple. Thing is, see, I hadda get rid o' *you* first." Sheena's head jerked up from the papers. Adán opened a tangle-toothed grin at her.

"What—you think I carry around your dismissal papers just for fun?" he chuckled. "You were shit tonight. You've been shit most nights all week. When the review comes out tomorruh mornin'— impartial reporter, major city, big newspaper—you're all through. Best lawyer in America couldn't beat this dismissal."

She grabbed her share of the papers and rammed them into the outside pocket of her suitcase. "Call me up when your people haven't been paid for two months. I'll come and do a benefit for you."

Adán picked up his papers and began tucking them into a folder. "Stick with modellin', swee'hear'. You couldn't get a job rubbin' your ass on a firepole in the West Thirties anymore."

"Fuck you!" Sheena slapped at him, but Adán jerked nimbly backward, and her hand fanned past his nose. "And you!" she screeched at Mary Ann. She stomped up, and I quickly stepped around in front of Mary Ann.

"I know your secrets, crybaby—you know, like washing out tampons?"

"Oh, Sheena, that's—" Mary Ann's voice cracked into a sob.

"And I'm going to write them all the way down Broadway in letters ten feet high." Then she turned and went back for her suitcase— but Adán grabbed her wrist and twisted it slowly and softly, making Sheena twirl around.

"Ow! Let me go, you motherfucking Spic piece of shit! *OW!*"

"Try it, hohney'," he murmured over her shoulder. "Just say one word about her. Tomorruh I'm gonna tell the media a little fairy tale about artistic differences between you and me: four good years, raised the cohmpany image, some great puhformances—a clean break. But I can always have a little girl from the *Voice* come over an' jog my memory about your pills and powder. So you watch yuh fuckin' lip, hear me?"

"I'll watch whatever I fucking well want!" Sheena snarled, writhing away from him. "You're history, get it? I'm going to fuck you over in ways you never even thought of."

But Adán was calling the receptionist to put the papers back in his deposit box.

When the street door had swung shut behind Sheena, I turned around, but Mary Ann had vanished. Across the lobby, the doors of the elevator were sliding shut, and in its mirror, I glimpsed her quivering green cashmere back.

6

So: was it love? Had Cupid shot his arrow?

To start with, I have a bad opinion of Cupid: his aim, his intentions and his sense of humor, which inclines to the slapstick. My divorce is one reason. Another is that love sinks into me slowly, like rain sinking into the soil. Maybe I have a thick sentimental hide. In fact, I'm skeptical of people who fall head-over-heels into a relationship, and frankly consider them immature.

I liked Mary Ann; she intrigued me; she wasn't the girl next door; she wasn't one of these sorry office workers for whom a relationship was a campaign, complete with risk-benefit analyses, short-term and mid-term goals, paradigms and quarterly reviews. The year before, I'd had a six-week relationship with a woman who never failed to give me a performance appraisal of our previous date, broken down into four categories: "niceness/humor," "gentlemanliness," "patience/understanding," and "sex/affection." (I scored best, incidentally, on the second category. In "sex/affection" I got a C and was told that I had "real prospects.")

Mary Ann had had an adventuresome life and seen rough times. She was incoherent now and then, she was innocent, she was baffled by a lot of things around her; and if Sheena Biggs could be believed, it had been necessary to take Mary Ann aside and explain more than a few of the common civilities. But Mary Ann had an edge to her—that was what excited me. She was searching, she was climbing a cliff in the dark. She was an artist, a person who interpreted sounds floating on the air. And on top of it, she loved; she radiated love. She had loved *me* in the abstract for seven years.

I thought a lot about her over the next two weeks. I wondered about different aspects of her story, about Adán's now-complete, Sheena-less dance company, about the new lessons New York was teaching her. She didn't call, but sent me a photo to read. It was of a note, written by her roommate, I figured, telling her to buy eggs and a few other things. I called her and recorded the message on her phone. I got a reply SMS: *OK*.

But I'm getting ahead of myself.

About the time I received the ticket to the dance show, a crisis came to a boil at AllPoint Engineering between it and one of its most important clients. The crisis would turn into an important element in my relationship with Mary Ann.

I won't name this client, though more out of courtesy than anything else, since you can count on one hand all the companies in America that build nuclear power plants. Anyways, let's call this client Chintsy Nuclear, an affiliate of Chintsy Inc.. As to the conflict itself, don't worry if you're a little fuzzy on matters nuclear, like high-neutral reactor flux or the finer points of steam-isolation valves, or why super-criticity brings out beads of sweat on the engineering forehead. No problemo. AllPoint's trouble with Chintsy was one that any kid running a lemonade stand could sympathize with: Chintsy refused to pay us for three months of work done—"done" as in "contracted for, performed, and delivered"—eighteen months earlier.

At stake, ladies and gentlemen of the jury, was a million bucks, and that's *before* late-payment penalties. A courteous emissary from our financial department, carrying strict orders to grovel, had gone to Chintsy to discuss the "pending invoicing matter," as we so delicately called it back then. They listened to her arguments, examined her documents, and replied, We do not wish to discuss the pending invoicing matter. They did, however, discuss it long enough to mention that "understanding" on our part would go a long way to assuring AllPoint future sub-contract work with Chintsy.

Incredible, you say? I'm afraid not. You would be amazed at how often big companies try to chip a few points off what they owe to the little guys; by which I mean, those of us who rent office space rather than build 70-story towers in Manhattan, like Chintsy Inc.. When the big boys are going through financial blues, the chipping can get pretty goddamn outrageous; and rumor had it that the good ship Chintsy was sailing close to the rocky shores of Chapter Eleven. Our emissary, with the last of her dignity, informed Chintsy that a high mandarin from her company would soon take up the matter with their own corner-office types, a comment met with polite smiles.

Enter your hero.

First I tried a chummy conference call with Chintsy Nuclear Project Development. I told them that "We do not wish to talk about it" was surely the result of, um, a misunderstanding. A failure of communication. An uncaught drift. I mean, hell, guys, let's just get this whole damn thing talked out so that I can go back to Financial and tell them that the money is in the pipeline, it'll fall in three or four payments, it's just a matter of when the spigot will open. We're still buddies, we're gonna do great things together and make a pot doing 'em.

We do not wish to discuss the pending invoicing matter, came the answer.

So I headed for the Big Apple. There was really nobody else for the task. Jean-Jacques had too Gallic a temper for dealing with a lot of smarmy New Yorkers; and Ralph was a purely technical man. We talked it out one evening in Stubb's. Ralph, who had five kids to feed, was inclined to take the longer view and remember that Chintsy was a heavy-hitter in the industry; in the early years they had accounted for half our billing. I reminded him that it was for precisely this reason that I had jumped on my horse and started drumming up international business, to diversify our portfolio of clients. This way we could keep our business model on track: one project on the drawing boards, one on deck, two or three potential ones in the dugout.

Jean-Jacques agreed with me. He knew what playing Mr. Nice Guy got you from his days in the French nuclear community. "One sing is zee late-payment penalty," he said, swinging his fork around in a tight circle. "Zat we can deescus; zee inflation has not been so bad zees last years. But one million dollars? No, no, my dears. Zat is our yearly profit. Zat is our profit-sharing bonus for our people. Zat is *honneur*. We have a contract, zey must to make good. *C'est comme ça.*"

I finally managed to get an appointment about two weeks after my first meeting with Mary Ann. I arrived in the morning, though the meeting would take place after lunch. Before going, I wanted first to talk to a former, disgruntled Chintsy engineer who had just left the company and was about to move to a competing company in L.A.. I was going to taxi to his house, but he phoned me the night before I went to New York, and said that he could see me in the airport itself, "just after putting my mother-in-law on a plane back to Boise with her stinking little chihuahua." We met in a JFK coffee joint. I found him sipping tea—"coffee tears me apart"—and eating a chocolate-chip cookie bigger than a hubcap.

An interesting chat.

The rumors about Chintsy Inc were true, if understated: their numbers were not red, but definitely pink, and Chintsy Nuclear's were a very bright vermilion. The main reason for the crisis was that two projects in a row had gone way over cost, including the Djakarta project AllPoint wanted its money for. The top dog at Nuclear, Edgerton Salk, had to get the financials back on track during the present and next fiscal years, or the whole unit was going to go on the auction block. The highlights of the conversation:

"He's absolutely why the heat on your million," said my contact. "He's got everyone working 55-hour weeks. Total chaos: days, nights and weekends, right down to the cleaning ladies. Place looks like a damn pigsty....

"What else? People are paying for business lunches and taxis out of their own pockets. Salk and the brass chalk it up to 'company loyalty,' but everyone knows the score: cough up and you keep your job. And people, they're gettin' sick from the pressure, I gotta tell ya. One girl—works in logistics, great legs but nervous, see, works like the possessed. Christ—gets up one morning, things look a little strange. Can't figure it out. Does the breakfast, the shower, gets in her car, starts backin' down the driveway. Thinks, 'The hell have I got my head cranked all the way around like this for?' Finally hits her: she's blind in her right eye. From the stress. Can you believe it? The stress!

"So to make a long answer short, yeah: Salk'll go to the mat for your mill—he'll go to the mat for a lot less. You wanna sue? Great. Salk loves a war. It isn't a *job* to him, see, it's a knife fight....

"My take? Cut a deal with the bottom-feeders in Financial. Take twenty, maybe thirty, on the dollar and count your blessings. But don't mess with Salk, my humble O. He takes all that blessed-are-the-achievers shit way too serious. Damned if the stock price is gonna fall on *his* watch, no way."

So much for that: by eleven o'clock I found myself much enlightened and free for two hours before the meeting.

I could have sat in the airport, portable PC on the table, clearing my In basket. But it was a bright April day, and what good is being boss if you can't go AWOL sometimes? I caught a cab and set sail for Sergio Adán's dance studio.

7 Sergio Adán, incidentally, was a Puerto Rican native with a Spanish mother. He had spent ten years in Madrid enjoying the rising homosexual freedom with the cultural renaissance of post-Franco Spain. He had lived on bread and olives, worked like hell at his dancing, slept with whomever he needed to, and ended up performing with some of Spain's top choreographers, who were starting to knock together staccato-heel flamenco and modern dance, with fine results. He returned to New York, now as dancer *and* choreographer. He blew his savings and his great-aunt's generosity on a Soho warehouse and turned it into a dance studio. After four years of hard work and skimping, he had achieved artistic recognition from the cultural high llamas. The year before, his company had been voted Best New Dance Company. A very New York story.

I read of these events in framed articles hung up in the lobby. It was also the office of Bertie, the business manager, a heavy woman with a rocky Jewish nose and whose dress could have covered a three-ring circus. She worked at four desks arranged like circled wagons. Two were covered with books and printouts. Another held a skyline of paper stacks with a green Central Park in the midst of them: a blotter to scribble phone numbers on. The fourth held the inevitable computer with a froth of cables skirmishing behind it. Beyond her were four red doors, two of which led to shower rooms, my nose told me. Another probably led to the dance studio; the thumps and slides of slippered feet simmered from behind it. The fourth door was a mystery.

I was awaiting both Mary Ann and Sergio Adán because Bertie had insisted that I talk with him. The conversation had gone like this:

"Yeah, help you?" she said, slapping the phone in place and banging out something on her computer. I waited for her to finish, but she went right on to something else and snapped at the screen, "Yeah? Spit it or swallow it. Busy day."

"I'm a friend of Mary Ann Jaalkov's," I began. "She invited me to stop by when I was in New York, and, well, now I am."

"I'll call her at coffee break. You stop Serg' in the middle of rehearsal, and you'll get a bad case of Spanish flu, lemme tell ya," she threatened keyboard-wards. She wore bottle-bottom glasses and seemed to be a little myopic, as she bent low to hunt and peck with two chubby, pointy fingers, the backs of which were showing pink scraggles of melanoma. Her dark hair bitten with gray flopped over her forehead like a mop.

Then she snapped up and slapped off her glasses, which were saved by the gold chain that lay over the back of her neck. "Wait a minute. You said you're a friend o' *Mary Ann's?* Not Hal." It was an accusation.

"Hal it is," I said, wishing it weren't. "And you are...."

"Bertie," she said flatly, as if that were hardly the issue. She examined me, meaty lips squashed together, as if I might be an enemy spy. She ran a mannish hand down her throat as if checking her shave. "O-kay," she said at last. "O-kay. You're listenin' to me, right, Mistuh Hal?"

Friendly, appeasing, not to say cowardly: "I sure am."

"That's the nicest little girl evuh walked the planet, unnuhstand? And I'd take it very personally if she were to come in here some mornin' sayin' that Hal had played her, let's say, a dirty trick. Do I have to tell you how dirty or how personally, or can we skip that pwot?" This with a casual murderousness that would have stopped Godzilla in his tracks. I might have been offended, but her devotion to Mary Ann seemed not less than motherly.

"I think we can skip it." I nearly added that I hardly knew Mary Ann, but then remembered that she had told everyone I was her boyfriend.

"Good." She smiled minutely with square teeth that were too widely set apart. "I'm a little protective. I'm also serious, and don't you forget it." She turned to her papers, then something occurred to her. "Hey—Sergio would talk to you."

"Well, actually, we talked briefly in Chicago."

"Yeah? He didn't tell me."

This was probably because the conversation had not been, well, exactly memorable. He had shaken my hand, asked if I was Mary Ann's long-lost friend Hal, and dashed to the elevators to "put her back on track."

"I'm sure he's busy. I just wanted to say hello to Mary Ann and—"

"No Serg', no Mary Ann," she said, swinging around and squashing a red button on top of the table. That was that.

Ten minutes passed as I read the articles and listened to Bertie argue with a printer about paper quality for the programs. Then a male dancer came through the door to the studio followed by a hot gush of studio breath: sweat, wood, polish, and talcum powder. He was wiping his face on a towel, and Bertie called to him: "Hey, Santi! Guess who this is. Hal."

Again my unusual name had preceded me.

He was Spanish, very dark, and very handsome, taller than me, and built like a cliff climber, with long muscles not showy but necessary. He wore a black tank top and leggings, black slippers, and the usual bulky socks of a dancer. With touching fastidiousness, he dried a hand on the towel before shaking mine.

"Hal! Fantastic! I'm pleased to meet you," he said with a sort of English-as-a-second-language stiffness. He had an enormous jaw and enormous smile to go with it. "I'm Santiago." He gestured at his sweaty shirt. "I'm sorry for this."

I waved that away.

"Mary Ann, she has said me a lot things about of you. Did you like the Chicago show?"

"Everything except for Sheena."

"Yah—everybody hate her. One time I had to talk, uh, strong to Sheena to tell her that she not bother Mary Ann. But now with that Sheena is gone, we are going to make a great show. Everybody is really excited—y'know, ah, *vibrating*. Can I say this in English?"

"I get the idea."

"Okay, well, I am happy to meet you. Wait a minute. I call her." He stuck his head into the studio and yelled something in Spanish.

"Serg' is gonna *kill* you-u-u-u," sang Bertie.

"No. Is okay, we're breakin' now, 'cause of the radiator."

Bertie scowled. "Well, it's been two good months this time. Tools?"

"Yes, I need the tools again. But I am getting more comprehension of the system. Maybe this time will be the definitive."

Bertie had swung round and reached into a desk drawer and, with a grunt, took out a long metal tool box. Santiago vaulted across the room.

"Wait! Wait, Bertie, my love! What are you doing?" Santiago snapped. With a graceful lean over the desk, he snatched the box from her when it was still on the upswing.

"Hey, you're drippin' Spanish salt on Mrs. Thuy's clean flo-uh. *And on my papers! Santi! Fuh Chrissakes!*" Bertie snatched them away from under his leaning body.

Santiago swatted his chest with his fist and snapped, "Chill, baby. Round this dump, I's duh *may-an!*"

I bit my lip not to burst out laughing. It's not every day you hear a Spaniard imitate a rapper.

"You don't move your ass and you're gonna find out what you are!" Bertie snapped.

"Okay, Hal, I'm gonna go inna dressing room before that Bertie take out her knife. Maybe you and me we take a beer one of these days, okay? Hey, Mary Ann told that you have a engineer company? Wow, it's really—"

"Santi!" growled Bertie.

"Bertie, my flower! Don't worry about the floor. It's very sexy that a man sweat on your floor, okay? Come, admit this." He leaned far over Bertie's desk and kissed her on the forehead. "And your doc-u-ments, too, eh?"

Bertie harrumphed. "It's very sexy cleanin' it up—that's what's sexy." But the kiss had left her dizzy, it was easy to tell.

At that moment, Mary Ann came out, wiping her face with a towel. She too was bathed in sweat, blue leotard soaked in a long swoop that reached as far south as her bellybutton.

"Hal! Well, I'll be—!" she cried. "You come to see me?" To Santiago, who was laughing like a maniac: "You rat!" To me: "He told me it was a policeman."

Santiago rippled off a few lines of Spanish, in which I caught my name. Mary Ann rippled something right back—it sounded damn authentic to me—and snapped her towel at him.

"You see this, Hal?" called Santiago. "It's what I receive for to teach her some insults in Spanish."

"That's what you get for bein' a big, fat creep! *Sinvergüenza!*" shouted Mary Ann gaily.

Santiago dashed to the door to the men's dressing room and grinned back at her. "This room is only for the boys. But I let you to come in if you want. You are our guest."

"C'mon back here and fight like a man, ya cowart!"

Santiago disappeared. Mary Ann dried off her face and threw the towel over her shoulders and put her hands on her hips. She was radiant—hardly the stumble-mouthed woman I'd seen in Chicago.

"Everyone seems to be having a good time," I said.

"Yeah, isn't this the funnest place y'ever saw?" said Mary Ann. "Ever since Sheena left, we're all just, just laughin' and gettin' along great. 'Cept now the radiator's actin' up again, and the guys gotta fix it 'fore we get cold and break our tendons. That's why we hadda break a little early." She grabbed my arm, and with a power that made me wince. "But gosh, it's, it's just great and fine and wonderful to see you again! You came out here to see me?"

"Well, that and a meeting."

"Oh. Yeah. Right." She glanced at Bertie, and I knew that my answer lacked gallantry. "We're rehearsin'. We're preparin' the big show—*Revelaciones.* But, ah, maybe if you get, like, finished, y'know, and, and, like, and *we* get finished—"

"Sure, let's do something this evening," I blurted, though I remembered a dozen things to do back in Chicago. They were all going to get pushed back now.

Another male dancer—a Brit with thinning, blond hair—came out: "Beg pardon, sunshine—Santi in the gent's then?"

"He just went in," I said.

"Okay. When he comes out, tell him Darryl went down the basement."

"Will do."

Mary Ann grinned. "It's for the radiator. Darryl and Santi are the radiator guys. Everybody's gotta do two jobs around here."

"What's *your* other job?"

"Makin' everyone feel good," Bertie called from across the room. "This little girl's the life o' the pwotty."

"Yeah, well, when I'm not makin' dumb mistakes, I am."

"Bull. And she dances like a dream—Serg' told me. Best American flamenco he's ever seen."

I wondered if she was advertising for Mary Ann, for she certainly sounded like a spinster's mother.

"Really, what I do here is make soups for ever'body," Mary Ann said.

"Soups?" I said.

"Yeah, we all live together in the same buildin', y'know. So I take soup up to the other guys sometimes."

"What kind of soup?"

"My homemade soups—best thing y'ever ate in a New York winter. I make meatball soup and cream o' chicken and, and heck, cream o' just about ever'thing. Alba—that's my roommate?—she told me this is the first winter the company's made it 'thout nobody missin' on account o' flu. And that's good, 'cause Sergio can only afford two extras for understudy stuff."

The studio door opened again, issuing another warm wave of air. Several other dancers, half of them either Spanish or Latin, had come out of the studio and entered the dressing rooms; the last was Sergio Adán. In his black tights, he seemed just a wisp of a man, with just enough bone and flesh to dance in. His salt-and-pepper hair, mustache, and goatee were dark with sweat, as was the gray strap that held his glasses on. The lenses, however, were perfectly round and perfectly clean, if misted at the tops.

Approaching us, he looked over at Bertie and nodded curtly: *You were right to signal me.* "Yeah, Hal from the hotel loh-by in Chicago! Great to see you again. Hey, you come to invest in the cohmpany? Get ya in on the ground flo-ah." The New York jab of his speech was almost as sharp as Bertie's, though softened by Puerto Rican vowels.

"You bet. My briefcase there is stuffed with a hundred thousand in cash."

Mary Ann's eyes opened wide. *"Really?* Goll."

"No, Mary Ann, I was only kidding."

Her face went bright red, and she swallowed.

To act as if I didn't notice, I told Adán of my meeting in New York.

"Chintsy, huh? They throw a lotta tax write-offs at the big New York dance cohmpanies—like Ray Radow's outfit, where Sheena went."

"You should check into that."

"Take corporate mohney? No way. Dance in the park for tips first. You take corporate, you gotta accept ovuhsight. Here we get a break ohn our cleanin' bill—my cousin's outfits does all our costumes. I give him a quarter-page ad in the program. After that, we work like bastards and save like old ladies."

"Like on radiator repair."

"Yeah. Hey, did Santi....?"

"In the men's locker room. And Darryl's downstairs."

"Good. See, we got about ten minutes before the studio gets seriously cold and New York's best dance cohmpany starts pullin' muscles."

Mary Ann shivered. "Darryl told me there's rats down there."

"Well, sohmebody's gotta adjust the water pressure, hohney. And speaking of pullin' muscles," Adán said, throwing an arm around Mary Ann—she immediately leaned her head on his shoulder. "Swee'hear', go get yourself out of that sweaty stuff pronto, okay? And tell the girls to put on heels and long skirts. We're gonna pound some nails."

"Okay!" Mary Ann cried gleefully. To me: "He means dance flamenco," Mary Ann said to me. She demonstrated with a quick drum roll on the floor with her heels.

"Pound nails—right," I said.

"So I'll see you, like, maybe, you know, this afternoon?" she asked shyly.

"Around six?"

"Well, normally I gotta stay late to work on flamenco stuff." Mary Ann looked questioningly at Adán, who said, "If it's for Hal, I'll let you go early."

When she had disappeared into the women's locker room, Adán grinned his train-wreck of teeth at me and said, "That means you owe me one. So c'mon up with me for a sec'. Gotta ask your opinion ohn sohmething. Mind?" Adán held open the fourth door, where a steep set of stairs rose into the dark.

S ergio Adán's apartment-office was that of a monk: silent, dim, functional, with the august smell of old books. These lined two shelves, dance videos another two. The bed was a monk's cot with a simple blanket folded at its foot. I glanced at a video box. The label read *Africa, primitive: !Kung Bushmen, Namibia*. Quite a collection.

"Make yourself cohmfortable, Hal," Sergio hissed, for his cell phone had started beeping with incoming messages the moment he turned it on. "Just wanna see if the world is ending heah."

"If it is, let me know."

I stepped over to the line of interior windows that looked down on the studio, which was the size of an elementary-school basketball court. Mirrors and wooden bars lined its sides. But what caught my eye were the steel rails in the walls that rose to the ceiling and, here and there, oddly-situated, rectangular skylights. Then I saw an arm-chair-sized block-and-tackle hanging from the girders: in a previous life, the building had been a warehouse; the rails and skylights had ac-commodated industrial elevators.

Just below me a jumble of seven or eight benches sat touching at the ends, forming obtuse Vs and Ws. Two women dancers were sitting there chatting, one massaging her feet, the other rolling her long, black hair in a bun. A male dancer, dark as coffee and straight as an oar, came in pushing a rack of clothes, which he parked halfway up the floor. He slipped off his leather shoes, rummaged through the clothes and found a pair of gray trousers with a wide black belt strung through them, and pulled off his shorts; only a canary-yellow jock strap protected his hon-or. One of the women whistled, and he laughed. Which, I supposed, said it all about the locker-room intimacy of dancers.

Santiago entered and walked to the far end of the room. That tool box was a hefty steel monster indeed, but it merely floated from that perfect limb of his. Now he knelt on one knee, took out a fat monkey wrench, adjusted it with a thumb, and said something in Spanish to the women on the benches. One got up and crossed the studio to a point in front of an air duct on the floor by the mirrors. I had the feeling this was the normal drill.

"Okay, Dareel, are you ready?" she shouted, rolling the Rs.

A disembodied warble: "Ready we are, old love."

I wondered if he was dodging rats.

"*Ya,* Santi."

Santiago put a hand on the radiator, gingerly at first. Several seconds passed, and he turned a bolt that I couldn't see. He took out a screwdriver and jammed it into the end of the radiator and levered up and down till a fussy little sputtering of water came out. He shouted something to the woman, who shouted, "More, Dareel!" to the vent.

Adán touched my arm. "See Santi there? Looks like he's fixin' a radiator, right? Really, he's holdin' up the finances of this cohmpany."

"Let's hear it for Santi."

"You can say dat again. I'll bet you remember him from the show in Chicago, don't you?"

"Vaguely. He's really majestic-looking."

"Damn right. Six-foot-six of grace, stage presence, whole package. I'm lucky he's stayed on with me. He could make it on the Madrid stage by now."

Adán walked back to his desk, a folding, metallic, military-campaign affair that was at the far end of the room beside the window. Amidst neat papers and files was a portable PC, which he now turned around for me to see, setting it down soundlessly, as if it were a baby; he was a careful man. "I want ya to tell me somethin', Hal. Rorschach thing. When you see this picture, what words spring to mind? It's the cohvuh of the program for our new show."

"All right."

"Okay, go." He tapped a few buttons, and the cover appeared. "What words describe this?"

Two graceful forearms and hands, one masculine and dark, one feminine and white, entwined against a black background; only the backs of their hands actually touched. Underneath, in cursive letters: *Revelaciones.*

"Elegance, strength, drama," I said. "Mystery, maybe."

"Good! Good, that's just what I wanted. Not too awty, is it? Pretentious?"

"Not at all."

He stood back and looked at it himself, smoothing his mustache and goatee, judging it. "Good. Took me two hundred shots o' hands to get that single one."

"You're a graphic artist, too?"

A laugh. "Graphic awtist, photographuh, choreographuh, cohstume designuh and the staging directuh. Used to be janituh, too, but Bertie went behind my back and hired Mrs. Thuy, nice Vietnamese lady."

"I guess it's that or you give Chintsy a seat on your board."

"You can say dat again. Oh, I'm also dance mastuh. But don't get the wrong idea." He turned off the computer, gently closed the computer's lid and came over to me by the window. "I don't run one of those cohmpanies where they weigh the dansuhs every mornin' and tell 'em to lose another pound or they can hit the road. Okay? My people know what they can eat and what they can't."

"Dance masters do that?"

"Oh, yeah—some are real full-blown bastuds. They want yuh to look like a runway mohdel these days. Got run through that mill myself in one cohmpany—after three months I looked like a fuckin' piece o' string. Jussa sec'."

Adán pushed open the window a little more, leaned out and yelled something in Spanish.

Santiago answered, then added in English, "Hal, tell him that not worry. I am the best plum-ber of Sevilla and half of New York."

"You duh man," I said, and he laughed.

Adán leaned back in. "Just ease it along, babe," he murmured. "Just get us to May—that's the promised land. Just don't fuckin' *break it*."

"Has he ever broken it?" I inquired.

"No, no. He's fabulous. But we need a new heating system, and that would be the end. *The* end." A glance at me. "That's between you and me, right, Hal? The cohmpany has enough to worry about just gettin' their steps right."

"Secret's safe," I said.

Which made Adán peer at me through his specs, thoughtful. "Yeah. It is, isn't it? I believe you. I have right from the get-go. Yeah: that's why Mary Ann talked to you ohn the plane, isn't it?"

"Could be," I said with a shrug.

"Interesting story, you and her. Remembuh Marilyn Monroe? Arthur Milluh said that in a crowded room, she immediately sensed who was an orphan, like her, and spent her time talkin' with 'em. Mary Ann's the same way. I watched her in two pwotties we've had since she got heah: she knows just who to trust. Guys tryin' to hit on her, she just laughs 'em off."

In the studio, Santiago lifted his head and called, *"Ya!"*, which must have great significance in Spanish, for the woman at the vent hollered to valiant Darryl that he could come back up.

Adán grunted a one-note chuckle. "I swear, if I have to light a bohnfire in the middle of the studio, we'll make it. All we gotta do is get to May."

"May."

"Yeah: *Revelaciones.*" He said it lovingly, as if pronouncing the name of his daughter.

"Sure that's the promised land?"

A distant smile. "Who's shu-ah about anything in this business? All I know is this is my best shot. Now that I got yuh girl up to speed ohn Spanish dance. She was just what I was looking for—my wild cawd, last piece o' the puzzle."

"What puzzle?" I asked.

"The right mix: the right eight dancers, plus two understudy."

"They're that hard to find?"

He nodded. "I've had *Revelaciones* in the drawer since I founded the cohmpany—it's *the reason* I founded it. Didn't bring it out befo-ah 'cause I didn't have the people. Sheena was okay—at the beginning— but about half the rest didn't make it." He shook his head in amazed frustration. "It was always something. Always. They could do flamenco but not tango. Or they could do jazz, but couldn't get the flamenco. Or the Spaniards—great flamenco, but they didn't know how to ham up the jazz."

"Yeah. I suppose that for—"

But he went on, and I realized that he was talking more to himself than to me, urging himself on, as he surely did in the wee hours, when doubt and his thin finances crowded around that narrow cot.

"And then I needed my court jestuh—someone who could make everybohdy laugh. I did have one that could, but she was Spanish, and it's got to be an American. People don't relate the same way to a foreigner. I kept goin' with audition after audition, hirin' and firin' and hirin' and firin'—you can't be sentimental when you're chasin' your dream. Then Mary Ann came along—boom. That was it. The last piece o' the puzzle."

"Mary Ann learned how to dance flamenco in Las Vegas?" I asked, amazed.

"No, but all I had to do was let her listen to the music and show her a few steps—you know, the heel work and how the arms go. Unbelievable. Okay, she was just imitatin', she didn't own it. But the clean execution came right through. So—we're still in the audition, right?—I put Santi up beside her poundin' nails. I said, 'Try that, darlin'—just hands at your sides. See how long you can keep up with Santi heah.'" He shook his head. "Matched him right up the scale. Beat for fuckin' beat. I said to do it in a fast three-four gallohp. No prohblem. Legs like a pair of jackhammuhs. Whole cohmpany's jaw droppin' on the flo-ah."

"Is that right?" I murmured.

Adán was still talking out the window, either talking or remembering; I couldn't tell. "I take her on, teach her—boom. She moves right up into the tough stuff: *taranto, sigirilla, martinete.* Like I say, she starts out imitatin'—like everybody does, that's fine—but she works like the possessed till she lives it, owns it, wears it. In just six months with her, I've got her up to speed. Even the arms."

"The arms?"

"Yeah, that's the really tough part of flamenco. Poundin' nails, okay, that's basically a quaystion of good training. But the arms have to flow, from your back and chest right up to the fingertips. Actually, Alba did the heavy lifting there. Takes a woman to take anohther woman through it, y'know."

"*And* she's your court jester, huh?" I said with an eagerness that surprised me.

"Yeah—*joy*. Starbursts of it. Joy born frohm pain. You know she ran away frohm home?"

I nodded.

"She told me one or two things about it—kind of embarrasses her, so I didn't dig. But the moment she told me, I thought, 'Yeah. Yeah. There it is—right there. That's what it is.' She dances, she dances whatever, and the room turns into gold—'cause she's so happy to have come through all that. That's why I got a hot show."

"So you're pretty –"

"'Cause this is gonna be one for the history books, when flamenco-fusion splashes dead center in American dance. This is the one they gonna hear about in Peoria. No stars, y'know—fuckin' *sick* o' stars. Everyone's gonna get his moment of glory. But Mary Ann—she carries the *story,* see. That big, big smile ohn stage, that joy. Someone that's just happy to be here. *That's* the element, *that's* the ingredient, see: the court jestuh. It's not the one getting' the laughs, not really: it's the one that's always just a little ohn the outside."

In the studio, Santiago had closed up the tool box, and now stood up and bowed elaborately to the others, who cheered. So did Adán: "Bravo, maestro!" he called. To me: "Man, what would I do without Santi? Came along two years ago—manna from heaven. Repaired half the goddamn buildin' for me. Won't take a nickel for it. Believes in the dream, too, y'see: typical Spanish Quijote."

Adán started away from me, but I asked, "He told me he had a talk with Sheena once about Mary Ann. What did he mean?"

"Some talk!" Adán laughed. "One mornin' I'm ohn the phone in here, and I glance out. Mary Ann is cryin'—Sheena'd been ridin' her again—and Santi is backin' Sheena against a bar. He reaches round and grabs that long blond hair and forces it down so hard that now Sheena's looking back inna the mirruh, see. Santi steps between her feet and presses his crotch right up against hers, and he's whispering down at her face. Whole cohmpany just standin' there watchin'—nobody lifted a finguh to stop him."

"Jesus."

"Aftuh that, Sheena stopped ridin' her—at least around the studio."

He went over to his desk and snatched a clipboard.

With a few others, Mary Ann came in now, wearing a pearl-gray leotard and thick-heeled pumps with which to "pound nails," and heavy socks like great clouds around her ankles. Everybody's shoes crackled as if they had tacks stuck on the heels. The coffee-colored man said something to her and made a fast thundering staccato with his heels. Mary Ann grinned and answered the same way. They went back and forth several times, the rhythm and execution immaculate. Then the man went over to a bar and began stretching, and Mary Ann stepped over to the clothes rack and began to look through its many long skirts. Already at the base of her spine a circle of sweat had started, like a daub of spray paint.

"Look at that back—Jesus!" Adán pausing beside me. "You could prohp a bridge ohn that." He swatted his thigh with the clipboard. "Well! Work to do!"

I was about to step after him to the stairway, and glanced one last time down at Mary Ann; I suppose I wanted to see which skirt she chose to go with the gray leotard. She took one, blood red, with a white tie-belt along the top. Walking across the floor towards the mirrors, she swung the skirt around her waist and tied it with a smart tug at the side, near her right hip bone; then, with both hands, she pushed her dark-red hair back off her forehead. Then she grabbed the bar, propped a leg on it, and laid her torso along that, stretching out.

"Comin', Hal? You're welcome to watch us, if you want."

"Love to, but I've got a meeting with Chintsy," I said, following him down the steps.

And yet...

And yet...

And yet a week later, on a night flight down to Sao Paulo, Brazil, I was seized—possessed, electrified—by that vision of Mary Ann tying on her skirt with that thoughtless little jerk and smoothing back her hair. It simply popped up in my mind in the middle of an *Economist* article on climate change in the Arctic. I had spent some time with her and Alba that evening in New York, thought of her during the week, even talked to her by phone. But my vision of her in the studio? Nothing. Not a hint, not a wisp, not a flutter. It returned to me on the plane, right out of the blue like someone's birthday I'd forgotten to buy a gift for. But when it did....

For hours, flying south across the starry Equator, I stared out the window, paralyzed. I could think of nothing except Mary Ann, that thoughtless jerk of the tie-belt, that shove of the hair. Only sleep would finally end my trance.

Strange.

8   But on to more mundane matters. Or at least they were mundane back then; they would turn out to be historic.

At Chintsy Nuclear, after a full-body scan in the lobby, where my tin of lip-moisturizing gel met with sneering grins from the security staff—real men apparently use it only for sex—I was hoisted to the twenty-fourth floor and seated with the disdain due an ever-moneyless cousin, at a glass table easily ten feet in diameter. Three ugly steel pyramidal contraptions supported it against gravity. On the far side sat three Chintsy reps of varying career stages, who assured me dangerously that if I could not be "swung round to a more reasonable position," a "big player" would come down and "turn the screws" on me. And two of them pointed up to the ceiling and nodded, implying that among the thirty or forty or so floors above us roamed a fearsome, screw-turning player-monster.

Such were the characters to whom I had to make AllPoint's color-less argument that it be paid for its work. If I had not shaken hands with each, I would have sworn they were images painted on plate glass.

First up—let me call him Entry-level—was an incoherent, pale man of around 25, still smelling of frats and beer bars, who wore his hair fashionably congealed in small stalagmites. He went over the basic po-sition: AllPoint's request for payment had "totally blind-sided" Chintsy.

"See where I'm coming out now, Hal? It's fundamentally flawed right from the start. I mean, it's like these monies don't even ballpark for us. They're like over and done with, read-my-lips history. All right, now you've got to admit we *have* sat down with you. I mean, we *have* talked you through this, which I personally think has been pretty, like, ultra-cool of us, especially in view of your total lack of proactivity. But hell, I mean, as per the actual *doing* of this thing—puh-lease you me! Your stance is just totally above and beyond the call of duty."

I smiled in apology of my stance, as if it were my three-year-old son who had trampled his roses. Then I laid a forefinger on the contract and observed—in a gesture of proactivity—that the invoice was for work done in the five months before Chintsy had signed the final construction agreement with Djakarta. Chintsy wisely wanted to jump-start the work, and the contract that AllPoint signed with Chintsy was valid, even if it was contingent upon the second, permanent contract, signed later on, once Chintsy had formalized matters with the Indonesians. Chintsy had paid AllPoint for the second, larger contract—and thank you very much. As fate would have it, however, the first contract had escaped Chintsy's notice, and AllPoint had brought this lapse to Chintsy's attention many a moon earlier.

"Oh, puh-lease you *me!*" moaned Entry-Level again. You might remember this was the latest business catch-phrase back then. "Jesus. We come. We sit down with you. We reason with you. If you don't get this, Hal, what can we say? Listen, I can't afford to spend any more time on this." He picked up his cell phone, pushed a few buttons on it, and to my amazement, walked out. Not angry, not in any sort of huff, nor with a syllable that signified farewell. He simply left.

The other two did not seem surprised.

"He's right, you know, Hal: you have to understand our position on this." This from a wrinkle-shirted, menopausal man in mid-career, whose dull wedding band made me think of unruly teenage children who drank on the weekends and wrecked his car. He had bulging shoulders and an artless tie that was held in place by an incongruously beautiful, diamond-studded clip. Mid-Career's approach was to bludgeon me with flights of specious reasoning, each topped off with a refrain of "You have to understand our position on this, Hal." I insisted that I did understand. No good. For Mid-Career, to understand meant to agree, and because I didn't agree, I didn't understand. This wheel creaked for fifteen minutes.

With tact, I restated AllPoint's position. He burst out shouting—literally roaring—at me: "That's the trouble with you guys in dip-shit little firms that we have to jerk around with in order to interpret a project. You're all a bunch of liberals who think that everything has a right and a wrong, and you're going to fight and scrape for your rights even if this whole fucking country goes down to hell. You're a liberal, aren't you, Hal? Huh? A fucking liberal. I can hear it by the way you talk. You don't give a shit if you have to come here and suck up the time of a huge, complex company like this extrapolated across a whole planet—you don't give a *fuck*. All you want is your money. A million— hell, that's nothing for *us*, you know. In fact, there are guys around here who'd just as soon *give* you the money as get rid of you."

In a tense meeting, the more upset my opponents become, the more I plod. I nodded, took a few notes, nodded over these, and said, "Okay, point taken."

"So are we down to closure on this thing, Hal?" asked Mid-Career, on the assumption that his bullying had thrust us down the road to resolution. He was leaning forward on his forearms, mountainous shoulders framing his stupendous indignation.

"Maybe," I said encouragingly.

"Great. Now: I'm authorized—and I hadda fight for it, under-stand?—to offer you ten percent payment, just on the recognition that there *was* some type of misunderstanding." He pulled a paper out of a file and passed it across to me; unfortunately, it stopped sliding halfway across the table, beyond anyone's reach. Mid-Career tried to blow it, and all he achieved was to waft me his coffee breath. Like an uncoop-erative child, the paper stayed where it was.

"Ten percent, huh?" I said as if I might actually consider it.

"That's right—and you have *me* to thank for it, too."

"Great. Well, before I do, ah, Ms. Passing: you're from Legal. What's your take on this? Surely an unpaid contract, with nonpayment pen-alties right there in black and white, must give you some concern."

"What the....?" Mid-Career fell back noisily in his chair. His big face adopted a mobile loathing of me.

Ms. Passing was a 33-year-old lawyer of the type I was eternally dating with the best of intentions. No rings on her fingers, pinstriped power-suit over an open white business blouse, hair too long for her aging, disappointed face, heavy bags under the eyes and the taupe patina of Career worked into her skin so deeply that neither makeup nor Caribbean resorts would ever efface it. Life was passing Ms. Passing by. With a stepping-up-to-the-plate scowl, she drilled her index fingers into the glass table—probably a body-language thing she'd learned at one of those vile assertiveness seminars from which I am constantly protecting AllPoint. She explained Chintsy's position, which was based on a minor contractual statement reminding SUPPLIER that while all project expenses were to be reimbursed by PURCHASER, preliminary studies and preparatory expenses—travel to the project site or consultation with specialists, for example—were not included.

I pulled out my copy, read the statement, shrugged, and politely asked, "Right. Now, how would this relate to the present problem?"

"*How?* Your preliminary work on the Djakarta job clearly, unquestionably, not to mention unequivocally, falls under this clause, Hal," she said. The tendons of her neck stood out like rigging for a tightrope cable.

"*Now* do you understand our position?" said Mid-Career. "I was hoping it wouldn't come to this, Hal, but you've really pushed us to it."

"The first contract was indeed preliminary work," I said. "It was a preliminary study of the Indonesians' changing from a PWR system to a BWR, which is what they *had* planned to build before they changed their minds."

"Mind speaking English here, Hal?" said Miss Passing.

"The systems? Pressurized Water Reactor and Boiling Water Reactor," I said, amazed that she didn't know. For anyone in the nuclear industry, it was like knowing the difference between offense and defense.

Sourly: "Thank you."

"The point is, they were separate jobs. The clause you're referring to, Ms. Passing, is a standard clause that you can find in both contracts. It simply protects your company from having to pay for what are properly our expenses. Why should you pay for our getting the skinny on the latest advances in a design? Or take, for example—"

"God!" Mid-Career threw himself back in his chair again, and so hard that its front hoofs lifted off the floor and he nearly fell backwards. It was only by throwing a hand to the side—he hit Ms. Passing in the breast—that he managed to right himself. So now he was more angry than ever. "Jesus H. Christ! I knew it was a mistake to talk about this. Hal, if you don't get our position the first time around, what good is all this?" Again he elaborated on the villainy of liberals like me. Quite a philosopher.

I wallowed in their anger for a while as Ms. Passing restated her stupid position. In truth, I felt sorry for them. They had been told to stonewall me, and being good company joes and janes, they were doing just that. A cross bobbed between Ms. Passing's too-parted lapels, and I wondered if meetings like these weren't the reason she needed religion.

"So if I understand your position here, Ms. Passing," I said, "you're calling three months' work by ten engineers—work for which we have a separate contract, work that was necessary for the real work to start, which was the purpose of the next contract—you're calling *all of that* 'preliminary studies and preparatory expenses'?"

"Well, isn't it?" she said, flipping her dry hair back off her shoulders. "End of the day: same project, same plant, same everything. You didn't design *two* control panels, did you?"

I pretended this was a joke. "No, we certainly didn't," I chuckled. "We had our hands full with just the one from the beginning."

"And you delivered it on ti-i-i-ime? Let me see," said Ms. Passing, swatting wildly through some papers in a file, for the sudden hope had occurred to her that AllPoint might be caught on that aspect. I saved her the trouble.

"*Weeks* ahead of time. See, we really *are* dealing with two contracts. The corresponding delivery papers were all filled out and signed by your company." I made a shrug before slipping the knife in: "And now it's time to pay the piper."

"Yeah, but maybe you'd better think a little about what collecting in full is going to *cost* that piper," Mid-Career pontificated to the ceiling.

"That's true, you know," added Ms. Passing sweetly. "Senior management takes a very dim view of suppliers that they have trouble with."

And so we entered the arena of veiled and not-so-veiled threats, which I resent; I suppose because I like to consider myself a gentleman in a gentleman's business. I listened, attention on my face and tedium in my soul. Nothing sounds more sappy in business than some salaried yes-man trying to play The Godfather.

Fortunately, the player-monster "from upstairs" came in; his entry was so timely that I wondered if the room wasn't bugged. He emanated a muscular, military calm, wore his silver hair split perfectly on the side, and as he shook my hand winked in a conspiratorial way that meant that, like him, I stood head-and-shoulders above mere salarymen: Edgerton Salk.

Head cocked apologetically, he listened to Ms. Passing for a while. He pulled out a chair, swung it around and perched on its back, his jacket open so that we could all admire his smooth gut. He wasn't some hack who was going to sit down across a table and horse-trade.

"Ah-huh, ye-e-e-es," he murmured at last, and Harvard trailed in his tone like a scarf. His mouth was lipless, just a maw where his face stopped at its shore. "Well now, seems to me we ought not to stand so much on legalities." A glance at me. "As I like to remind business groups, we're all brothers in business, at the end of the day. Mr. Dormund, what do you say to our paying, say, fifteen percent on total? Let's just get this behind us and do *business,* shall we?" It might have been a good movie he was inviting me to see.

"At AllPoint we'd certainly like to keep yours," I said evenly.

"You've got a helluva way of going about it, Hal," snarled Mid-Career.

"So as a gesture of good will to an old client," I went on, "we'll forget the surcharges for late payment. But we do expect one hundred percent payment on the contract itself."

Both Mid-Career and Ms. Passing barked a *Hah!* in harmony.

"That's certainly not much of a discount," Salk observed.

"On the contrary: it's over a hundred fifty thousand dollars. Interest is ten percent per annum, compounded, and payment is now late by eighteen months."

Mid-Career took this blow in the stomach. "That is so totally—that is just such fucking *bullshit!* Hal, if you can't see our point of view, can't you please send us someone who can?"

With a rueful laugh: "We're all a little myopic at AllPoint, I'm afraid."

"Then how about if Mr. Salk sends you a goddamn pair of glasses?"

I was surprised that Salk admitted that kind of language, and I should have taken note: his standards would come to surprise me a lot more.

He contemplated his shoes like the old man he refused to be. "Well, that's just a shame, really too bad. Yeah. Well, I guess we're done, then. Can I walk you to the elevator, Hal?"

So we were finished for the day. Ms. Passing shook my hand; Mid-Career snapped open his cell phone and bounced out, grinning at me like a little kid: *Now you're going to get it, smartass.*

Salk and I walked out to the elevators. The floor was carpeted with the usual flat, functional material, though coffee stains broke its business-blue integrity.

"Hal, may I give you a word to the wise?"

"I'd appreciate it."

"Or maybe two words." Salk stopped abruptly. We were in the middle of the building, near the elevators; all was quiet. From the side pocket of his suit jacket, he pulled out a military medal about the size of a bottle cap, which I quickly recognized as the Bronze Star. "Got this in Nam in '72. I was just 19. My team got orders to intercept a holding point for two dozen American POWs about to be shipped north. And we did, mister. Did it the hard way, too—hand-to-hand through eleven of the enemy. We didn't want any strays hitting our boys. Didn't lose a single prisoner." He put the medal back in his pocket. "Always been very proud of that operation."

Apparently he was making a point about his toughness. I wondered how many people he'd given that same little lecture to.

"The other word is this. What you're trying to pull—it's not worth it. Press the matter, and we'll drop AllPoint right off our speed-dialer, I guarantee you. For-ever. I'll give you fifteen percent—no, hell, call it twenty, you *did* do the work. But get used to the idea right now that we make our own reality here. You want to roll with that, fine. You don't, you're going to cost your firm a lot of business."

I pulled a little shrug.

An unexpected laugh, for which he opened that ragged, lipless mouth—the only poor feature in his trim face. "You *can't* think we need you! We can get your services from Hungary for pennies. Think about basic necessity here."

"What if we think about the basic principle?" I snapped. "You contracted out the work, we did the work. And now you pay."

He laughed again. That mouth, a rough-hewn hole, might have been taken from a killer scarecrow in a slasher movie. "Hal, principles are only as good as the money they're printed on. They have the value that the market assigns them. And don't give me any lectures on cynicism—you think the same way. Do any of your people get up every morning, five days a week, for a principle? No, they do it for a paycheck and a good car."

"Is that something you tell business groups, too?" I shot back, and from his cold stare I could tell I'd hit a nerve. Perhaps that was why Salk would take our conflict so personally.

"You just remember who you're dealing with, buster!" he growled.

"Never forgotten." The elevator arrived, and I stepped in. "If this goes to litigation, it does," I said, punching the ground-floor button.

"You're a silly man, Mr. Dormund," said Salk. "Silly and innocent. If you'd've been with me in 'Nam—"

He stuck out an arm to stop the elevator doors from closing, but was standing too far back. So I never found out my hypothetical fate in that tortured country. Just as well.

9　　In the New York Public Library, I composed a careful memo for AllPoint's legal counsel and cleared my e-mail, then visited a superb exhibition of Rodin's sculpture at the Metropolitan Museum. In the evening I caught a cab and picked up Mary Ann and Alba, her roommate, at the dance studio and went to their apartment.

The apartment building was Sergio's, you remember, part of his aunt's largesse—and here he housed his company, making up for the thin salaries he paid. The dancers joked that he controlled his dancers' weights with their pay. Only joked, mind you: they knew perfectly well that Sergio operated on the thinnest of shoestrings. Bertie, I found out, was not an employee at all but a retired currency-market pit-boss.

She'd had thirty suit-and-tie soldiers at her command. Having made a pleasant pile of dough, she now ran the company's business side literally for love of (the) art.

Mary Ann and Alba's nest in the Big Apple was about what you would expect of two dancers on the payroll of a best-new-dance-company-of-the-year award-winner. Alba was among Sergio's original hires for the company. Van Gogh and Velasquez prints hung on the living-room walls. The towels were little better than cheap cloth, the furnishings classic Goodwill, the tiny closets jammed with clothes and concealed behind yellowed drapes. Washed leotards hung in front of the radiators.

Alba, who like Picasso was from Malaga, on the south coast of Spain, had put up beach tourist posters in the bedrooms. She seemed to have learned everything about New York's crawly and furry housemates: not a scrap of food existed outside the refrigerator with the exception of a salt shaker, and the trash was taken out right after our dinner. A clean, well-lighted place.

I would have invited them to a restaurant, but Alba offered a home-cooked Spanish dinner, and Mary Ann one of her soups, and those convinced me. Now, as Alba hung out yesterday's leotards and threw today's into the washer, Mary Ann dashed into her room to "put on somethin' pretty."

"Oh, Mary Ann, you look all right!" Alba growled.

"I look like an ol' ragbag," Mary Ann shouted. "Hal, you come in here, and I'll put a dent in your butt! That's what ya get for sneakin' up on me today."

Alba yakked a few lines in Spanish to her and, to me, rolled her eyes. "Mary Ann," she said, "wants to look nice for you."

"She's fine as is."

"She is twenty. Well, it is good practice like this for my future as mother. Okay! Dinner." She walked around the low bar-style breakfast counter, which was all that divided the living room from the kitchen, and pulled some frying pans out of the oven, which was apparently their storage space.

"Can I help?"

"You, Señor Hal, can be a good guest. If you want something, I will bring it. You are the guest, I am the host." An artful curtsy. "Now you will sit on this breakfast stool and have a conversation with me, okay?" She raised her voice: "For example, tell me about how you plan to get Mary Ann into bed."

"I heard that, ya rat!"

Alba had a more conventional body for a dancer than Mary Ann: slender, bony in arms and chest, and shoulders whose long muscles bounced to attention whenever she raised her arms. It was her I'd seen making a bun of her hair in the studio, I now realized, for her fine-stranded, black mane fell below her shoulder blades. Her face was thin with high cheekbones—wolfish maybe when she pulled her narrow lips back in a smile.

"Would you like a beer or a glass of wine? I still have a bottle of Rioja from when my fiancé came to visit last month."

"Wine sounds good."

She pulled out a bottle from under the kitchen counter. From an ugly plastic plate rack she took a wine glass, checked it for transparency, washed it under a torrent of water, and put it on the counter front of me, still wet. "In Spain, it is the man's job to open the bottle," she said, taking a corkscrew from where it hung with a lot of cooking utensils above the sink.

I settled carefully on the stool—its joints were dodgy—and got to work with the corkscrew. "So if we can't talk about my plans for Mary Ann, what can we talk about?" I said loudly.

"Both of ya—rats!"

"Talk with me only about the most normal, everyday things: the weather, how impolite the people are, how terrible the traffic is, or the government, or soccer, or clothes or your boss. With a Spaniard, the point is to complain. It is necessary to complain about everything. If it is possible, you must to stay talking until three in the morning and go to work tomorrow with big bags under your eyes."

"I'll give it my best shot," I chuckled.

Alba poured an inch of olive oil in a frying pan and began peeling potatoes.

"It must be hard to keep a relationship with your boyfriend so far away," I said.

"No, no problem. He is flight attendant for Iberia. He comes each two or three weeks and stays for a few days before flying back. I am sure he has a girl to, ah, *fit his needs* there in Madrid, but I don't care. This is my last year with the company, and then I will go back and marry him and make his life miserable."

Mary Ann ran out of her bedroom and into the bathroom, and slammed the door. "Alba, can you come and, y'know, do somethin' for me here?" she called.

To me, quietly: "She means that I put her makeup. I do it always for important events." Louder: "No! I am making dinner. You look fine, Mary Ann! Fine, fine, fine, fine!"

"Please!"

"And we have a guest, which I am entertaining. Have you not noticed this?"

"Alba, you can't do this to me!"

"Yes, I can! I am going to seduce him and take him to my bed if you don't come out. Then you will be sorry." Alba winked at me. "Sorry. I should to have said that in Spanish."

"You're a big ol' rat and a creep to boot! If you aren't gonna, y'know, do this, I gotta start all over again!" Mary Ann ran back to her room and slammed the door shut.

Alba shouted a single word at her. "That means 'dumbass,'" she explained.

"Mary Ann," I called, "just a decent shirt and jeans will do. Or your bathrobe. Whatever."

"Hey, I'm no harlot!" she called through the door.

"Hal, what is a harlot?" Alba asked quietly. "Mary Ann often uses this word."

"A prostitute. But it's an old word. You don't see it much outside the Bible."

Alba reached slowly for the next potato. "Aaah! A *prostitute!* And in the Bible! This is interesting."

"Alba, here's a question for *you*. When I was in Chicago, I met Sheena Biggs briefly, and she said something about—"

Alba spoke quietly. "Yes, Mary Ann told me. She was *so* embarrassed. She has worried every day that she would never see you again."

I also lowered my voice. "She said that Mary Ann used to pick her nose or something."

Alba cut up the potatoes and tossed them into the frying pan, now with hot oil. "That will be done in a few minutes. I am making a Spanish tortilla—potatoes and eggs and onions."

"It smells great."

Alba took another wine glass, checked it for spots, and washed it. I poured three fingers for her. She sipped—and glanced towards the hallway where the bedrooms were. "I have teached her everything, you know. Everything. She came here with one plastic bag—a garbage bag. It had her clothes and everything—they were not clothes, they were only rags—two, ah, gym suits and a sweater and a jacket."

"Jesus," I said. I remembered Ruth: *Okay, I treated her pretty much like shit, too, actually.*

"Her hair was a rag, also. I took her to a good hairdresser, helped her to buy nice clothes, taught her the make-up, everything. She didn't know what a subway was or how to read the map!"

I took a slow slug of the Rioja. "And how to hold a fork and knife, too, right?"

She nodded. "It was a very embarrassing time for her. *I* was embarrassed also."

"I'll bet." I didn't ask for any more specifics; Mary Ann wouldn't have liked it. "Well, but what about at school?" I asked. "Didn't her friends kind of steer her along a little?"

"She only went until high school. Then, ah, she *renounced?*"

"Dropped out."

"Yes. She said that she had many problems there and that the other children laughed at her." She frowned. "Perhaps she has a type of dyslexia also." She sipped her wine, looking in the direction of the hallway to the bedroom. "She is a dancer, nothing more. All her life she only has danced. Very little television also. She doesn't know Rachel from *Friends*—you know, Jennifer Anniston?—or, or for example, Matt Damon, the actor. It is as if her life have started six months ago when she came to New York."

"Well, thank god she found someone like you to help her out," I said.

Alba shrugged and stirred the potatoes. "At least she is a fast learner. Did you know that she has a memory almost perfect? I tell her a word in Spanish, or how to conjugate the verbs, and she remembers. She has learned in only a few months! The other Americans in the company only learn the commands that Sergio gives them."

Mary Ann came out of her room. She wore a bathrobe and held up two different tops, a white shirt with straps and a blue stretchy tee-shirt. "Hey, you aren't sayin' anything bad about me, are ya?"

"I am saying Hal that you have learned Spanish very fast."

"She says you're a genius."

"Oh, that was easy," Mary Ann said. "'Mesa' is 'table.' Easy as pie." She shook the shirts on their hangers at me. "Hal, you decide. Which—"

"Oh! And Vietnamese," said Alba.

"Vietnamese?" I said.

"Yes, Hal—Vietnamese! From the cleaning lady in the studio. Mary Ann started by asking her how to say this and that, and now when she has a conversation with Mrs. Thuy every evening."

"Well, it's just to be friendly, y'know. Mrs. Thuy don't speak much English, and she's just so sweet and she works *so hard!* Ever watch her? Bertie says she's a little angel."

"Yes, Mary Ann, but Vietnamese is very hard," Alba insisted. "These words don't sound like words. They are—"

"No, ya just gotta think of Ping-Pong balls, I mean, but soft: *bao bao bao.*" Impatiently, she shook the two shirts at me, one blue, one white. "Now which one o' these should I wear, Hal? Which one do you like?"

"The blue."

This disappointed her. "Really? The blue? You think?"

"Better the white."

"Right!" And she twisted away at incredible speed towards the hall. "And don't laugh at me, ya rats! I just wanna look okay. B'sides, I got a soup ready in the 'fridge, and Alba's makin' tortilla de patatas. That takes a while." She slammed the door behind her.

Alba grinned at me and stirred the potatoes. "It only is one more day of living with Mary Ann."

I wandered into the living room. On the coffee table, I came across a glasses case—I recognized it from the restaurant. It had a sticker on the bottom with Mary Ann's address and phone number. I opened the case, for a question had suddenly popped into my mind. If Mary Ann, without her glasses, couldn't even read the big letters of a note written by Alba, her eyesight must be pretty bad. Yet, to my surprise, the lenses were normal, thin crystals, a long way from bottle-bottoms. What correction they had was minor.

I put them back. The bookcase held about twenty books, half English, half Spanish, and a smaller number of DVD movies.

"Okay, I'm ready. Ta-da!" Mary Ann said, sweeping into the room and striking a pose, arms raised proudly like a flamenco dancer.

"Wow, you look like a statue," I blurted.

"Okay, but how's my blouse?" she said impatiently.

I tossed out a compliment, but I wondered if she had any idea of how beautiful she really looked.

We had dinner—Mary Ann's cream of asparagus was unbelievably good—chatted and sipped wine and played a noisy game of Parcheesi on the coffee table, which was really two boxes covered with a table cloth. Alba soaked her feet in icy water, her nightly custom, she told me. I took the opportunity to tell them about Frank, who, I've forgotten to tell you, had been calling me every few days.

"Well, if you talk to ol' Frank again, you just tell him I'd like to talk to him the same way I'd like to talk with, with, with a big ol' smashed squirrel in the road or somethin'. Gosh, how the heck did Frank get hold of you?"

I reminded her of her PIN number and my message.

Alba threw up her hands. "Mary Ann! How can you be a girl so silly? Anybody can guess 1111!"

She blushed. "Oh. Yeah. Sorry. I guess I'm kinda dumb, huh?"

"Stop feeling sorry for yourself!" To me: "Excuse me, Hal, for a moment. There are some things that are better to say in Spanish." And off she went, yammering and gesturing—half the time at me, as if to say that nobody likes a crybaby—and shoving Mary Ann's face around till both ended up laughing. Alba was certainly the best thing that ever happened to Mary Ann.

Meanwhile, an idea had occurred to me: "Why don't I call your number again, leave another message that sounds like we *haven't* gotten together, and—"

"Oh. Sorry. Can't. I don't have the phone no more. I canceled it—'cause, well, you called, and like I had to pay on it every month, y'know."

So much for that.

Both Mary Ann and Alba were pretty bushed, since Sergio was working them hard for the big show he was putting on, and rehearsals were tough—the equivalent, Alba said, of doing the show twice a day. Mary Ann laid out some blankets on the sofa with a quite natural, unembarrassed air. For pajamas, I had those of Juan, Alba's fiancé.

The sheets tucked well in, she faced me. "I'm really glad you came today, Hal. When I saw you there in the lobby, heck, I was, that was, it was like, I mean it's just about, like, the gladdest I ever been about anything."

"Me too."

"Yeah? Gosh, that's great!"

Alba came out of the bathroom, said good-night, and went into her bedroom.

"Hal, do you think I'm older than the last time I saw you?"

I tested the word: "Older."

"Yeah, like, more, more...." Her brow wrinkled. "More like Alba, I mean, more, more like, y'know, a woman...." She fluttered an arm towards the ceiling, and at the end snapped her hand shut in a fist. "Like that."

Like that. It was as lovely a description of womanhood as any I'd ever seen, so I said yes.

"Oh, good! 'Cause y'know, I'm, I'm gettin' better. It just takes me longer 'cause there's a lotta things I don't know yet."

"Well, Rome wasn't built in a day, either."

This either made no impression or she didn't hear it; she was thinking now, planning, her brow deeply furrowed. Her hands came together; one was gripping the thumb of the other and twisting it as if to unscrew it. Her hands certainly expressed her better than words did. "And I never had a boyfriend, either, and, um, and I'm not, like, all the things you have to do, it's like... I don't really know what I'm *supposed* to do."

"You mean with me?"

Softly: "Yeah, sure. Sometimes I hear the other girls in the company when they're talkin', and it sounds kinda, like, fun and nice, but I mean, like, like, what I *mean to say* is: I want us, y'know, I *only* want us to have a, a, a *loving, caring relationship."*

Well, it was the thought that counted with Mary Ann. I reached over and took one of her hands in mine. "Well, Mary Ann, everything in its time. We've only—"

Mary Ann stared at our hands. "Oh, that's so nice, Hal. That's so nice."

"We've only seen each other a couple of times, and—"

"Yeah, that's right, ain't it—isn't it?" Mary Ann exclaimed in surprise.

"And, well, we don't really need to aim for anything, or any type of relationship. It just happens. It's only when you look back that you see what you have."

"Yeah—like improv. Like when we do improv and Sergio films us. He get ideas that way, he says."

"A lot of just living every day is improv," I said, remembering my meeting with Chintsy Nuclear.

"Yeah! That's right, isn't it?"

"And who knows? Maybe after a while, we'll get tired of each other and we won't want to continue."

"Not continue?" Mary Ann cried.

"That happens, sometimes. In a relationship, you never really know what's going to happen."

Mary Ann's brow wrinkled deeply. "Yeah, that happened to Diana— this one girl in the company. She broke up with her boyfriend, Sonny, and gosh, he was just as nice a guy as you'd wanna meet. Gosh. Gosh. You wouldn't forget about me, would you, Hal?"

"It's a possibility. I mean, love is a—"

She was looking around with such horror in her eyes that I stopped. This possibility had never occurred to her. On one hand, I felt like a shit for having scared her with it—and wasn't I just knocking a hole in the wall in case I needed to escape? On the other, *she* was the one who wanted to grow up.

"It's happened to *me* with girlfriends. What I'm saying is, having a relationship with someone is a rough game, and you have to be ready for everything."

And again Mary Ann surprised me. "Yeah. Yeah, I forgot that: you said that on the plane. You told me you'd had a wife, and she turned into a traitor and did stuff she'd never done before you got married." She looked at me. "But you were nice to her, even then, too, weren't you? When you broke up. You said, 'I can't treat someone badly who's meant so much to me.'"

I shook my head: she was exactly right. "You sure have a good memory."

"You'll be nice to me, then, if we, y'know, break up?"

"I promise. And you'll be nice to me, too, right?"

"Oh, Hal, I'd never break up with you. That's why I kept buggin' Ruth to keep lookin' for you. 'Cause we have to be together. I've always thought that right from when you got off the plane in Chicago."

"Well, things happen, Mary Ann. Heck, there are a lot of good-looking guys in your company. One fine day, you start thinking—"

"Oh, Hal, don't say that! *Please* don't say that! They're all great guys and I love 'em like they're family, but they don't have, y'know, they, you can't, they can't, really, like, *tell* you anything. I mean, those guys, they know where to buy nice clothes and stuff, and they know how to make a big party and cocktails and they're great, wonderful dancers, but... I mean, none o' those guys are ever gonna work in a nuclear power plant."

I stared.

"Well, you know what I mean." And her hands shaped a ball that the meaning occupied.

We sat down on the sofa, silent for a long time, our hands joined, feeling the shift and shudder of the building around us and the distant sizzle of street life. Now and then Mary Ann, brow wrinkled, examined our hands. I finally suggested that we hit our respective hays.

Mary Ann agreed; we got up.

"Hal, there's a, can I, um, would you mind if I sort of gave you a, sort of a, a kind of question?" All this in a blurt, and it was clear that more was coming, and it was making Mary Ann's face red.

I checked my shoeshine. "Sure—ask away."

"Like, about, I mean, it's a *sex* kind of thing, like."

I made a mental note that my oxfords needed new strings. "Anything at all."

"Okay! Ah, do you ever, is it, when you want to hug somebody a lot—do you get that, ever, like?"

"What—want to hug somebody?"

"Yeah, like. Yeah."

"Sure, I like to hug people."

Annoyed: "Hal, I'm talkin' about women! You know... Huggin', like, a woman, I mean, pretty much a woman."

"Well, sure. Women especially."

The answer didn't satisfy her much, but damned if I had a better answer. "So, like, what do you do? The hug, I mean."

Plodding assiduously: "Well, if it's the right moment and the right place and the right person—er, *woman*—I hug her."

Mary Ann's brow wrinkled into a thousand waves now, and she sucked in her bottom lip, thinking. "Boy, that's a lot o' *right* stuff! Gosh!" she gasped.

"So how about it, Mary Ann?" I said finally. "You ask me, this looks like we have all the rights just where they have to be."

Slowly, checking off my list on her fingers: "Yeah, I mean, we got the right place—I mean, that's no problem, 'cause it's my own house—with Alba, I mean. And we got lotsa time. And golly, I'd sure like to hug you—and not, y'know, just quick, like in Chicago."

Had I hugged her in Chicago? I knew better than to question her perfect memory. "Well, then, let's get to it," I said, holding out my arms.

She frowned. "Now that ain't quite what you're s'posed to say, is it? I mean, the guy."

"Ah, right—sorry. Something a little more, ah, in the mood."

"Yeah, even in dance, you know, Sergio, he's always talkin' about *textura*. And that's kinda like, y'know, like, *feeling.*"

I put my hands on her shoulders. "Mary Ann, I really want to hug you, and really hard."

"Hey, that was great! Okay!" She shuffled closer. Then the uncertainty flared again. "Well, now, you gotta, like, rehearse this a little with me here. I mean it's my first time and all that. It's not like I, there's just, I don't, like...." She huffed angrily. "Well, I mean, to *start* with, do I put *my* arms under *your* arms, or do you wanna do that, like in Chicago?"

"Mary Ann, c'mon! You've hugged people before."

"But not a *man,* Hal! Not a real man. Please, Hal. Just tell me how, this first time."

I shrugged. "All right. Well, there are no rules, exactly. Ah, but generally *I* prefer to put my arms under the woman's, and you can kind of put your arms up around my shoulders." I took hers and put them in place. We were still a hand-width apart.

"Oh, yeah—we do that in this one jazz step where the guy lifts the girl by the waist."

"Right, and now we kind of squeeze together, nice and slow."

We started to, but Mary Ann jerked back. "Now, am I gonna be on the right or on the left? My head, I mean."

A choreographic question. "Tell you what. This first time, you pick a side, and I'll just follow you."

"Yeah. Yeah. Right. Improv. That's a good idea. So I'm leadin'. Okay." She was nervous. "Oh, and can I unbutton some o' your shirt?" she whispered. "Not many. Just one or two. Or maybe three."

"Help yourself."

The collar of my business shirt was already open one button. Fumbling, Mary Ann undid the buttons down below my chest and pushed apart the lapels a bit. "Oh wow! This is gonna be great!" she cried nervously.

"Okay, now raise your arms and put them around my shoulders."

She did. Mary Ann's shoulders were tight, and I told her to loosen up her arms. "That's it—loosen everything up. In a good hug, you press everything together."

This alarmed her. "Everything? Hal, I'm not a harlot, you know."

That word again. "No, of course not. Just enjoy yourself."

We hugged. I was taller than Mary Ann by a few inches, and I leaned my head against the side of hers—on her right, by the way. God, what a body! It was like embracing a tiger. She shifted, and her back muscles leapt like soldiers jumping to attention. My left hand was near the base of her spine—though I had an instinct not to explore any lower—and even there I could feel the perfect definition of her buttocks. Her shoulders moved forward, and they embraced me too. Now she seemed to grow into me a few inches. Warm waves fell of indescribable joy fell over me one after another as if I were at the very gates of heaven. I clutched her closer. A short, single note vibrated in my throat. I lowered my head and kissed her neck by the shoulder, amazed at how deeply felt this was.

"Oh! Oh, Hal!" She raised her head, and I kissed her more, even part of her throat.

Suddenly, she vibrated, the muscles along her spine rose and shivered under my palms, and she wrenched the length of her body, easily wrenching mine along with it. Again, again, again. And then she went slack again, molding so deeply into me that she might have gone unconscious. A sigh sped past my ear.

"Oh, Hal, you're wonderful, you're everything, you're the greatest!" she panted.

For the life of me, I could have sworn she'd had an orgasm.

I got up a little after five A.M. to catch a flight for Chicago. I had taken a shower, put on yesterday's clothes, and folded up the couch blankets when Mary Ann came out of her bedroom. She was wearing a white bathrobe, and even with her morning hair and the lumpiness of sleep in her face, she looked like a million. White always was her best color.

She came straight to me and put her arms around my waist and pressed her head to my chest. "Well, so I'll see you, like, some day, but maybe not like too long, okay?"

"Sure. We'll work something out. I'll have to come here for business anyways."

"Maybe you can come for a weekend some time, or, like, whatever." She clutched the sleeves of my suit jacket. "'Cause I'd really like to see you again, y'know, Hal. I mean, see you really often. Heck, I'd like to see *you* every day o' the year!"

"Me, too. So don't—"

"Really? You too?" she screeched. Then: "That was dumb—sorry." She straightened up and pulled away slightly. "'Cause that'd be great,

y'know, like, if you wanted to see me too."

"Sure. Heck, I want a free ticket to your big show."

She slapped my shoulder. "You rat! You big ol' double rat!"

"Ow! That hurt!"

"Oh, Hal! I'm sorry! I'll never do—"

"Mary Ann, I was just kidding." Which was a lie.

She walked over to the bookshelf, took a small pair of scissors there and, to my amazement, snipped off a lock of hair on the back of her head.

"Your hairdresser is going to smack you one," I said.

"Don't matter." She held out the lock of hair to me. "Alba gave one to Javier, just so he'd have a part of her to take back to Spain with him. 'Cept hers was longer."

"That will do just fine," I said awkwardly, looking around for a place to put it. My pocket wouldn't do. Finally I opened my briefcase, shook a CD disk out of its envelope, and put it in there.

Then, before I even knew what I was doing, I pulled her face to mine and kissed her. She melted against me.

"Oh, Hal. That was so nice!" she gasped. "I mean, you didn't even tell me that was comin'!" Then she began to throw her arms around me.

She stopped.

"Wait. Sorry. I mean." She jerked her arms straight at her side, fingers flaring out. "Hal, can I please give you one more kiss before you go?" she said with great control. It might have been a dinner invitation to the White House.

"Why not? You're my girlfriend, aren't you? That's what you've been telling everybody, at least."

Her brow crumpled into an ocean of waves, and she looked down, thinking. "Yeah, that's right. I got a boyfriend. Alba's got a boyfriend, and so do I. Yeah." And she nodded floorwards in a couple of tiny jerks and stared for several seconds.

"Mary Ann, I've gotta run. How about that kiss?"

"Oh! Right, yeah. Sorry."

After that:

"Please come back soon," she said, still holding me. "We got a couple performances in Boston this weekend, but that's a pretty near city, I guess. After that, y'know, we'll just be rehearsing for the new show."

"I will. I'll come soon—promise," I whispered, and kissed her coarse, red hair. It scraped my cheek as she nodded.

Ten minutes later, in a cab, I was amazed at what I had done—sheepish. I felt as if I had taken candy from a baby or seduced the neighbors' daughter. How had I got so caught up in a moment like that? How could I lead her on? "You fool, she's only twenty!" I muttered. I had a few more things to tell The Beast Inside of Me, but the taxi driver was trying to get my attention:

"Hey, yo. M'man. *M'man!*"

Shaking myself: "Yeah. What's up?"

"You want me to slow up for this party followin' you? Or they know the way?"

"Someone's *following* me?"

The man nodded. "Yeah—what I figured. You didn't know, did ya?"

"No."

"Big-ass four-by-four, five-six cars back, left lane? Noticed 'em just after flag-down."

I had a notion to turn around and take a look, but checked it. "You sure?"

"'Member that dippy-divin' shit we were doin' ta get onna the freeway ramp? Your man hustled his ass right along with us."

"You make a habit of watching for people following you?"

He laughed darkly. "Make a habit o' watchin' out for any large-type mo-fos lookin' to put me onna six-o'clock news, 'cause turns out maybe my fare's carryin' two keys o' angel dust in his briefcase. Happened just last month, middle o' day shift: stopped the cab, cold-blasted the fare, did the brother right in his seat. Ain't gonna happen to me, no sir."

I shrugged. "Maybe they're just going to the airport."

"Yeah, and my momma's from fuckin' Norway."

I turned around and looked. I could just see it, a Jeep Cherokee fifty yards back, one lane more over to the left. The windshield was tinted.

"Here's the deal, m'man," said the cabbie. "I'm gonna change lanes—like I'm gonna go down Hutchinson P-way? He changes lanes too, you out a hunnerd bucks."

"And if he doesn't?"

"JFK onna house, m'man."

I looked back again at the Jeep. "You're on. Go."

I lost a "hunnerd," but it was worth it: I knew now that Edgerton Salk played for keeps.

Others were playing for keeps, too; over the following week I found out how much.

I called Mary Ann in the evenings, though only for a minute; the phone is fine for business, but as a medium for romance it works about as well as, say, full-dress sex. Once she sent me another photo of a note left by Alba to say that she was going to a restaurant for lunch after rehearsal. Why she couldn't put on her glasses and read it herself was beyond me; maybe there was something to what Alba had said about Mary Ann being dyslexic.

I received the picture of that note was in Los Angeles, where I was talking to Chintsy's two competitors, covering my still-exposed backside against an eventual elimination from their projects; AllPoint could make it on foreign projects, but it was good to keep contact with the American side, who sub-contract nearly all of their control-room designs. Each firm received me cordially; nobody called me a fucking liberal. They explained their points of view—they were uncomfortable working with us while we were contracting with Chintsy, and I told them that I understood that. Both companies said that they would keep me informed of their upcoming projects, one of them neutrally, the other seriously.

That night, when I arrived back in Chicago, Mary Ann called. She had been attacked by two men that evening outside the subway station, walking the fifty yards to her apartment building. Nothing terrible—at least in the sense that she wasn't injured; Mary Ann had fought them off, and the attackers got the worst of it.

"These two guys came up behind me, and one grabbed me around the neck and kept me from screaming, and the other guy bent down to grab my legs, but I got a leg free and kicked him right in the face, and I think I broke somethin', 'cause his mouth went way off to the side like it was just, like, hangin' on by the skin, y'know? Anyways, he ran off to their car in the street holdin' his mouth, and the other guy dropped me and ran after him. And I was on the sidewalk and got up, and I was kinda crying, but then a real nice couple came runnin' up, and they helped me. They didn't take anything—the creeps, I mean."

"And you're okay?"

"Yeah, 'cept my toe hurts a little from where I kicked that one guy. I got a good aim on him, y'know. I musta knocked his mouth clean off."

I could imagine. A kick from one of those perfect legs would have stunned a rhino. I asked a few more questions, which gleaned little. One thing that struck me, though, was that the "creeps" had not said a word the whole time, and their car had pulled up alongside the cars parked at the curb. These two facts, together with the idea that they had not gone directly for her bag indicated that they were experienced in the work and that the objective was Mary Ann, not her money. For rape? For ransom?

Or for the blackmailing of the boyfriend? Would Edgerton Salk go that far?

I asked if she had gone to the police.

"Oh, Hal, Alba said I shoulda—so did the couple that walked me to the apartment. But I don't know. All that stuff—police and all—just kinda scares me. Besides, those guys just drove away. I didn't get the license number or nothin'. And I didn't see their faces. They wore these masks over their eyes—you know, like Zorro?"

Too bad. It wouldn't have been too hard to trace a man with a broken jaw. And to work the trail back to Edgerton Salk and some quietly-retained security service would have been worth the effort—but only mine, not Mary Ann's.

"So anyways, from now on, if I have to walk alone to the apartment, one o' the guys is gonna come get me or somethin', since we all live there, y'know. I'll call from the subway."

"What about going *to* the subway from the studio? That's a rough neighborhood."

"Oh, Sergio always walks with me."

"Good."

In the background, I heard Alba calling. "Hal! Mary Ann was magnificent! She was Superwoman! She turned them into little bits! She is invincible! 'Invincible'—is that correct?"

"Ah. Just a sec'. Um, Hal? Is 'invincible' a word? 'Cause, y'see, that's what ya say in Spanish."

I left for Iceland the next morning and returned Friday afternoon; Frank had called the office again—for the first time in a couple of weeks—and I couldn't stand the idea of spending the upcoming weekend pushing away the thought of him. So I called him. I hoped that just maybe I could get rid of him once and for all.

I wasn't so ready as Mary Ann to tell him to go to hell; if I could figure out his interest in Mary Ann, I would. Not for nothin' had Frank swung "ol' Bessie" up to Chicago and left her "suckin' up rates" while he played touchy-feely with me. He didn't seem so interested anymore, as I could tell by the lower frequency of calls. But it was better to get to the bottom of this than to let it slide.

I called Frank from AllPoint's silent office, the cleaning lady just starting her round.

He answered. In the background, Bessie droned along. I told him that Mary Ann and I had gotten together and had a long conversation over drinks. I said nothing about her profession or whereabouts.

"So when was this?" Frank demanded.

"A few days ago."

"Not before?"

"Nope."

"Right." This with a husky trenchancy, and I suddenly had the notion that he knew I was lying.

So I added, "We set up the meet well before that, of course."

"And you didn't tell me?" he snapped. "Didn't I call you just two weeks ago? Fuck, mister, we're here sweatin' bullets to hear from her."

"We?"

"Me and the Reverent—her old man."

"Well, I'm sure you can understand that I wanted to talk to Mary Ann first to be sure it was all right to talk with *you*."

"What the fuck?" He spat, and I cringed, thinking what his truck must smell like. "I told you not to tell her I'm checkin' up on her. Can't you follow simple directions? What kinda motherfuckin' skunk are you? I'm her brother! Why wouldn't she wanna talk to me?"

"Why? Frank—let me tell you a story. Guy walked into my office a while ago, said he's checking up on the joker his sister is going out with. All right—little eighteenth-century of him, but I went along with it. The funny thing was, though, I hadn't met the sister yet, and I didn't know the guy. What's more, the guy insisted that he didn't want his sister to know about his visit. Okay, he leaves, time passes, and I get to thinking: Is she really his sister? Or is she just some poor kid who witnessed him, say, turning the mailman into a lampshade?"

Frank changed a gear and grunted doing it.

"Don't get me wrong here: I don't mind helping you out," I went on, "but it's got to be on the up and up."

"What ain't on the up and up?" Frank cried.

"Well, since you asked: turns out Mary Ann isn't all that crazy about touching you with a ten-foot-pole ever again. In fact, she got a little pale when the subject of you and her family came up. First she wants to know why you want to talk with her."

"Well, she's my—" He stopped. "The Reverent wants to see his daughter. He gots a right. Ain't that enough?"

"Not in this case, it isn't. Mary Ann told me a few not-so-nice things about life in Arkansas. Sounds to me like her donkey Bolts took better care of her than anybody else."

"That... Don't that just... Fuckin', fuckin' little *Stupe-face!*" he rasped through gritted teeth. After some unmentionables: "Well, hell, *I* didn't do anything to her."

"That's true. The way she tells it, you didn't come off too badly."

A pause. "Just what'd she tell you about?"

"That you and your brothers worked her to the bone. That if she stepped out of line, she got locked in the barn."

"That all?"

"Isn't that enough?" I snapped—instead of listening more closely to what Frank was saying; but hindsight is clear and cruel. "I said you didn't come off badly, Frank. I *didn't* say that you ever gave her so

much as a bedtime story. If I'd have come across Mary Ann ten years ago, you'd be in jail for child abuse—the Reverend, too."

This amused Frank. "Yeah—try that with *him*," he chuckled. "Look, we're gonna get this done one way or another. You playin' ball with us or not?"

"That right? And just how would you get it done without me?"

A silence. "We got means. Point is, you got no right, keepin' a man from seein'—"

"No, but Mary Ann does. In the first place, she's twenty, she's an adult, and she can see whomever she damn well pleases. Second—"

"She's my goddamn sister and—"

"Shut up. Second, she trusts me. And third, I'm your only connection to her, Frank, and you know it, so you'd better play nice."

I listened hard for his reaction to that, but heard only the scratching of his cigarette lighter. "Nice... fuck."

"Now—last chance: you convince me there's a good reason for Mary Ann to sit down across a table from you, and I'll talk to her about it."

A puff on the weed. "All right—a good reason." Another huff. "See if this is good enough for you: the family farm is gonna get broke up. Mary Ann gets a share. We're talkin' eighty-ninety grand apiece, dependin' on how the auction goes. And that's *after* the fuckin' government takes its bite."

An inheritance. That would explain both the urgency and Frank's selfish selflessness. "Someone died, is that it?"

"Yeah. Grampaw. Farm was in his name. Everybody gets a piece—me, the Reverent, ever'body."

I stepped carefully, and not only because Mary Ann had never mentioned a grandfather. "So what's the deal? You need Mary Ann to sign papers or something?"

"That's right. Lawyer says nobody gets nothin' till ever'body puts down his John Hancock."

I listened to Bessie sing for a few seconds. "Okay, Frank. That sounds reasonable. Tell you what: I'll run this by Mary Ann. Why don't you give me the name and number of this lawyer, and—"

"I told ya more 'n some outsider's got a right ta know! You get her on the line while she still got a shot at her eighty thou!"

"Forget it," I said simply. "And get it into your head right now, Frank: Mary Ann doesn't take a step without me."

"You ain't her husband! You got no right! What—now she's got some money comin', you think you're gonna get in on the action and take your—"

I interrupted, wanting to get to my weekend a little sooner. "I'm her friend and that's good enough for you. I'll talk to Mary Ann and *if she wants to,* set up a meeting with you. Call you in a few days." I didn't trouble with a good-bye; Frank wasn't worth an expenditure of courtesy. I just hung up.

And heaved myself back in my chair, staring out the window at a mixed, overcast downtown Chicago. Across the way in other offices I saw more cleaning people, heads down, concentrated on the detritus of the workday.

"Why the hell am I doing all this? Why?" I blurted. "For a twenty-year-old girl I hardly know, not exactly worldly, kind of a pain in the ass, and definitely lots of issues behind those big, dark eyes. *Why?*"

It wasn't for her good looks or her body. The relationship had no such heat. Yet the longer I sat there staring into the gray, what echoed in my mind was that sight of Mary Ann in the studio jerking tight the tie of her skirt and pushing back her hair. I didn't know why, and really still don't. Maybe it was, if not Cupid's arrow, his tap on the shoulder. For that memory had a whispered promise to it, like a quiet word to the wise that Mary Ann was rising, rising like one of those new Pacific islands surging steamy from the sea, and in her good time would rise to the occasion. As she said over and over, she was getting better, there were just a lot of things she didn't know yet.

10 A few office odds and ends—performance reviews, which I've always hated but which Ralph insisted upon—finished me off for a Friday. I was putting on my jacket when my office phone rang, and to my galactic surprise, it was Sheena Biggs. She was downstairs in the lobby. She had been

in the offices of a cosmetics company down the street from AllPoint. She wanted to apologize for her scene in the hotel. How about a drink?

Well, what the hell? I figured. If she wanted to apologize, the least I could do was listen to her. Besides, it warmed my heart to think of my brother Henry, the bigshot Hollywood lawyer, envying me a drink with a famous beauty.

But as with most famous beauties, Sheena Biggs exuded a vaguely absurd persona. It was as if she were two people: Sheena on the left, her beauty on the right. She wore a splashily flowered knee-length dress and chunky pearls at her ears and around her neck—part of the "back to the 50s" look that was popular that year, or at least that week. Shaking hands, I wondered if the cosmetics company had given her a make-over; or perhaps she had prepped herself especially in order to win another endorsement contract. Whatever. Through all those layers, I doubted she could feel her quarterback's kiss.

She steered me across the street and down half a block to a club I would happily have paid not to enter: a disco-type bar decorated in minimalism and loneliness, with corporate music designed to hammer your chest. The lyrics described all the invigorating things bad girls will do for you if you'll only open your heart to them. The walls consisted of back-lit photos of illuminated cities, all lined up as if they were one, and maybe they were; all cats are black in the city night.

I followed Sheena through the writhing dancers to a glass-walled-off space where ferns drooped from ledges around the sides. Here the music relented just enough for conversation to take place. Above us was the glass-floored entrance to the place, so that we had a fine view of the public sole as it trotted into the joint. Call it art.

"You're sorry about what, exactly?" I asked, once the waitress had left our drinks and I could get down to business. "Kissing me? Or saying shitty things about Mary Ann?"

My experience with women aware of their beauty has inclined me to severity. Women take this in two ways. Mature women are grateful; they understand from the start that business will be business. Immature women don't like it at all because they realize their looks won't carry them over the potholes. Sheena was the second.

She thought this over and apparently considered the effort of thinking not worth it. "Oh, just everything in general?" she said, and I realized with dismay that she was one of these tiresome women who spoke in questions. "Like just sorry in general?"

This was bad news. Sheena was after something else. A heads-bowed couple across the way was stonily sharing a last drink before divorce. Another couple was eagerly talking sports, the man's coat sprawled over the table. Telma had told me once that the place had a reputation for good strawberry margaritas; I sampled mine and found she was right.

"Well, maybe you should apologize to her, too," I suggested.

Sheena grunted and sipped her cocktail. "I only apologize to guys," she said with a mock-flirty grin.

"I have a feeling that you don't do that much to us, either," I said.

Hurt: "Hey, I *said* I was sorry. I saw AllPoint Engineering on the building directory when I passed by, and like, all during the meeting with those people in LikeLuscious Inc.? I was trying to remember where I'd seen it? And then just at the end of the meeting, I remembered: 'Yeah! Hal from AllPoint Engineering!' So I thought 'Why not see if he's free?'"

I gave this a 40-60 chance of being true. LikeLuscious did have a big building just a block down from AllPoint, but Sheena didn't sound remorseful. "What were you doing with LikeLuscious?"

"Oh, they pitched me for a promo job—on moisturizing facial cream and night mask stuff? I was like, 'Yeah, sure, I'm going to rub this shit on my face for a piddly hundred grand. Come back when you have some folding money to offer.' Did you know that Mary Ann can't read?"

Apropos of nothing. It took me a moment to catch up. "No."

"That's right. Can't read her own name."

So *that* was the reason for her visit: to do more dirt to Mary Ann. "Everybody's got a problem," I said carefully.

"She ever tell you about the Bee Gees thing?"

"No."

"Figures." She took a heavy slurp of her manhattan; she had the alcoholic's habits. "We were in this mall—in Fort Lauderdale? We had a performance there."

"Poor Sergio." I had an urge to leave—it was clear which way the conversation was going, and I didn't like it. But I stayed: I was suddenly hungry to hear about Mary Ann.

"Mary Ann said she liked a song that was playing from the ceiling—Musak, you know? She'd heard it a bunch of times but she didn't know the singer. Know who it was? The Beatles. McCartney singing 'Let it Be.'"

My head rose slightly in surprise. Sheena's painted mouth burst wide, and that reedy, world-shattering laughter exploded like bats out of a cave.

"That's right, sweetie—the Beatles. I said, 'I'll show you where it is, Arkansas, c'mon,' and I took her over to a shop? And then I got an idea. Instead of the Beatles, I pulled out the Bee Gees? I put it in her hand, and I say, 'This is the album.' She looks it over and says"—Sheena imitated her, and well—"'Oh, thank you, Sheena, thanks so much!' and she runs off to the counter to buy it." Another rictal laugh.

"She have her glasses with her?"

"Honey, the words 'Bee Gees' covered the whole CD. Mr. Magoo could've read it."

I was thinking about being in the restaurant with Mary Ann. *What do you have that's really good?* she'd said. Then she ordered not from the menu, but from what the waiter had suggested.

"And you have to take advantage of a person's weakness?"

But Sheena had been on the cover of *Cosmopolitan* and didn't need to answer questions from peons. She took another swallow of her drink, plucked out the cherry, and slid it off the little sword with her teeth. "We get out in the hallway of the mall, and I nail her. I said, 'You can't read, can you? That's not the Beatles. I handed you the Bee Gees!' And she gets all pissed—ever seen her pissed?"

"No."

"Pulls back her fist way back like this"—she demonstrated—"and she was going to hit me! The fool! Right there in the mall, can you believe it? And I say, 'Oh my! Y'all gonna hit me with yo' big bad fist? Go ahead, Arkansas—and I'll tell the whole world you can't read your name.' *That* fucked her up good. She goes all teary and says, 'Well, golly-gosh, Sheena, I cain't help it. I got dyslexia. I was born this way.'"

"You're lucky she didn't hit you," I said, just to slow her down. "A few days ago, a couple of guys mugged her coming out of the subway, and she broke one guy's jaw."

Sheena stopped chewing her cherry.

"God's truth. Left it hanging on by the cheeks. Sounds like she should have cleaned your clock, too—like Santiago. He sure did a job on you."

"He's a motherfucking rapist."

"At least he got the message across. They tell me that after that, you left Mary Ann alone."

Sheena had let me speak only as long as it took her to guzzle the rest of her manhattan. "The trouble I'm having now, though," she reflected, "is, should I mention that in interviews? Arkansas with her little reading problem. I mean, since the whole New York art scene has gone like ape-shit about me?"

"It has?"

"Yeah, about me moving from Serg's little outfit to Raymond Radow. Me, I don't know if I should talk about Mary Ann, but I mean, it *is* true."

"Ah, so *that's* what this is all about! You're with *Radow* now. Backed by Chintsy Inc."

Sheena wrinkled her nose. "What's *that* got to do with anything?"

"What—did Edgerton Salk put you up to this?"

"Who?"

"Salk—head of Chintsy Nuclear. Slender, silver-haired, military comb-over?"

Sheena leaned forward and caressed my cheek. A just-between-us wink. "Actually, sweetie, it was like *my* idea? I thought, 'I have to be in Chicago. Why not pass by Hal's place and give him a little warning?'"

I pushed her hand away. "A *warning*."

"I talked it over with Ray, and he said, 'Great. Nothing like a little controversy to raise ticket sales.' You know: a little joke? A little taste of what show business is all about? Y'see, Arkansas needs a good lesson in who she's messing with. You'll find out on Monday morning."

I thought about this. "Bullshit. Salk put you up to this. He's trying to squeeze me. That's why he tried to get Mary Ann snatched on the street."

"*What?*"

"You know what I'm talking about—and if you don't, you'd damn well better find out what you've fallen into the middle of."

"Edgerton Salk," Sheena murmured. It made no impression on her. "Well, now that you mention it, dearie, Ray and I *are* having lunch with some top Chintsy execs next week. He thought my presence would help to pull like another hundred grand out of them? I'll ask him."

Was it a case of *me and my big mouth?* I couldn't decide. "Do that. And tell him for me that I'm not backing down. He'll know what that means."

"Okeedokee." She got up. "And don't forget what I told you: Monday morning. A nice, big surprise for you and little Miss Arkanshit."

"Fine. I'd see you out, but this drink is terrific."

"I wouldn't let you, shitface."

And she waltzed out, wiggling her hips like the whore she was. A moment later, above me, I saw the soles of her scarcely-used shoes.

I sat puzzling over her warning and sipping my pleasant margarita. I took out my cell phone and, after going through Information, called LikeLuscious Inc. Somebody cranky answered, and I asked if Sheena Biggs was still there.

"Nah, left an hour ago. Hey, you her agent? Listen, about these head shots you sent over. I didn't say anything to Sheena, but you can clean your crotch with 'em. They must be five years and ten kilos of coke old. Okay, we gave her a make-over for the screen test, but that face has 'I oughta be on the wagon' written all over it."

I said I wasn't her agent, and the man apologized, saying that for endorsing the product—just a few posters in shopping malls—Sheena had asked for two hundred thousand dollars.

I hung up, feeling like a fool. Sheena had come to Chicago for the LikeLuscious contract and thought she'd make a little mischief. And I'd put her on to Edgerton Salk.

I wondered what Monday would bring.

11

Monday was not old by the time I'd found out. At nine-thirty, I got a call from Mary Ann, which was odd, since she would have been starting rehearsal. She told me about the Boston shows, and especially her well-received solo at the end of it, much applauded. The newspaper review was glowing. "Sergio's still makin' some changes about how we're using some black screens at the end, but it's real good. I just disappear right off the stage at the end."

But that was the high point of the conversation. She sounded uncertain, almost sad. Finally, I asked her if anything was wrong.

"Well, yeah. Alba said I oughta, like, just, talk to ya. I mean, it's kinda dumb, and I'm not even sure it's you, but—"

"Not sure that *what's* me?"

"Um, well, Hal, this is kinda, I don't really wanna--" A pause while she gathered herself. "Can I ask you a kind of personal question?"

"Sure."

"Do you, is there, do you think... Well, what I mean is: do we, like, have a *full, interpersonal commitment*—like, to each other, I mean?"

I slumped in my chair. I coughed up some feeble, imbecilic, manikin-worthy reply now lost to history.

"Um, well, one of the other girls—Janice, she's a real, real nice girl, she's from Vermont—she was talkin'—well, not today, but one day when we were on the bus goin' to a performance?—and said that it was important to have it."

"Well, I guess, we have what we have," I replied helplessly.

"Oh, Hal, that's not an answer!"

"Well, the question isn't any great shakes, either."

"I mean, well, gosh, Hal, am I, are we like, like—gosh—are we *okay?*"

I looked with longing at my computer screen, which showed ruler-straight rows of numbers. The windows beside me held back a cruel, rainy Chicago morning. Out in the office, Jake Skilling and Darla Valpajjee, who carpooled 65 miles each way, were shaking rain out of their umbrellas. Jake pressed his hands together and bowed an Oriental apology, which I accepted with a wave of the hand.

Finally, I gathered my sanity. "Mary Ann, I like our relationship, and you like it, and that's enough."

She said nothing, and I blurted, "But I hope it's going to grow, Mary Ann. I really do. I'm really glad we met."

"Yeah? Well, gosh, me, too! Hey!"

"But—try to understand here, Mary Ann—hopes and dreams and commitment all of that cheap romance-novel stuff—come *on!*"

"Oh, yeah, right, but...." She swallowed noisily. "So, like, you and Sheena, you're not...."

"Sheena. Sheena Biggs, you mean?"

"Yeah. And, like, your picture in the newspaper today? It's not like I bought it or nothin', you know. It's just that, goin' into the subway there's this kid handin' out newspapers to everybody."

"Uh, yeah," I said slowly.

"I mean, it's free, like. And there's this picture o' you and Sheena sittin' at a table, like, talkin', y'know? And Sheena's touchin' you on the cheek? Alba told me the headlines—'cause I didn't have my glasses on me. And she said the headline says, 'Who is Sheena's new lover boy?'"

"What?" I snapped.

"And Alba said this article, like? It said that you had a, um, like a cocktail with her on Friday."

"Yeah, that's true. Sheena just kind of showed up at my office. Look, this is the story." Briefly, I explained what happened, adding the bit about my call to the cosmetics company. "You see, she wanted to make you jealous. She wanted to give you a shock. She was hoping that the photo would make you think that we're having an affair or something." Meanwhile, I was working out whos, whys, hows, angles: the table Sheena had steered us to, the couple sitting off to my right, the odd coat on their table. *Yes,* I thought. *Bravo. Nice work. Radow's company got a nice shot of P.R. He probably paid for the photographer and the extras himself.*

"Sheena did that?" Mary Ann said in disbelief.

"Well, she was pretty angry about getting fired, and she's probably trying to take revenge on you and Sergio."

"Oh. Yeah. Yeah. I get it." A pause, and I could imagine her brow wrinkling up. "She always was a pretty sad person. She's like a person who can't get a splinter outta her finger."

"So don't worry. You're my girlfriend, and I only want one at a time. I only agreed to the drink so that I could tell my brother Henry and make him jealous."

"Oh yeah, the one who was a football star and now he's a rich lawyer in Hollywood, right? And he broke two o' your ribs once playin' in the yard?"

"You know about that?"

"From the plane, sure."

Jesus, what a memory! I thought. "Right. Well, anyways, there's nothing to the drink. It was just a drink, and she called me a shitface at the end."

"Yeah. Yeah, that's just what Alba said. I'm sorry, Hal. Golly, I am so *stupid!*"

"Mary Ann—stop that!" Alba squawked from somewhere close.

"Okay. Well, Hal, I better go. We're gonna pound some nails here."

"Mary Ann, I have to go out to New York again this week, so—"

"Oh, great!" A whisper: "Can I give you another hug, just a little one?"

"Actually I'm hoping for a great, big one."

"Yeah! Okay! You got it!"

"I'll let you know the day. Do you have a performance this week?"

"Just in a high school tomorrow afternoon. And Sergio says it's not too far—in Yonkers. Isn't that a funny name?"

After the usual, I hung up and called Edgerton Salk's secretary. She worked me in for a ten-forty-five meeting for Wednesday. I also asked her if she was hoping to meet Sheena Biggs later that day. She said Sheena was coming tomorrow, on Tuesday, but they were all going right to Chintsy's executive restaurant for lunch: "No time for us little people who just want an autograph," she sighed.

Damn.

Come Wednesday, Edgerton Salk wouldn't talk to me till I'd been softened up by the underlings again—just Mid-Career and Entry Level this time; Ms. Passing, it seemed, had found lawyerly things to do. Entry Level entertained me with more campus clichés and his spiky crew cut, Mid-Career declaimed in wonder that I *still* couldn't see Chintsy's point of view. On and on for an hour. I won't bore you with the blow-by-absurd-blow, other than to note that they did raise to twenty-five percent the proportion of the debt outstanding that they were willing to pay. And yes, Mid-Career had had to fight for it.

I expressed disappointment, and added an archaic homily on the theme that work performed competently ought to be paid for in full, on time, and without negotiations. This was considered "just so not today" by Entry Level, and "a total lack of understanding" by Mid-Career.

At noon, Salk ambled in behind his avuncular, 32-percent-tax-bracket smile to hear how things were going. Entry Level informed him in four or five jagged phrases.

"Hal, can what I'm hearing be true?" he said incredulously. Cheerfulness scratched like fingernails down the chalkboard of his silver-haired distinction. That vicious mouth of his—no sign of lips that ever kissed a girl, just a hole in his head—would gladly have ordered me chained in the dungeon till I rotted.

"What can I say? I always seem to be the bad guy here," I said with a smile.

"'Bad guy' is putting it mildly," said Entry Level. "Genghis Khan same-pages more than you do."

"'Same-paged.' He's dead," I pointed out, which was the least I could do if he was going to toss out verbs like that.

Salk smiled and shook his head as if he were dealing with an unruly five-year-old. "Here's an idea, Hal. I'm hungry. How about joining me for lunch up on the fifty-eighth? Maybe a decent steak will help you see the light."

E dgerton Salk, unlike most men who had served in "Nam," enjoyed talking about the experience. He had risen to lieutenant and had delicious memories of the "free-fire zone":

"Those were the days, friend. No rules, no holds barred, civilians long cleared out—the way it ought to be," he breezed over his rare-to-medium. "Just us and them and the terrain. You get so much in weaponry, and you have to get from Point A to Point B. Orders: take down as much personnel as your trigger-finger's worth. You're too slow, you get shot—tough titty. Everybody knows the rules, no need to explain or apologize. Got three radios shot off my back. Don't care. We did it, and we won."

My fork, full of impaled salad, stopped short of my mouth. "Conventional wisdom has it we *lost* the Vietnam War."

"Housewife crap," he scoffed. "History for the fast-food manager. Not the reality, not by a long shot. Listen: we knocked Commie Vietnam right out of the ballpark. Took it thirty years to come back as a functioning entity." He put down his utensils and laid his hands flat on the table, eyes wide in mirth. "And when it did? It was a *capitalist* country, for Christ's sake! Bill Gates ticker-taped through the streets! Marvelous."

Military life clings to a man or woman long after they have left the service—I know this from my days working on our nuclear arsenal—and Edgerton Salk, who had worked in the Pentagon for twelve years after the war, was a classic: the part in the hair straight as a compass needle, the brittle manners, the elegant lunch he gave me accompanied by jolly tales of heads blown off right through the trees they had hidden behind. His billfold—he paid for the meal by waving his Chintsy i.d. card over a chic little gizmo held at a respectful distance by the maitre d'—had a combination lock that he activated by thumbing a sequence of buttons on one side. I asked if a thief couldn't simply open the billfold with a knife—by its folded side, for example—and Salk launched another ugly giggle.

"Yeah, he could—with luck, might lose an eye." He flapped his wallet in front of my puzzled face. "Israeli. Has a wafer. Point is to blow up the plastic, but if collateral happens, more power to it."

The steak was very good, as was the wine, but I warned Salk as we finished that they had done little to change my opinion.

"The lunch is a consolation prize, Hal, tell you the truth. Figured you deserved something for putting up so much pushback." He raised his glass in honor of my pushback, so I did, too. "Damn fine negotiator—y'ought to work for us," he added.

"Uff! You could never afford me," I said, mock-seriously.

"We'll see."

He signaled the waiter that we were going upstairs and to have our coffee brought up.

"Upstairs" meant the roof of the building, which we reached by a special elevator that connected it to the dining room. Beside a heliport and slightly below it, since the heliport was actually a raised platform on the roof itself, a pleasant private café-bar was marked off by a lawn of artificial turf, nice and bouncy like the kind Henry used to smear running backs into. A little thicket of Parisian-café-type tables and chairs populated it, and Plexiglas in a semi-circle cut most of the wind. A deferent Romanian waiter brought up our coffee with a tray of sugar cookies, left the pot on the table, and walked back to the elevator and disappeared. We were alone under an April sky of great, bulky clouds whose shoulders the sun peeked over like the short guy in the crowd. The military man was testing my mettle, trying to hurry me by getting me cold.

"Is this where you heave off your disagreeable suppliers?" I asked, admiring the view of the Lower East Side and, through the interstices of cement, the brooding sea beyond.

"We use the chopper," Salk replied evenly. "Middle of the night. Haul 'em a mile out to sea." From behind the bar he took out a pair of binoculars as big as two half-liter beer bottles and stood scanning the skyline.

"Anybody making love?" I inquired.

"Carrot and stick, friend. Carrot: thirty percent of contract and two new offers—Scottsdale and Yucatan—within ten months, biz-as-per-usual, our eternal gratitude to a supplier for helping us through a rough spot."

"Thank you, Edgerton," I sighed, "but AllPoint has a full schedule of work straight through till—"

"Stick. Your arrest in either Ukraine or Turkey the next time you set foot on their soil."

"Arrest? *What?*"

"For rape, and don't you try to deny it, friend. Both girls have the semen to prove it." Salk pulled his eyes from the binoculars long enough to leer at me. "How could you be so dumb as to leave your load behind in the condom? If you were my employee, I'd fire you and give you a boot in the can on your way out." He went back to scanning the skyline.

I froze, frightened. In both countries, AllPoint was finishing projects. Even if I could beat the charges with greater bribes, the process would take months, maybe years. But no—I could send someone. Maybe Perry, a young, new engineer who had recently entered the firm: he was eager to travel, sharp too. I could bring him up to speed on those projects; Jean-Jacques and Ralph would understand. But they would also understand that we were getting into serious blackmail and would have to deal with the police.

"Now, you can probably work around me on those projects, one way or another. They're just a warning—let you know I'm serious."

"So there's more."

"Uh-huh." He turned the binoculars towards the airport. "Know what I learned in 'Nam? Never torture the guy you want information from. You want cooperation? Put his comrade on the rack. Or his brother. Or his *girl*. Then you get answers." He adjusted the focus. "And let's get one thing straight: I never, never, no matter how much I had to fight for information, I *never* finished a guy off after I got answers. Patched 'em up and threw 'em back in the pond. If he killed one of our guys a month later, more power to him."

"How admirable. Hey, your mother never taught you not to play with binoculars when you're holding a conversation, did she?" I asked, as Salk continued to scan New York real estate he didn't own yet.

"See where we're going with this about your girl, or do I need to spell it out?"

"No. It's just too bad she got away from your boys the first time."

"Who got away?"

"My girlfriend. When those two thugs grabbed her in the street. Sounds like she kicked the one guy's face clean off."

Salk lowered the glasses. A snarl: "I don't know a goddamn thing about that!"

"Oh, sure. And you don't know a goddamn thing about the car that followed me after our last meeting, either, do you? Not even your mother would believe that."

Salk's jagged mouth began to form a word and then stopped. "No. No. Chrissakes, this isn't some ad hoc... I never said...." But he was thinking, and deeply, hands on his hips now, the binoculars dangling from his neck. His mouth drew together in a wrinkled little pucker, as if closed by a duffle-bag's string. Finally: "At least that's what *orders* were!" he growled. "Wait here. I'm going to see if someone got *creative* on me."

He walked away to the bar, dropping the binoculars on it with a bang, and out a back door and up to the heliport, where he talked on his cell phone for a good ten minutes. He came back much relieved.

"Looks like you're making more enemies than are good for you, Mr. Dormund. Answer's no—no snatching, no following, no girl, no nothing. Now, do we have an understanding, or do I have to make use of Miss Biggs's excellent information? And by god I will. Nothing physical, mind. That's for amateurs. But we can make her life pure hell."

It wasn't a moment for understandings—my mind was in a tornado—so I put him off, saying I had to speak to my partners, and left.

What was going on? If not Salk, it had to be Frank behind the kidnapping attempt. And not just Frank, but someone with big money—enough to pay people to follow me around till I led them to Mary Ann.

For the first time, I felt the presence of fanatical evil.

12 I booked a midnight flight to Chicago—things were getting a little too hot for my liking, and I didn't want to use the next morning getting back. I worked with my computer through the afternoon in a Starbucks. Among other things I signaled Jean-Jacques and Ralph that we needed to talk seriously about Chintsy. I also told our office manager to call Felix Weikert, our security contractor, and tell him to meet me the next morning in the office ready to sweep and sniff and jerk up the rugs. Too many people knew about my movements and doings and kissings, and I wanted to know how.

That evening, I picked up Alba and Mary Ann in the studio and took them out for dinner. Mary Ann didn't make a fuss about what she was wearing this time. "But this looks all right, don't it?" she said as we waited in the restaurant lobby to be seated. She was looking down at her jeans and high heels and a light-blue blouse, which had a colorful Indian embroidery on the shoulders.

"She chose this because we expected you," Alba said with a wink.

"You rat! You weren't s'posed to tell him. I wanted to seem more grown up."

"Then tell him the truth, *cariño*. This is to be grown up," Alba said, squeezing her around the shoulders and kissing her on the cheek. "And don't worry—you are growing more and more every day. Don't you remember the silly things you were doing only last month?"

"Yeah, but... don't tell Hal, okay? It's like, that would, that kind of things just makes me all, like—"

"Shut up! I don't like to hear these sentimental things," said Alba who, by the way, was effortlessly graceful in black slacks and a white-and-green New York Jets jersey, black hair hanging lazily around her shoulder like a shawl. "Hal, are you a man or a asshole? Find us a table before that I die of hunger!"

Over dinner, I told Mary Ann about Frank and the inheritance. It seemed to me that the best step was for us to meet face-to-face with him, look over whatever documents Frank brought, and give him some kind of answer. I don't know which argument actually convinced her: that she could make a chunk of easy money or that this would be the last she would ever hear of Frank. At any rate, she agreed.

Alba left us at the restaurant, on the excuse that she had joined a Spanish-American discussion group, sponsored by the UN, on ways to improve relations between the two countries. "It's really just a good place to pick up lovers," she said with a wink. So I took Mary Ann home by taxi, though I would have barely a half-hour there before having to run for my flight at LaGuardia.

She snuggled against me in the cab, informing me that Alba had said that she shouldn't ask if it was all right to do that—just do it.

"Good advice," I said with a chuckle.

"Don't laugh at me, Hal. Alba laughed when she told me, an' I know she's a sweetie and don't mean nothin', but it, y'know, kind of makes me feel, y'know, squished up."

"Sorry."

"There's just a lot of things I don't know, that's all."

"I don't care." And I kissed her, kissed her for all I was worth. It simply leapt out of me.

"Oh, wow, Hal. That was great, really fantastic!"

So I did it some more, with swiftly improving results.

After a while, I lowered my voice, for the taxi driver, and said, "Mary Ann, do you know how to read? Remember I told you I talked with Sheena Biggs? She told me you had dyslexia."

No answer.

"Actually, she said *you* told her that," I said.

Still nothing.

"I didn't know what to think. I remembered seeing you read the menu at the restaurant, when we first met, remember?"

"Uh-huh."

I waited, this time determined to leave the ball on her side of the court.

Finally: "Well, no, now, y'see, it's just that, most of the time I just for-get my glasses. I always leave 'em at home, y'know, 'cause they're, they cost me a lot of money, and I don't want to lose 'em."

"Good idea."

"Or then I take 'em on the subway and I leave 'em at the studio."

Another block passed.

"Mary Ann, if you can't read, it's okay. It's nothing that—"

Mary Ann pushed away from me. "Hal! I said *I can read*. I don't know why that bitch Sheena is sayin' these things about me, but if I catch her somewhere I'm gonna grab one o' her legs and twist it right 'round till it snaps off! Now *I can read*—I can read just as well as the next person. That sign over there says 'stop,' okay?" A pause. "Okay, that was a stupid thing to say, I know. When we get home, I'm gonna read and read to you till ya miss yer ol' plane, okay?"

"Bitch," I noted. Not *"creep"* or *"rat."*

I said nothing, wondering what sort of excuse she would make once we got home, and wondering if I shouldn't try to head off the situation before she made a fool of herself; clearly, it was really a sore point with her. And it seemed to me that Sheena's story was true, if only because she had even less imagination than kindness.

But as things turned out, Mary Ann made no excuses at all. I hadn't even got my coat off before she had thrown her own jacket over a chair, pushed me onto a kitchen-bar stool, put on her glasses, and snatched *The Great Gatsby* out of the book case; it was a chewed-up second-hand copy, made for the movie version of *Gatsby* starring Robert Redford and Faye Dunaway.

"Chapter One. 'In my younger and more vulnerable years my father gave me some advice that I've been turning over in my mind ever since.

"'Whenever you feel like criticizing anyone,' he told me, 'just remember that all the people in this world haven't had the advantages that you've had.'

"'He didn't say any more but we've always been unusually communicative in a reserved way and I understood that he meant a great deal more than that.'"

"Okay, okay," I said, but she waved me away and kept right on going.

After another page: "All right, already!" I said. "You win."

"No, no, no. You just sit there and listen a while, and the next time you see ol' Sheena, you tell her I didn't look at the cover of that Bee Gees CD 'cause I just figured it was the title of the album or somethin' like that. That's what I get for trustin' someone who just wants to play me a dirty trick."

She went on reading for two more pages—the entire prologue of the book—narrating beautifully, voice rising and falling like sea waves, though here and there she mispronounced a word.

"'...the short-winded elations of men,'" she finished. "Want me to go on a few more pages?" she challenged.

"No, that will do it."

"Okay then: can I read or can't I?"

"You can read."

Mary Ann writhed a gaudy, ornate curtsy. "Thank you, kind sah," she said with a British accent. She went back to the bookshelves and put the book back. "Isn't that a beautiful story? And it's so sad when Gatsby dies—I just about split my guts cryin'. And Daisy turns out to be such a creep, and that Tom—heck, he's just a big, dumb chunk a brick. He's worse 'n' Frank is."

"I've read it a couple of times. By the way, speaking of Frank—"

Mary Ann turned around. "Now I ain't—darn! I'm *not*—gonna tell you that I read all the time, or that I buy a lot o' newspapers or nothin'. And there's a lot o' stuff that I just don't know, 'cause I didn't go to school as much as I should've. But like, well, when I need to read, I read. I don't have—"

I pulled her to me and put my arms around her. "Mary Ann, I believe you, okay? I believe you. Case closed: you can read." I kissed her a long time, to make sure she got the point.

Mary Ann's lips eased into my own firmly but softly; already she had learned. Was there anywhere an imperfection in that body? Still, after a moment, I had to stop and tell her to loosen up her arms before she crushed me like an anaconda.

"Well, I've got to go, Mary Ann," I said, pulling back sadly. "Not that I want to."

"Yeah, I wish you could stay." Her forehead fell against my chest, and a tiny sob bubbled out of her.

"Listen. I'll set up the meet with Frank and we'll get together then."

"Soon, right?"

"Soon as I can. If he's really interested, he'll come 'round."

"Okay, well, be careful."

"Careful and short. Frank tends to see things his own way or not at all."

Mary Ann looked at me thoughtfully. "Yeah," she said softly. "That's the way you talk to people: just, just, just real tight and clean, like a fan kick. I mean, not like you gotta, like, tug 'n' scuff with somebody or call him a rat or nothin'. Just be clean and straight." She ground her palms together, and under her blouse a sierra of muscles leapt from her forearm up to her shoulder and across her chest. "That's the first thing I noticed when I talked to you on the plane—you talk so clean and straight ahead and, and, like—" She made a slow, scooping movement with her hand, fingers closed, and extended her arm to the horizon.

"I do what I can," I said—for lack of anything better. "Say, what's a fan kick?"

"Oh. It's a jazz step. Like this." Turning her back to me, she threw one straight leg sideways and upwards, and made a perfect circle with it—a fan—which passed over my head like a shooting star. "See what I mean? It has to be real tight and clean, and you can't fake it by swayin' back or nothin'." She smiled shyly. "Just like you."

I wondered what it would be like to have that kind of power and skill in my body, ready at a whim.

"'Cause I think you're just, just great, Hal, I really do. I know you're not s'posed to say things like that, but it's just that, y'know, sometimes I'm just, I just wanna...." She steadied herself. "Hal, y'know, can I give you, like, just another quick kiss—please? Before you go?"

"Didn't Alba tell you not to ask?"

I jerked Mary Ann to me and, though nothing happened that you haven't seen in a John Wayne movie, I can assure you I gave her more than a quick kiss. As my airplane lifted off the runway two hours later, my body was still with her, feeling the taut press of her breasts against my ribs, the valleys and hills of her back, the sharp concavity of her waist, and my fingers in that coarse red hair. This was heat. Real heat. She was the most transparent and most mysterious woman I had ever met. And she could read.

13 The next morning, Felix Weikert appeared in my office, dressed in gray chinos and a flannel shirt, bowing and shuffling shamefully as if it were his duty to hang you or drill your molars. He was about fifty and had a son in Harvard, "only on half scholarship, though"—which he mentioned every single time he handed me a bill for his labors. You would never suspect him of running a high-tech anything, much less a high-tech security firm.

But he did, and in five minutes found a half-dollar-sized listening bug—on the underside of my meeting table, right where Frank had sat. Its battery had worn out and no longer transmitted. Felix made some guesses based on the type of battery and the type of equipment it ran—it was a high-buck model made by a Japanese firm, which he said indicated "some very no-bullshit, hard-ball types." He told me that it probably sent a signal about a quarter-mile to a secondary relay, which, attached to an AC current, strengthened the signal and sped it on its way into the stratosphere to wherever it slaked curiosities.

Which didn't surprise me, for it surely came from the fine folks who had hired pros to trail little ol' me—for days? weeks?—at the cost of mucho dinero, till I led them to Mary Ann's apartment.

Of course, by "fine folks" I mean "Frank's folks." And there was the rub. How did a stinking, dumb, Neanderthal-browed, chain-smoking, chain-wearing over-the-road trucker fit into something like this? What he was spending to track Mary Ann down and grab her would use up whatever he might make on the farm inheritance. No, the answer had to be the Reverend.

So I put a lot of thought into setting up the meeting with Frank and his father for the following week. I called Frank and told him they'd have to come up to Chicago for it, which he didn't like, but I wanted the home-court advantage.

I selected a cafeteria of the type I particularly dislike: a downtown "food court"—a sort of filling station for humans whose only redeeming virtue was that it made no pretense to fine, or even tasteful, dining. It catered to the midday ties-and-heels crowd, who fed from food stands with screechingly catchy names like *Why-Oh-Wyoming* and *What's Your Beef?*. The purple-and-yellow tables and chairs were designed to be easy to clean, the imitation-oak floor easy to mop, the pop-art beach scene stenciled on the wall easy to wipe. Worst of all, two digital clocks high on the wall at each side, big as hockey goals and with lime-green numbers, stared at you like your boss's Post-it: *Time might not be money, champ, but it sure as hell ain't lunch.*

A steady and well-dressed clientele lunched there for about two hours every day, however, and that's why I chose it. I wanted a lot of lapels and nylon hose nearby to make the trucker and "the Reverent" conscious of their voices and their manners. It was also easy for an out-of-towner to find, being just a step away from the John Hancock Building, which is a hundred stories high and visible from any truck stop where Frank might tether Old Bessie.

I had met Mary Ann at the airport an hour earlier—I had had a ridiculous craving to show her my Porsche, which in her nervousness she didn't notice at all—and brought her into the city.

The meeting was at one, but we got there fifteen minutes early. I wanted to get a Coke Lite paid for and delivered into her nervous hands to give them something to do. I also wanted a table along the wall and chairs with our backs to the beach-scene wall so that Mary Ann's red hair showed up against the blue sky.

I had told Mary Ann to put some care into what she wore that day.

"Yeah. Yeah. I get it. Like, one look at me, and they'll know they're not dealin' with ol' Stupe-face anymore."

They certainly would not. Mary Ann took off a light spring jacket, and half the lunch crowd lowered their forks. She was wearing a white leotard top with wispy multicolored stitching over the bosom; it was cut high and wide, framing her clavicle and perfect shoulders. Her long rough-cloth skirt was a dramatic burnt orange. Pearls at the earlobes peeked from under her swirl of deep red.

"Do I look okay?" she asked. "Take a good look now." She turned one way, then the other, pushing up the sleeves up her forearms.

I laughed. "'Okay' is not the word that springs to mind."

"No?" she cried.

"No. More like 'incredible' or 'perfect' or 'stunning.'"

She huffed in relief. "You big rat. Hey, you're not just sayin' that, are ya?"

"Are you kidding? You're the most beautiful lady in the place."

"Lady," she repeated. We sat down side by side, and she mouthed the word to herself again and again. I had intended to buck her up, but, not for the first time with Mary Ann, the chance comment sent down a taproot into that churning mind of hers, spread out, touched new roots, touched old ones, fed one and fed from another. She sat quietly for a while, sipping her Coke, her brow wrinkled deeply, mouthing the word, and her eyes made shy little tours of the room. "Yeah, I guess I look all right," she murmured. And she crossed her legs at the knees.

Right on time, recognizable at a distance by his haystack of comic-book orange hair, Frank tottered in from the street-end of the food court, where the shops were, frowning and swearing to himself. You would have thought he had been forced to pay an admittance fee. He seemed to be alone.

"Okay, Mary Ann, curtain's up. So remember: take everything nice and easy."

I started to get up, but she touched my arm and looked at me. "I'm okay, Hal. Really. I'm a lady. I'm, I, that's what I am."

I had conferred a title on her.

I was beside Frank before he realized it. He looked at me with resignation and didn't bother to shake hands, so I kept mine at my sides. "You really hadda come, dincha?" he muttered. He was wearing a scruffy dark-green chamois shirt and jeans, with the same scarred leather belt that couldn't keep his belly from overflowing the waistband. He didn't smell so much of tobacco this time; the Chicago spring wind seemed to have blown it out of him.

"Wouldn't miss it for the world," I said.

"Yeah, fuck you. Where's Stupe—where's Mary Ann?" He was fishing a cell phone out of the hip pocket of his jeans and punching keys with a dirty thumbnail.

I pointed across the room. Mary Ann raised a cautious hand.

"That's her?" Frank blurted, tiny eyes growing large. "That's *her?* The *fuck!*"

"She's probably changed since you saw her last," I deadpanned.

Frank's world rocked beneath him; till that moment—and it was a long one—he had never envisioned Mary Ann as a young woman. She was still "Stupe-face."

"Hey, you doll her up like that?" It wasn't a question but an accusation.

"I don't dress her, if that's what you mean."

"You mean she *always* looks like that?"

"Frank, for Pete's sake. Are we going to have a meeting or talk about spring fashions?"

Whomever he'd called was now shouting for attention, and Frank answered him fast. "Yeah, she's here. So is he. Okay." To me: "She's s'posed to come out to the parkin' ramp. He's got a minivan." He saw my frown and said into the phone, "Can he come too?" The answer was affirmative, for Frank nodded and winked broadly, as if doing me a favor.

"Tell him this isn't a Jackie Chan movie," I said. "We'll wait here for him."

Frank laughed. "Yeah, like people can tell *him* what to do."

But I was already walking back to Mary Ann.

*T*welve minutes later by the lime-green numbers, seven of which Frank spent arguing into his cell phone, the Reverend appeared, big and fiftyish, unhappy to have been roused from the comforts of the minivan, and unhappy in any case. You know the type. As with pro-basketball coaches, traffic cops and midwives, happiness was an emotion unworthy of his face, and made only brief, humiliated visits. He was tall and capacious in the torso, like his two children, but had none of the deep complexion that showed up so nicely in Mary Ann. Nor did his hair show any red; it was strictly shaven salt-and-pepper crew cut that announced disdain for a whole dimension of human life that included fancy cocktails, art more modern than cave paintings, foreign countries, and young women shopping for great clothes in New York.

The Right Reverend Richard T. Jaalkov. I had tapped his name into an Internet search engine three days earlier to see what the gods of information could tell me. And got plenty of reading for my efforts.

Reverend Jaalkov had a Sunday-morning religious TV program broadcast from Tulsa, Oklahoma—part of a national religious broadcasting network. Its top preacher, Humbert Swellton Jr., was well-known for tending the spiritual needs of Senate conservatives over the past forty years or so in Washington.

Jaalkov's program had a Web page. Here's a quote from the FAQs section: "First thing I'm gonna do when I get to heaven? Easy! Tell St. Pete he's fired for slackin' off! The gates o' Heaven just got narrower, and I'm the guy doin' the weldin'!" Additional entries in the search engine, however, indicated controversy. Jaalkov, it seemed, had quaint opinions about women, homosexuality, the family, and an impending Final Apocalypse that he was looking forward to: "Good Christians need not fear. For us, it's gonna be the Super Bowl, the World Series, and Christmas all wrapped into one."

Back to the present. Frank was still arguing—or begging—and Jaalkov was shaking his head. His little eyes grew wide as he scanned the area, and they said that this was not the plan, not at all. He was near to panic, it seemed to me—like a man with a mortgage on the brink of losing his job.

Mary Ann was alarmed, too. "Oh, God A'mighty, the Reverent, when he's like this...." she whispered. "Oh, golly, golly, gosh." Her face had lost all its jaunty cheer and gone gray as a winter sea. Her shoulders were tight, and her fingers were gripped together like tangled ropes. I told her not to get up when Frank and the Reverend approached; she nodded in two robotic jerks.

At length, the Reverend bowed to reality, hardened his face, and began to wind his way through the tables to us, Frank trailing. He wore a three-piece suit of innocent blue, a white business shirt, and a tie whose stripes scarcely dared to show themselves against the navy-blue background. His black shoes were polished to a righteous shine.

I stood up and introduced myself, received a perfunctory handshake and was instructed to address him as "Reverent Jaalkov." To Mary Ann he offered neither a handshake nor a hello. He simply looked down at her, hands on hips, his suit jacket pushed back to reveal his tightly-packed vest. Slowly he nodded, as if he'd always figured she'd end up like this.

"All right, you got me up here, Mr. Slick. Happy? Lotta wasted trouble, seems to me. Let's go, Mary Ann. Car's waitin' down the block. C'mon."

"My last name is *Dormund,*" I said. "Now there are a lot of things to talk over, so why don't we just—"

But for the moment, I was not part of the conversation. Mary Ann stayed where she was—though only that seemed to require an effort—and Jaalkov didn't like that. "Mary Ann, is this man your husband? Is there something I don't know here?"

"Hal is my"—she swallowed—"my good friend."

"Then you're gonna do exactly as your *father* tells you. Now let's go." And he reached over the table and actually grabbed Mary Ann by the upper arm, and her eyes went wide in fear.

"Now just hold on a second here," she said appeasingly. She was not pulling back, but not standing up, either. "Why can't everybody just sit down here—really!"

"I am your father, and I am directin' you to get up and come with me. You backtalk me one more time, and the consequences will be—"

I had something to say and had taken a big breath to say it with. But a woman at the next table down the beach-scene wall screeched it far more eloquently:

"Take your hand off her arm, sir. I said 'Take it off.'"

Jaalkov jerked. He stared at the woman, frozen.

"*Off!* The hand is *off!*" said the woman, who was African-American, graying elegantly and in her forties. Her business suit had pinstripes and *lawyer* written all over it. "Unhand that young woman right now. I mean it! *I mean it!* Or I'm going to be your worst nightmare."

Jaalkov let go, though not because he was afraid of a scene. "No stranger's gonna give me orders," he bellowed, "and especially crossin' racial lines in the process. Man's got a right to rescue his daughter from the forces o' darkness, and that's what I'm gonna do!"

The woman smiled coldly. Her hands went to her hips, too. "This young woman is exhibitin' no desire whatsoever to stand up or go anywhere with you, sir. Now you will not handle her in any way, shape or form, or you and I are gonna spend the rest of the day crossin' our *racial lines* in front of the judge."

Frank whipped around to the other side of his father. "You listen up real close, bitch. We don't need some nigger shit stickin' her nose inna the business o' my family and--"

But now the lawyer's two lunch companions, a man and a woman, were also on their feet shouting, as were a few others once they had had time to swallow their food. The lawyer was calling "Guard! Guard!" and motioning across the room for the security guard, who hovered in the area between the food and shops sections, and now strode over to us rolling his eyes with superiority, as if people ought to be able to sort out their differences by themselves. He had heavy, sloping shoulders, like a rugby player, and an ugly mustache like a shredded string across his upper lip. His utility belt held leather bulges and stainless steel, which he fingered as if counting them to be sure he had them all.

"Is there a problem here?" he asked, as if he had no clue, which he probably didn't.

"A father is tryin' to get his daughter back home at long last and back on the way to the Lord, and Satan's agents are impedin' my progress at every point!" Jaalkov exclaimed.

The guard looked at me, wondering if I might interpret.

"Rick, is it?" the lawyer read on his nameplate. "Rick, these gentlemen are trying to take away this young woman against her will. That constitutes abduction. Are you going to be party to that?"

This was all far beyond poor Rick, who had to look around a moment to find the young woman; finally Frank moved aside. For lack of anything better to say, or perhaps just to look at her longer, Rick asked Mary Ann, "Ma'am, do, uh, do you wish to go with these gentlemen?"

"No. Now, now, I don't mind *talkin'* to 'em, but I just want everybody to sit down and, and talk nice," Mary Ann said.

"Well, all right then. Now everybody just sit down and, uh, keep it down. Any more problems, and I'll have to ask you to leave, sir." Duty done, Rick walked off, his utility belt plucking one way and the other.

He would have had more to do if the brittle silence had cracked at that moment, but by a miracle, it didn't. With a final glare at the lawyer, who glared right back, the Reverend jerked a chair out and dropped his bulk on it. "Ask me to leave, ask *me* to leave!" he fumed. "Come a day when the good Lord'll throw ever'body out *but* me."

Frank took up a place behind his father like a praetorian guard. "Want me to call 'em?" he said, cell phone in hand.

The Reverend scowled and nodded. Plan A, evidently, had failed.

14

What I remember most vividly about this conversation was Frank, who hardly spoke at all. Standing behind the Reverend, he kept staring at Mary Ann, and only looked away so that she wouldn't catch him. He couldn't get over her. Apparently, it had never occurred to him that Mary Ann might have aged since her disappearance, and the reality had left him spellbound. Twice he fumbled with his cigarettes before remembering, to his disgust, that he couldn't smoke there.

Jaalkov, however, had business to do, and Mary Ann's good looks and adulthood changed nothing. He was bent on taking Mary Ann with him. "Is that what we're coming to in this country?" he accused her; for the moment, I didn't exist. "A man can't get back his disappeared daughter after lookin' for her so very long? Man can't lead her back to the Lord? No sir, he's gotta sit here listenin' to ol' Mr. Slick, and a Northerner to boot."

"Reverent, I'm honestly real happy just the way I am," said Mary Ann. "I'm just fine, honest."

"Mary Ann, you are a long-lost lamb, you have a long history of mental problems, and we're gonna take the best o' care of you from now on."

"Mental problems? But, that's, you're sayin', like, hey—I'm not stupid! I'm not!"

I stepped in: "Reverend, let's confine the conversation to the matter of the inheritance, shall we?" I said, though I now realized that neither he nor Frank were pulling out any papers.

"Well now, nobody's callin' you stupid, dear, and nobody's sayin' it was your fault, either. That's why we took care o' you so special on the farm. We just wanted you to progress and grow up in your own good time." He was now leaning forward across the table with "humanity," and you would have needed a barrel to catch all the grease that slid off his big face.

Mary Ann watched him, her fingers tightly interlocked. I decided to let matters ride. If Mary Ann could get herself out of this by herself, so much the better.

"Now that we've found you—praise the Lord—we just wanna take you someplace and get you the help you need. Now we've got a little more money and we're doin' a little better, so we can afford these good things. C'mon, we got a nice, big van with a TV just waitin' for ya."

"Hey! If ya want, I'll take you halfway in my truck!" said Frank. "Since I'm goin' down that way. 'Member how I used ta promise you I would?"

"I'm not stupid," Mary Ann repeated sternly. "And I'm not six years old. I'm a *lady*. And I'm not going nowhere with you in some ol' truck."

"I *said* nobody's callin' you stupid, Mary Ann, dear," said the Reverend as if Mary Ann were an intelligent two-year-old. "But we just wanna help you get over a few problems that—"

"And I don't got... I mean, like, like, on the farm, I was sure smart enough to do all the washin' and cleanin' and cookin', wasn't I? I was like those poor kids out in sub-Sahara Biafra, where they're all starvin' and havin' to carry their baby brothers ten miles to a doctor!"

"Y'see?" the Reverend said, now to me. "That's the problem. This poor girl—it's so wonderful to see her again, and lookin' so pretty, praise the Lord—this poor girl can't distinguish between what's real and what's not."

"Funny—I thought her grip on reality was pretty darn—" But that was as far as I got.

"I remember sittin' there on the back porch, shellin' peas with Mary Ann, and she's tellin' me long stories about how dragons attacked her and she stabbed 'em to death with a sword. Everything was always attackin' her. I thought she was possessed—I did! I musta prayed every night for ten years straight for Satan to let go o' her soul."

"Telling stories seems to run in the family, doesn't it?" I observed. "A while back, Frank told us a good one about Mary Ann coming into some kind of inheritance. I guess there was nothing to that, huh?"

Frank grinned.

"There was as much to it as need be," the Reverend breezed. "After all these years, we finally have Mary Ann in front of our eyes. Praise the Lord!"

"Ah," I ahhed.

"I used ta think, well, who knows? Maybe if it weren't for her mother dyin' so young—maybe that was it. Traumas—well, that's what the long-hairs in universities call 'em, but that's the devil right there, what it really is, pickin' off an easy target."

I had given Mary Ann's leg a squeeze, and perhaps that was what rallied her. "What about you stickin' me in the barn all night?" she said, slapping one hand in the other. "I make that up, too? And the mice crawlin' on me and the bats screechin' around? Nothin' but ol' Bolts to keep me warm? All that weren't no *story,* Reverent."

"Bolts died just last year," Frank said as if we were just remembering old times. "He was great, ol' Bolts was."

Two men in dark suits, ageless and bald, loomed up at our table. Wordless as ghosts, they sat down to Jaalkov's left; the Reverend hastily scooted his chair over to give them room. He presented them as "Mr. White and Mr. Besby." They folded their hands on the table and nodded curtly; handshakes were beneath them. For a wild moment, I had hoped that they were lawyers here to talk about the inheritance, but clearly they were the Reverend's bosses, lacking only Gradgrind's bowler hat. Their moon faces hovered like Judgment.

The Reverend now stretched his humanity—so far it creaked. "Well, now, Mary Ann, dear, I'm not sayin' I was a perfect father. Maybe I've got some prayer-work to do on that. Maybe I was a little severe, and maybe I'll end up askin' God's forgiveness." That said, he propped an elbow on the table and pointed a finger straight as a drill punch at her. "But at the end o' the day, you gotta admit a father's word's law in his house, and I don't see that you're any the worse for it."

"Well, I *am* the worse for a couple o' things," said Mary Ann.

The Reverend drew a breath. Even Frank was roused from his adoration of Mary Ann. "Like what?" the Reverend said.

Besby shifted his shoulders. White uncrossed his urbane legs.

"Like, like, like I was sayin'," Mary Ann stuttered. "There just, there was times I wasn't... Like I remember bein' pretty miz'ble. Why don't you just go pray about that and maybe the ol' Lord'll give you a few answers?"

The Reverend smiled sadly. "Mary Ann, every parent makes a few mistakes along the road. You gotta be forgivin', darlin'. Worst thing you could say about me wouldn't turn a head in a church. Scripture says that a man who—"

"Scripture!" Mary Ann groaned. The word fell over her like a wet blanket. "Oh, Reverent, can't you just leave me be, *please!*"

It was time for me to take up the ball. "Reverend, let me try to throw some light on this conversation, since we don't seem to be getting anywhere." And to my surprise he let me. "First, can I ask you why you are interested in Mary Ann? You could have traced her easily when she ran away years ago, and you didn't."

Besby's and White's eyes darted to the Reverend.

"Didn't look for her? Why, we were worried sick. Weren't we, Frank?"

"You kiddin'? We—"

"I didn't come here to listen to a load of bullshit," I interrupted rudely. "To find a twelve-year-old girl with bright red hair is not a hard task for the police. Years passed—*years*—and you never lifted a finger. Now, six, seven, eight years later, whatever it is, you're suddenly concerned for her. You trace Mary Ann's phone number, and you guess her PIN number. This means you made a considerable effort. You listened to her messages—probably for months—till mine came up, and you had a chance to find her. Now what's going on here?"

"A man's desperate to find his daughter. Is that so hard to—"

I rolled my eyes in irritation, and he didn't like it.

"Are you a Christian, sir?" Jaalkov bellowed, and Besby and White seemed to appreciate his charge.

"We're here to discuss my theology?" I said.

"That means no, you aren't. A real Christian would be on his feet proclaimin' his faith at the top o' his lungs. Now I wanna know what in tarnation a damn Yankee outsider like you is doin' sittin' here and runnin' the affairs o' my family?"

Mary Ann spoke up. "Reverent, Hal speaks for me, and he hasn't ever been anything but the kindest, sweetest friend a girl ever had."

"He ain't your husband, young lady. And I'll be doggoned if I'm gonna let Mr. Slick—"

"I don't care. I'd marry him right now if I could. Anything you have to say to me you can say it in front o' him."

The Reverend poured on more oil. "See? He's turned your head, dear. The carnal delights are Satan's own web o' sin. They bind you up till the spider comes along and sinks his fangs into you."

I didn't know if I had an ace or not, but I played it. "Does all of this miraculous *concern* have anything to do with your TV show?"

No answer. Alarm, however, lightened Frank's mug.

"Reverent, you're on television? *Wow!*" Mary Ann blurted.

"Because that's all I can figure out," I went on. "I mean, you *are* Richard T. Jaalkov on *Holy House of God,* on KTMA in Tulsa, Oklahoma?"

Jaalkov swung a leg over his knee and clasped it with thick hands. I noticed that he wore a thin leather band tied around his left wrist. "That's right: most-watched local Sunday morning show in the Southwest."

Frank, still standing behind him, seemed to swell. "And soon as we get a few things cleared away, he's gonna be coast-to-coast, and on satellite to Asia, Europe and Australia," Frank added proudly.

Ah, from the mouth of babes. Jaalkov's face froze. Still as a reptile, Mr. Besby allowed his tongue to flicker out and wet his lips.

"'Cleared away,'" I repeated. "I get it: 'cleared away,' as in 'mistreated daughters cleared away and set up for life in, say, a mental institution.' *That's* where this is going, isn't it?"

"What? What?" chirped Mary Ann in alarm, grabbing my arm with both hands and nearly pulling it out of the socket. "Hal, I don't understand. Don't let 'em... golly-gosh!"

"Your father, Mary Ann, is about to land the job of a lifetime preaching to all America, sounds like," I said, using some force to loosen her grip before she dislocated my elbow. "The top preacher of his religious broadcasting network is getting on in years and wants to retire—it's that Humbert Swellton, spiritual advisor to half the Senate, right?—and the network wants Reverend Jaalkov to go in his place. Is this on target, Reverend?"

Frank spoke up. "Yeah, 'cept he's gonna bring in audience like they ain't never seen before!"

"Frank!" snapped the Reverend.

"Problem is, Mary Ann," I went on, "your father says a few things that piss people off. And newspapers might want to investigate him— y'know, see if he really practices what he preaches?"

"I'm as righteous a man as ever—" Jaalkov began, but I ignored him.

"So your father needs to tidy up his past—mainly his daughter, whom he treated like a slave for so long that she had to run away." To Jaalkov, as I jerked a thumb at the Messrs. White and Besby: "Isn't that it, Reverend? No green light from the network brass till you take care of Mary Ann?"

No answer, but Jaalkov's loathing eyes said it all. Besby and White, silent as photos, watched ruthlessly, as if observing insects copulating.

"These must be the people who put up cash for listening bugs and the heavy-handed stuff, huh?" I went on, and saw White's shoulders shift again. "And right now, they're warming a bed for Mary Ann in some nuthouse at the end of a long, long valley, am I right?"

126

At this point, the Reverend pummeled us with a speech, which you needn't erode your eyesight on, about how he was one of the forces trying to turn "this godless country" around, how America had had a glorious future until it turned away from God to "materialistic i-dolatry" and "entertainment worship." "It's this lot o' thieving, lying, godless Satan's agents that are gonna bring this country to its knees!" he finished. "And I'm the man to turn 'em back!"

I like to use silence against my opponent when I can, and I ladled out a few helpings now while I thought things over. Mary Ann was terrified, but I couldn't give her any time. I re-fitted my voice for negotiation: "All right, I think I have a better understanding of the situation now. What do you say, gentlemen? Can we deal with it? Talk turkey?" I asked, blatantly directing my words to Besby and White.

"I gotta sit here dealin' with Satan's Sec'tary of Defense," grumbled Jaalkov. But Besby had nodded minutely.

With a reasonable chuckle: "Well now, Reverend, if you're strong enough to stand up to Satan, you shouldn't have much trouble with Mr. Slick. Let's see: the problem here is that you're worried about the public discovering your past with Mary Ann, right?"

"I got absolutely nothing to be ashamed of! I have always wanted what every man wants for—"

I raised a hand to stop him. "All right, all right, all right—point taken. Put it this way: the general public would not understand *how* you brought her up." The Reverend tipped his shaven head to either side, testing this euphemism. I moved ahead while I had a chance. "You would prefer that this matter stayed out of the public light. Mary Ann, on the other hand, wants nothing whatever to do with either of you."

"Oh! Oh, you can sure say that again," Mary Ann said in a grateful rush.

"All right then—we have the makings of an agreement, don't we? Can't we just say that Mary Ann will say nothing about her past, and in return, you—*all of you*—will leave her alone?"

"Yeah, like you can trust ol' Stupe-face," Frank muttered.

"You—!" Mary Ann started. "Frank, I am a lady. Now you just remember that."

Frank leered and began to answer, but Jaalkov told him to shut up.

He stared at me for a long moment, then glanced at his masters—again Besby nodded millimetrically. The Reverend plunked his meaty forearms on the table; I was glad to see it—that's how people compromise.

"Where the bottom line comes down," Jaalkov began, "long as we're makin' deals with the devil here, is: what happens if some muckraker comes round askin' Mary Ann about me? Gonna pretty well happen, y'know, where my name is goin'. You try 'n' take on sin wholesale, and Satan starts workin' overtime." The bastard had a cliché for every occasion.

"All right," I said. "If any reporter comes around asking Mary Ann about her famous father, Mary Ann will say... what? The Reverend was a great dad, she just wishes that she'd been able to spend more time with him, but he was always away from the farm doing the Lord's work. Nothing about barns or Bolts or doing your wash—not a single word that could be held against you. Mary Ann, is that okay?"

"Yeah, sure, absolutely. Long as they leave me be, I'll say anything they want."

"And none o' these makin' up tales outta school, eh?" said Jaalkov suspiciously. "I know what you're capable of, young lady, and it's none too—"

"Mary Ann will have nothing else to say on the subject of her father," I said. "If asked for details, she will have no comment."

"Yeah, right: no comment," said Mary Ann. She rehearsed: "'I got no comment on that.' Yeah. People say that all the time on TV."

"Okay?" I challenged them.

"Well, that's somethin' to think about, anyways," said Jaalkov.

"And you, Reverend, are going to forget Mary Ann. No mention of her anywhere, got it? Not in—"

"Wait a minute. What about my website? It says I have three sons and a daughter."

"Fair enough—too late to change it now. But that's *all*, understand? Nothing about Mary Ann in interviews *or* sermons *or* writings. And no private dicks, no spying—electronic or otherwise—no hassles, and no rough stuff. Any communication with her goes through me or whomever Mary Ann appoints."

The Reverend scratched his neck, looking sideways at Besby and White. I added a threat, which I dislike doing in general, but in an adversarial negotiation, it's a prudent measure. "Break the rules just once, Reverend, and I'll make sure the media has your ass well-done with mushrooms. Think I can't, right? Well, couple times a year, local Chicago reporters come to me with questions about nuclear power, and I put down my work and explain things and give them a few quotes. See? They owe me favors. All I have to do is light a match, and pretty soon you'll find yourself in the middle of a forest fire."

"Yeah! Yeah, that's it," Mary murmured, gripping my arm again till I writhed in pain and had to jerk it off. She was sheer muscle.

"Better watch what you're sayin', Mister High-Hand, 'cause the hottest places in hell are reserved for the sinners that take it lightly!"

"I'll keep it in mind," I said blandly. "All right: do we have a deal?"

"Well, now there's an interesting point," said the Reverend. He was playing for time, watching his two masters again. "Don't know if a man has to enter into contractual agreements with his own daughter. Scripture says—"

"Your own daughter didn't show up with a minivan and five guys inside to hold you down," I replied, and from Frank's smile, I could see I had guessed rightly. "You keep up your end, Reverend, and Mary Ann's the least of your worries. Now: have we got a deal? Stick your mitt out there."

The day had not gone according to plan, but the Reverend knew that it could have gone much worse. He glanced quickly at silent White and Besby, who looked at each other. After a long moment, as if they had read each other's mind, Besby looked past White and nodded to Jaalkov. Both men got up.

Jaalkov wiped his nose on a clean handkerchief—I wondered who had ironed it. "All right. Deal." And the bastard stuck out his hand as he was putting away the handkerchief in his back pocket so that he wouldn't have to look her in the eye—and only looked up because Mary Ann's grip, like the rest of her body, was as solid as a wrench's.

"Nice doin' business with you, Reverent," she said with a grin.

So of course, he had to finish one up on her. He wagged a finger. "Just you be careful with your end, young lady! The great train o' God's work is rollin' along, and it is not going to get held up for any funny stuff."

"Reverend, one last thing," I said. "You're a Christian, right?" We were all getting up. White and Besby, heads together, were already out of the food court.

"Sir, I am the most Christian Christian you'll ever lay those sinful eyes on."

"So how about apologizing to Mary Ann? Asking forgiveness? Closing out the whole thing properly?"

The Reverend face went stony. I might have asked him to apologize to the dog whose shit he'd stepped in that morning.

He never answered, because Frank grabbed his arm and swung him around. "C'mon, Reverent. Parkin' in this town costs a fortune."

Actually, it was Mary Ann who had the last word, for she suddenly took a step after them. "Reverent, wait. I wanted to ask you somethin'."

The two men turned.

"Look, it's just that, y'know, with my, that is, our family name, Jaalkov, where'd that come from? Some folks have asked me about my bloodline some times, and I don't know what to say."

It was a profound moment: a daughter grabbing her one chance to learn something about her ancestry. Frank, however, found it funny, and began laughing quietly, his belly bobbing, as if there were some private joke. And the Reverend answered with a big grin on his face.

"Czech," he said. "My granddaddy arrived in 1911 from Hamburg, and he married a Hungarian girl from Budapest he'd met on the boat. Name was Jaalkovich back then. Got changed in immigration. That's about all I—" Then he too broke down laughing, slapped Frank on the back. "Let's go, boy! We got what we came for. Lord's work's a-waitin'!" And the two tripped through the tables and away past the shops, giggling like girls. Then they saw White and Besby waiting for them at the street entrance, and hustled towards them like fifth-grade basketball players to the coach.

"Czech," Mary Ann murmured, disappointed. "Czech and Hungarian. What in the world is that?"

15 If it was a thin deal sealed with a handshake, the Reverend felt it was secure enough to begin his worldwide ministry. Just ten days later he started on national television, and in a big way: on his first show, he announced that a large portion of society—homosexuals, liberals, designers of video games, the unemployed, the unwashed—were not only sinners condemned to hell, but bloodsuckers on the national economy, agents sent by the devil to undermine human civilization, which America was "slated"—his word—to redeem. Even some moderately conservative senators distanced themselves from him. He attacked a psychiatrist on a competing channel who offered advice to troubled families, calling him a "homosexual facilitator." He branded as "sexual filth" a big toy ball with handles for tots to jump up and down on. A leftist Latin American president was "the Devil's bird droppin's on the windshield of the New World."

Well, it was show biz, and the Reverend was a hit. He created a traveling tent show, like the old-time preachers. (Frank, incidentally, bought a dozen trucks and had the exclusive transportation contract—according to the show's website—which satisfied my curiosity about his end of the bargain.)

It was a brilliant gimmick. Everywhere, from Alaska to Maine, wherever *Holy Tent of God* planted its two circus tents—one for the religious service, the other for the techies—it was greeted by multitudinous protesters who gave headaches to the police and juicy publicity to Jaalkov. You had to give Frank credit for prescience: the Reverend was indeed bringing in audience like they'd never seen before.

Maybe the political atmosphere helped, with a conservative president—and former Marine general—in the White House. Never one to disappoint his political base, President Wayne told a crowd in Arizona that, if re-elected, he would ask Jaalkov to give the invocation at his second inauguration. The Reverend's Wednesday Bible-study group—also televised—became a requirement for any conservative, even conservative Democrats.

Jaalkov presided over his legislative flock with severity, even goading members of Congress who voted afoul of what he considered Biblical precepts. "Would Jesus have voted for a bill to increase fundin' for those cretins at the U-nited Nations, Senator Gidarsky? Huh? Doggone right he wouldn't've. When good people everywhere see that, they know exactly why this country is in the parlous shape it is."

Bully for him. Jaalkov kept his word on Mary Ann, and that's all I cared about.

One thing puzzled me about the meeting with the Reverend, however, and I tried without success to get an answer out of Mary Ann. I'm referring to the Reverend's relief that Mary Ann had obviously not told me all of the trials of living on the farm. Mary Ann dodged when I asked her about this. I let it slide—the moment wasn't right.

For three reasons. First, opening night for *Revelaciones* was now only weeks away. Rehearsals, costume fittings, and PR photos were turning into a twelve-hour-a-day job: Sergio was tweaking the program, had every aspect on a schedule and got very testy about interruptions.

As I waited in the studio lobby for Mary Ann late one evening, Bertie whispered to me what was at stake: the show could break the company. Sergio was going deep into debt purchasing top-notch costumes and reserving nothing less than the huge Bellevedere Theater on Broadway. He would not listen to Bertie or look at her numbers: it was all or nothing. If the show did not run at least twenty performances to houses filled to 78 percent of capacity, by Bertie's calculations, Sergio Adán Dance was finished.

Even worse, as soon as the news got round about the Bellevedere, Raymond Radow set up his own new show to debut on the same day, not two blocks away down Broadway. Everywhere he put up posters with a sexy Sheena Biggs on it announcing the new show. A tiny bit of her left nipple showed on the first posters—they now sell on E-bay for more than a thousand dollars—and the publicity was so great that even Sergio admitted his admiration.

The second reason was that I got really busy at work, traveling a lot. I had a long talk with my partners about Chintsy, and we decided to stand up to Edgerton Salk. I was surprised that Ralph agreed—he has a big family to worry about. But when I mentioned Salk's blackmailing me, he was outraged. We decided on a course of action: train someone to replace me on the East European and Turkey jobs, tell our lawyers to go through with a lawsuit they were preparing against

Chintsy for the outstanding payments, and meet with the FBI to advise them of the blackmail; I did that the next day. When Edgerton Salk called me a few days later, I told him that we were still reviewing the situation. "What for?" he chuckled. "Measuring for curtains in a Ukrainian prison?"

Very funny.

There was a third reason, too. It turned out that I didn't need to ask Mary Ann about the mystery with the Reverend. I discovered it on my own.

As I said, I traveled intensely in this period, but I would fly in to New York from Brazil or London, spend a few hours with Mary Ann, then move on to Chicago or wherever I had to be next. We usually went out for dinner, then took a walk through the New York spring evenings, squeezed cheerfully together under her little folding umbrella. Mary Ann always had both arms around my waist or hung on my shoulder. I told her I wouldn't fly away if she released me—which was again stupid of me; it embarrassed her—and she said, very shyly, into my ear, "It's just that you're always comin' and goin', Hal, and when you're here, I just wanna, y'know, be with you, like, together, touchin' you."

One anecdote, painful but memorable, in this period:

I made the huge mistake, which to this day twists like a knife in my gut, of taking her to a dinner show with a stand-up comedian. He was terrific, so much that I scarcely even noticed that Mary Ann wasn't laughing. After ten minutes, in a claustrophobic panic, she jumped out of her chair and flurried out. When I caught up with her in the lobby, I found her incoherent—palsied—with confusion. An elderly usher even came over with a glass of water. Mary Ann couldn't say a full sentence, and her hands trembled. At first I put it down to the place being too crowded; and some of the humor was pretty off-color.

Finally, when we'd walked a good three or four blocks, she told me, "I just didn't understand that guy, Hal. He'd be just talkin' away, and then ever'body'd bust out laughin'. And it's just when ever'body's laughin' except me, and I don't know why, it's like my stomach just squishes right up so much I can hardly breathe."

Because you wonder if they're laughing at you, I thought bitterly. *How could I have been such a fool as to take you to see sophisticated New York stand-up?*

Then one night we entered her apartment and Mary Ann, brow wrinkled, was kneading her lips, which meant that some heavy-duty thinking was being churned up. "Hal, you wanna sleep with me tonight? I mean, Alba does with Javier, and she thinks it's kinda funny, you always sleepin' on the sofa."

"If you'd like," I answered. "Don't worry about what Alba thinks, though."

"No, it's just that, I mean, she has a big double bed and I just have the single, and we might not be too comfortable, but, y'know, like, I've been thinkin'. I'd really like to, y'know, make love with you again."

Again? I wondered. *What was the first time?* But it was no time for semantics. "Okay. Great."

"And we could, y'know, like, you could kiss me in more places and we could take more of our clothes off. And make love better."

Ah, now things get interesting, you're saying. Sublimities lie on the next page. Well, friend reader, you are in the same position as I was, hustling off my pants and not being too neat with the creases in hanging them up; pulling on a tee shirt and a pair of boxer shorts—my New York pajamas. Like you, I had forgotten that, where Mary Ann was concerned, reality had a few curves. Yes, love would be made and sublimities sublimed—stay tuned—but as in the building of a nuclear power plant, procedure and documentation would have to be respected.

"Just one thing," she called from the bathroom. "I'm, I'd be, well, I'm just a little... You mind not seein' me in my pajamas? I was thinkin', maybe, I could just get into bed first, and turn off the lights, and then you can get in, 'cause you can't see in the dark, or not so good. Is that okay?"

I said it was, and a few minutes later, we did things just that way. The room was quite dark, though there was a blue light beating a tattoo on the wall above her little writing desk. I slipped under the covers of the bed and at once she body-pressed me, kissing for all she was worth. That body! It was perfect in every contour, the spine deep in the back muscles, the shoulders tight in the neck, round and firm. After a while,

I adjusted our positions. I unbuttoned a top button of her pajamas and felt her tense.

"Is that okay, Mary Ann?" I whispered. "Or would you like to do it yourself?"

"Ah, no, that's okay."

And I kissed her neck and chest—covering new territory line by line, as if clearing land, waiting for her to relax. "Okay?" I whispered.

"Hal, you know what to do better 'n me. Just go ahead."

I unbuttoned more. Again she tensed, but then as I dabbed her nipples with small, quick kisses, she came back to normal. A gust of moans swept through her—orgasm?

"Oh, Hal, that is so, so nice. You're so sweet."

She sighed and swooped, touching my hair and shoulders, panting, sweating at the base of her spine. Everything I did seemed to sink into her, and the heat was rising fast in me. I sent my tongue round and round her broad nipple, her solar plexus flexed and she cried out, "Oh, Hal! Oh mah gosh! Oh!" That *was* an orgasm. Excited myself, I wondered what would happen when I explored further south.

To these regions I sent out that veteran scout, my left hand, while my tongue kept the fires warm for its return. Again her tension grew, but instead of dissolving with new caresses this time, it stayed. So, propped on my right elbow, I held my position a long time—relatively, for time stops during sex—kissing her breasts and stomach, her pajama top fully open now. I pulled her onto her side facing me, and my left hand went into a slow holding pattern along the thigh, always over her pajama pants, then to skim back north over her behind along her hip. After several circuits, I drew her knee up to let my fingertips trail along the underside of her leg, and after a while the inside, swerving away just before entering the valley of her buttocks. She seemed to accept this, though with greater reticence.

This would surely be slow going, so I decided that my first caresses between her legs would be best done with her pajama bottoms still on. *Very* lightly, I pushed her down flat again and palmed—skimmed—the top of her leg, and slid it up and down, then my hand straddled both legs, thumb on one thigh, pinky on the other. Again she tensed. So I returned my attention to her breasts, and another long shudder, like wind through a tree-filled valley, rumbled through her. Now she was ready. Complimenting myself on my astute lovemaking, I finally let my hand, now far down by her knees, slide north and north and north—no pressure, just barely grazing—to where her legs joined together.

But doesn't pride precedeth the fall every time?

"Hal! *Hal!*" And she was out of bed in a blink. She threw herself against the far wall, covered with the bed sheet. "What the heck do you think you're doin', puttin' your hand down there! That's private!"

"Mary Ann, what's the matter?"

"What's the matter? *What's the matter?*" She was crying. "Just who do you think you are? You think I'm some kind o' harlot? I never thought you'd do somethin' like that! I trusted you."

I got out of bed, and she squealed in panic.

"Mary Ann, calm down. What's the—Look, I'm not going to touch you. Just let me turn on a—"

"You doggone right you're not touchin' me! Hal, you! *You!* Treatin' me like a harlot! You think I'm some kind of just any old girl, like a dog or a cat!"

After a long, tangled moment, and after banging my toes against everything in the room, I managed to turn a light on.

I shouldn't have. She was shaking, tears running down her face, her mouth jagged. "You, you big pig. you're just like a lotta guys, all they want to do is touch you where they got no business bein'!"

"Mary Ann, *you* wanted to make love. It was *your* idea!"

"Makin' love is what we were doin' all along!"

"What?"

"I just thought it'd be nice if we did it in bed, like complete-adult people, like Alba and Javier, and there you are, tryin' to touch me in my—" She broke down crying—a force-ten storm.

I stared at her, speechless.

"I'm not a harlot, I am *not* a harlot, and I never will be!"

"*A harlot?* Where the hell did you get that?" Which of course only made things worse.

It took me ten minutes to calm her down and regain enough of her confidence for her just to talk to me. Pajamas on, I sat on the floor in front of her, giving her Kleenex, assuring, reassuring and promising

136

that we'd had a misunderstanding. She answered that not even in the dance studio did anybody touch anybody in the groin, "and if anybody does, like, just by accident, why, he apologizes plenty real quick. Even if you're in the shower, nobody even looks at you there, and we're all girls. And then to go *touchin'! Hal*, what, I don't know, gosh, what got into you?"

"That's making love, Mary Ann," I insisted, knowing that it was foolish to insist. But what else could I say?

"Yeah, that's making love, and I'm the Mississippi Queen!"

So I tried biology, but that horrified her even more.

"All you big pigs are the same. Soon's a girl's back is turned, there you are, up to your old tricks! And don't think I didn't feel that big ol' fat thing o' yours touchin' my knee down there. You were gettin' ready to do somethin' with it, weren't ya? Huh? Answer me, goddammit! Weren't ya?" She hit me on the arm—an afterthought, but it hurt. "God, I can't believe it. Even you, Hal! Even *you!*"

Finally, Alba knocked on the door. Both of us told her to come in.

"*Dios mio!* Mary Ann, you look terrible! What happened?" she cried, coming into the room.

"Ask that guy," she muttered.

I explained matters elliptically. "Now, is that normal, or is it not?" I asked Alba.

"Yes, very normal."

Mary Ann stared. "Yeah, that's normal like I'm the Mississippi Queen!"

Alba said, "Hal, perhaps I must to talk with Mary Ann alone. I, I didn't know that she—"

"No, no. Hal, stay here. It's, I'm... Just stay. Maybe you're not, I don't want to be, like, throwin' you out or nothin' just 'cause... well, you know."

So we went out to the living room, where Mary Ann tumbled onto the sofa, and I busied myself with hot chocolate for everybody. Alba, with truly poetic gentility, knelt down and explained sex to Mary Ann: erection, lubrication, copulation. It was a magisterial performance, partly in English, partly in Spanish.

"He sticks his, his, his *dick* in there?" Mary Ann said. "Are you

137

sure? And that's okay? Always? It's always okay?"

"Yes, Mary Ann, yes. Always. This is the part of your body that is made for that you share with a man. Don't worry—it is very beautiful when you are, ah, *united,* in this way." Alba explained that there were different ways of making love: the man on top or on bottom, in bed, in a chair, standing.

And now Mary Ann's hand hovered high by her cheek, and something new came into her alarmed face. She looked down, eyes wide, her mouth made a round O. I knew that look, and surely Alba did, too: Mary Ann was tying loose ends together. A comment here, a picture there, and finally things were making sense.

"And this isn't just, like, harlots? Good girls, too? Girls you'd marry? Everybody? *You?*"

"Yes, of course. Me with Javier. It is very good, very good—I told you. Mary Ann, what is a harlot? Why do you say that?"

"Oh, you know," she said with a sneer. "It's these girls you see all the time who just do whatever they want with guys, and they don't care about anything, like how they look or anything, and they never wash, like, the back of their neck or their ankles or nothin'."

Alba nodded. "Yes, this is interesting."

By now we were at the kitchen bar, and the hot chocolate was slipping down very nicely indeed. Mary Ann sat with her elbows on the counter, thinking. Finally, she raised her head.

"And you're sure this is all really, like, really nice, just like you're sayin'? I mean, it's a *good* experience, not a bad one?" She said it as if someone had told her otherwise.

"Yes, Mary Ann," said Alba. "With someone you love, it is—"

"Because you're my best friends!" Mary Ann blurted. She was between Alba and me, and threw her arms around our necks. "And I love you more than anybody in the world! You wouldn't lie to me about something like that, would you? I mean, you're not just gonna jump out at me and say, 'Surprise, it was all a joke!' 'Cause people've done that to me so many times, and I'm just so embarrassed, and it's 'cause there's just a lot of things that I don't know yet. Right? I mean, all of this is true, true, true, true. Right? All the time?"

"Yes, Mary Ann, it is *all true*—all! Mary Ann, you are hurting me!

Let go!"

She was hurting me, too—you would not believe the force she could muster in a single limb.

"Well, okay," she panted. "I'm sorry, Hal. I guess I—" She bit her lower lip. "I'll bet y'all think I'm stupid, too, now."

Alba snapped something in Spanish, but this time it didn't really do the trick.

"Yeah, but I'm always, I'm just always.... I'm always the last one to find out," she griped bitterly. "I thought I wasn't a virgin no more! I thought when Hal hugged me and I felt so, so *ZZZZZZZZZ* all over, that was—gosh! Okay, maybe I didn't study enough in school, but I, I—doggone it!—I just wanna know how everybody knows all this stuff except me! And be a lady! It just ain't fair!"

Alba hugged her and spoke Spanish for a while. "But Mary Ann, did you not hear about the sex from your friends, or have sexual education in school? Or just in watching a movie—you saw people making love. What did you think that they were doing?"

Mary Ann wiped her tears away with the sleeve of her bathrobe. "Well, gosh, I don't know. I just figured they were kissin'. 'Course, and then there's a harlot on every street corner!"

By now it was two A.M. Alba finished her hot chocolate and yawned, swept back her long hair, elegant even when messy, and got up. "Mary Ann, tomorrow I will explain you how the babies are born. For now I am going to the bed."

"Oh, I heard about that. Mrs. Kent—she was the mother of my friend in Vegas. She told me once. I mean, with the woman having eggs with their period and the guy having seeds and ever'thing like that, right? That's it?"

"Yes! But, but Mary Ann, how did you think that the seed arrived to there?"

Mary Ann's mouth made another O. "You mean every mother... does that?" Before Alba could answer: "So, it's like everybody does that when they have a baby. Wow."

"Good night," Alba sighed. "Mary Ann, tomorrow we will talk more, and I will answer all more questions, okay?" She took Mary Ann's hand and kissed it. "Okay?"

Mary Ann looked up, disturbed from her meditation. "Okay. Okay, thanks, Alba."

"And don't be a crybaby. Go make love—your boyfriend is very handsome. Hal, if she don't make love to you, come to wake me up. I am two weeks without sex, and I am dying."

I laughed, and Mary Ann said, "You big ol' rat."

Alba left, and Mary Ann sat hunched over the chocolate milk, brow knitted deeply. I had nothing to say and said it. I returned to Mary Ann's bedroom and re-made her bed. She had thrown the bedclothes all the way across the room; one pillow had ended up on her writing table. Then I went for my sheets and blankets for the sofa on the top shelf of her closet. I was beat—and angry with myself. I could have avoided the whole scene. All I'd had to do was consider the likely possibility that what Mary Ann had called "making love" might not be the dictionary version.

What a fool I was, I chided myself. *I humiliated her.*

I had used a chair to get my sofa bedclothes down, and as I reached the floor, I felt Mary Ann's arms go around me. Her head thunked against my back.

"Hal, I don't know what to say. I just didn't know. There are just so many doggone, *doggone* things I don't know yet! It just makes me—"

I put the bedclothes on the chair and turned around. "It's really my own fault, Mary Ann. I should have talked it over with you first."

"You don't have to talk it over first with a normal, grown-up woman—*do ya?*" she said bitterly.

I shrugged. "So what law says you have to know everything by the time you're twenty? Hell, I remember explaining to my ex-wife how to fry a hamburger. She'd never done it before. And she was older than you are now."

Mary Ann's eyes went wide. "Really? A dumb ol' hamburger?"

"That's right. B.A. degree in Sociology, Master's in Psychology, Doctorate from Duke University, head of the Mayor's Task Force on Education. And she'd never cooked in her life. Always had her mother cook—or ate out." *And damn the cost,* I might have added. And damn me if I had to do the cooking after a sixteen-hour push at work, for in those days, AllPoint Engineering wasn't a job, but a lifestyle.

"Wow. That's just about unb'lievable."

"Well, it's true—one hundred percent. And I had to eat a lot of burned hamburger before she got any good at it." How she'd screamed and accused me. And made me go out to a nouvelle-cuisine restaurant with her every day for the next week. No cheap Chinese affair for our Dana, not when she was in her little mood. "Everyone develops in their own good time."

"Yeah—*developin'*. That's important, I heard somethin' 'bout that." Her brow wrinkled, and she nodded gravely to my chest and pulled me close. My erection started against her hip bone again, and I tried to pull away slightly, but she wouldn't let me.

"The point is, Mary Ann...." And then I didn't know what the point was at all. My hand suddenly rose and cupped her cheek. I looked into those liquid eyes, and it was like looking down a well. "My god, there is no end to you, is there?" I whispered. "You're just this ocean, and every time I think I'm about to reach bottom, I realize I haven't gone halfway. "

She watched me for a long moment, then took my hand and pulled it under her bathrobe to her breast. "Well, I think I kinda got this now, like, y'know—figured out. So you wanna just go ahead?"

"Making love."

"Yeah—makin' love, and like, with your, y'know, like, with your, y'know, your dick and all."

"You're sure?"

"Yeah, let's do it now while, y'know, we're together and, like, on the same tempo here."

But I could tell it all frightened her. "We can wait if you—"

"No, if Alba says it's normal, well, it just is, and that's that." She swallowed. "I just gotta grow up, Hal. I really do. I can't have you waitin' for me forever. I gotta be complete. I mean, just, just, like, now when you come to that part, with your dick and all, you tell me, okay? So I can be ready."

"All right—if you're sure."

"Yeah, yeah, I'm sure. And you don't even have to turn out the lights or nothin'. And you can look at anything you want. Look."

And to prove it, she slipped out of her robe and pajamas in two swift movements and slipped into bed—though if I'd blinked, I would have missed it. She wasn't too comfortable about my being naked, either, so I got into bed quickly.

I turned out the light, and we made love—dick and all.

16

She was not a virgin. She was a harlot.

In the year, perhaps a little more, before she ran away from home at the age of twelve, the Reverend had raped her. On a regular basis. So did her older brothers, Ham and Ted—though, curiously, never Frank.

The sex began in circumstances Mary Ann could only sketchily describe as we lay in her single bed staring at the tattoo of blue light. I told Mary Ann that I knew she wasn't a virgin—and then explained how I knew. After that, the story came out, and I learned what the Reverend's soupy grin of relief—back at the Chicago meeting—had been about.

It seemed that the Reverend had been going through a bad streak: he was frustrated that he couldn't break into television evangelism, probably had money problems, and the death of his wife some years before must have been, in sexual terms, a burden. Home from his traveling preaching one day, he saw Mary Ann dancing around the living room, aping the dancers she was watching on music videos, which she watched all the time. The next thing she knew, he had jerked off her shorts, and hung her over the coffee table. The session ended in the bathroom, with the Reverend bitterly apologizing and grabbing every towel in the house to stanch the bleeding. Mary Ann, though horrified, seized her one chance to please, and told him that it was all right, that she was okay, and forgave him.

"I just wanted him to love me, Hal, and I told him that it was okay, 'specially if it was a help to him."

That night he came to her bedside and told her that he had committed a terrible sin and that he would never do it again; Mary Ann again replied that she would help him whenever he wanted. Her kind word, it turned out, trumped anything that the Bible said, and the sessions soon became regular. He treated her gently, it is worth adding, without kisses or caresses or humiliating foreplay, just a scoop of Vaseline for each of them, bang-bang, done. Mary Ann doesn't remember suffering any pain. The Reverend was grateful to her, even hugged her afterwards, and for once she felt like something more than a hired hand. He even brought her sweets.

"Heck, that was the only nice time I remember in that house. I didn't care about the rubbin', I just wanted—"

"Rubbin'?" I asked.

"The, y'know, the bedroom and the Reverend and everything like that."

"Right."

Silence, and the blue light beat across the room, flayed by the blinds; I could almost feel its impact on my eyes. "See, I didn't know there was nothin' wrong with it till I was livin' in Vegas, and I heard about this one thing on the radio."

The "rubbin'" continued for some months, Mary Ann thinks. Then, somehow, the brothers discovered the fun. When the Reverend went away on his preaching travels, Ham and Ted worked a tag-team against her. Once, they wanted oral sex, but Mary Ann, aghast, threw up on one brother's penis—to the other's great merriment, she remembers. The Reverend eventually got wind of events and he was not happy. He accused Mary Ann of being a harlot—of actually enjoying this and of cooperating with her brothers in order to get more sweets. Mary Ann replied that they had forced her, but she cut no ice with anyone. From then on, the Reverend began shoving her around, swatting her into position, bellowing, "Harlot! You're nothin' but a damn harlot!" as he slammed into her from behind. "You love this, don't ya? You can't get enough of it, so you're on to Ted and Ham!"

Maybe it was for this reason that Mary Ann's orgasms came as much from her vagina as from her breasts.

"Y'see, Hal? That's why I got so, so squished up when you touched my, y'know, touched me between the legs and all. I heard about makin' love and all before, sure, I just didn't know it was, y'know, the same as a rubbin'. I thought that's what harlots did. Hey, is there anything else you can do, I mean, to make love?"

"No, only what we did—though like Alba said, you can do it in different positions."

Silence. The light beat on the wall: so many beats, so much time, is all you get. "Heck, not much to it, is there?"

The punishment for harlots, even cooperative ones, was the same as for other transgressions: a night on the straw with Bolts. But after some particularly grievous offense—Mary Ann couldn't recall just what—she was to be banished to the barn every night for an entire week, and Mary Ann decided enough was enough. She escaped through the loft, stole a wad of Frank's truck-savings money and ran away.

I managed to turn off the alarm clock before it rang, but no sooner did I swing my legs out of bed than Mary Ann wanted to make love again, and I will never forget the sight of her in the pearly light coming in through the blinds. She sat on top this time, sweat running down her temples in rivers, and I sat caressing and licking her nipples, which with even a little work inflated and turned as hard as unripe peaches. When she reached orgasm, she twisted her head down and away from me—so far that it was grotesque—her left arm pressed into her solar plexus till the muscles in her shoulder stood up in waves and troughs. Her other arm rose skyward in super-slow motion, vibrating with rigidity. She growled from deep in the throat as her arm extended, rose, turning, caressing God's beard. Then came a long sigh as she slid back to earth. Then again, and again, before she was done. My own orgasm, by comparison, was the merest coda.

Except for the tears. As after the first time, she lay silent on me, and they trickled into my hair at the temples and joined some of my own. After tending to hygiene, she fell deeply asleep.

I slipped out of bed, took a shower, and shaved with the cheap electric razor that Javier left for his visits. I dressed in the living room, though I had left a few things in Mary Ann's room—my watch, keys and change. I crept in and scooped them off her little writing desk, where I had cleared a postcard-sized corner for them at the edge of her growing forest of sprays and perfumes and lotions. I noticed a stack of CDs in an open desk drawer. Mary Ann had taken a package of Kleenex from it after our first go-round that night. What drew my eye

144

was the oddity: she and Alba had all their CDs and DVDs in the living room, on the book shelf. What CDs were these, kept in a drawer?

Audio books. With growing dread, I quickly picked through them till, at the very bottom, I found the one I was looking for: *The Great Gatsby*.

17

It occurs to me, this late in my story, that practically all I have presented to you about Mary Ann relates to her life outside the dance studio. During the period that our gradual coming together took place, she was working on Sergio Adán's new show, *Revelaciones*. So, ladies and gentlemen, without further ado….

In late May, Sergio Adán gave me two second-row-center tickets and told me mysteriously, "Get to your seat a little early. You'll enjoy the show more." I had heard the same from both Alba and Mary Ann, though not a soul, not even Bertie, would tell me why. Having two tickets, and rather than invite Frank, I flew my mother up to New York from her Florida retirement home; my father, incidentally, had passed away a few years before. She dusted off an ancient black gown, pearls, and some high-heeled shoes; and walked into the Bellevedere with such authority that a couple of Japanese tourists snapped photos of her, lest they miss some 1960s Oscar-winner.

And inside—"My word! Well, isn't this something, Hal? It looks like Ed Sullivan is going to walk out right out and introduce us as eminent persons!"

The Bellevedere's stage was the kind you see at the Academy Awards ceremony, with three steps running its curving width and connecting it to the seat area. To my surprise, the stage was empty. A dozen antique dressing-room mirrors, placed at irregular intervals and inclinations, formed a semi-circle at the rear, and amidst these stood tall tables and stools, as in a café. Behind them were rolling racks of clothing—the kind pushed down Fifth Avenue by Italians and Chinese. No curtains, neutral lighting, black floor. That was all. As we sat down, two male dancers came out carrying boxes of liter bottles of mineral water. They put them on the tables and walked off.

A few dancers came out. They wore simple leotards and tee shirts and stretchy tops with thin straps and gym shorts and heavy socks—just the way I'd seen them in Sergio's studio. Some were barefooted, some wore the thick, medium heels for "pounding nails." They chatted and stretched, palming the floor, bending backwards until they fell and ended up doing handstands. Some did "fan kicks."

To the far-right side of the stage were five ladder-back chairs, low tables with water, and microphones on spindly stands. Here two copper-skinned guitarists sat down and began tuning up. One was smoking, after a few puffs, he dropped the cigarette and crushed it out with his foot. Santiago came out carrying a stack of white towels. He hung them on hooks under the tall tables. A group of young women up on the second deck yelled at him and he grinned enormously and waved.

"Well, this seems rather *informal,* doesn't it?" my mother murmured, and I wondered if I shouldn't have brought my sister Beth.

And now Mary Ann, wearing a light-blue leotard and slippers, back straight as a rake, strolled out of the wings. She took a long, black skirt off a rack at the back of the stage, stepped into it, and pulled it up to her hips. Then she put on a pair of nail-pounding pumps, using an arm-long shoe horn so that she didn't have to sit down. Spotting me, she came down the stage, down the three steps to the stage floor, and knelt on the first-row seat in front of us.

An odd start to a Broadway show.

"Hey, Hal! Well! You made it, huh?" she giggled.

"So, you're all ready to go?" I said uncertainly.

"You bet. And this must be your mother, right? Hello, Mrs. Dormund, I am so happy to meet you."

"It's very nice to meet *you,* Mary Ann," said my mother, shaking her hand. "Is this, ah, this is the show?"

"Oh, yeah. Sergio said he wanted to, y'know, not just raise the curtain and away we go, but, kinda, like, y'know, get everybody comfortable and then just ease into it."

And now I noticed that other dancers were doing the same thing as Mary Ann. To our left, Santiago had come out to the edge of the stage and was calling to the women up on the second deck, also Spaniards.

"Oye, Mariana," he said to Mary Ann, and added something else in Spanish, pointing at his friends.

"Oh, those guys. They're Santiago's fan club," she muttered, grinning and waving up to them. "'Course, half of 'em's his doggone sisters. I met 'em yesterday. They're nice, but, y'know, kinda like, squeaky. Excuse me a sec'."

She walked over to Santiago, put her arm around his waist, and shouted something at the balcony. A girl replied, and Mary Ann called something back, pointing at Santiago, and the girls roared with laughter. Then she came back to us.

"Oh. Oh my. Do you speak Spanish, dear?" Mom asked.

"Yeah, after a while, you kinda get the hang of it." She turned and pointed to the musicians. "And you see those guys? They're Gypsies—real, live Gypsies from Spain. *Gitanos,* they call 'em. And they don't speak a word o' English, I swear to God. They just came this week, 'cause we been practicin' with live music and fixin' ever'thing up. Sergio wanted to bring 'em sooner, but he didn't have enough money."

"Ah, a pity."

"And they sure like girls, golly-gosh! That one guy there on the accordion—Juan Carlos? He doesn't know too many words in English, but the ones he does know—holy cow!"

Twenty feet down, a woman was waving to her, and Mary Ann wandered over there and began to speak with a tiny Vietnamese woman—Mrs. Thuy, I assumed, for whatever they were speaking sounded a great deal like mushy Ping-Pong balls making *bao bao bao.* After a minute, she returned to us and said, "Oh, Hal, I forgot to thank you for the flowers you sent to my dressing room."

"My pleasure. Smell good?"

"Are you kiddin'? My room smells like the perfume department in Macy's! Just the kinda thing you want to smell after a performance." She lowered her voice. "'Cause me, like, I get so doggone sweaty. 'Specially this show—lotsa poundin' nails and no innermission."

"Sounds pretty grueling," I said.

"Oh, heck, once we get started on a program, last thing I wanna do is stop. Alba says Sergio's tryin' to kill everybody, not givin' us any rest. But she's just an ol' ragbag."

My mother put her hand on Mary Ann's. "Are you nervous, dear? I used to have a whole flock of butterflies in my stomach before a concert. I was a harpist, you know, with the Chicago Symphony Orchestra."

I had to smother a smile: Mary Ann looked about as nervous as a merry-go-round in full flight.

"Yeah, Hal told me. I sure woulda liked to hear ya. But no, no, Mrs. Dormund—nothin' like that. Heck, it's a lot more fun doin' a show than gettin' worked to death in the studio. 'Specially *this* show. It's gonna be so much fun! And it just doesn't stop till the very last second. Oh, and you're just gonna laugh till your sides split, too, when Sergio gets goin'."

"Sergio dances, too?" I asked.

"Oh yeah—a big ol' solo. It kinda gives everybody else a break. I'm kinda worried about him, though. He didn't sell out tonight—not nearly—'cause that big rat Raymond Radow moved up his openin' to tonight, tryin' ta swamp us. But he ain't gonna. You just wait and see. We're gonna kick his fanny up and down Broadway." She turned around and pointed to the center of the stage. "That's Alba right there. Hey, Alba! Hal's here with his mom!"

Alba waved.

"I'll see you later, okay, Hal? You know, like after that show in Chicago? Count to a hundred?"

"Will do," I replied, hoping that she couldn't see the tears that sprang into my eyes.

"My goodness, what a lovely young lady," said my mother. She jerked me to her ear. "I'll certainly have a good story to tell the boys and girls at chorus practice tomorrow evening. That my son's girlfriend is a professional dancer on Broadway?"

"At least this week she is. If they don't sell more tickets—"

"And they're already talking about marriage, too, dear?"

Mom used to be more subtle.

For several minutes, as the last of the audience dribbled in, the dancers on stage limbered up, drank water, and chatted with the audience. The *Gitanos,* with shoulder-length hair and dressed in black shirts open well down the front, came out one by one, as if reluctantly.

There were five of them, two with guitars, one singer, one with an accordion, and the last sitting on a box that looked like a dresser drawer stood on end, whose bottom he tapped or banged between his open legs. He wore a black bandanna over his forehead and was laughing about something with the singer, who suddenly burst out with a heavily accented, "I am se-e-e-enging in the rain, just se-e-e-enging in the rain." People laughed—but uneasily. I think everyone was wondering if they'd come way too early or way too late.

The guitars began tuning up with the accordion. One of the guitarists griped something, and the accordionist played a different note. Then he made a few riffs up and down his keys, and the guitarists followed him with astonishing lightness.

Sergio came out—now dressed in janitor's togs—and spread a sweet-smelling powder over the stage and worked it in with his shoes. A few people applauded, and he shrugged and called something in Spanish, and then, "C'mon! I haven't done nohthin' yet!" and walked off.

Alba rolled her hair into a bun and put castanets on her fingers. Santiago played a drum roll with his heels. Gripping a table with one hand, Mary Ann raised her leg sideways right up to vertical a half-dozen times, then did the other leg. Darryl, he who had braved the basement mice, slashed the stage with his feet like a hockey goalie prepping the ice. Two dancers swung each other around, another made a test series of flips across the stage and was mostly satisfied. The one black dancer leapt and touched his feet. Santiago stretched his magnificent frame and clapped his hands, then another clapped his between Santiago's beats to form a staccato. A guitarist played a riff. Almost imperceptible, a silent collaboration was growing, like an ambush about to take place, a cord about to be snapped taut. The dresser-drawer drummer tapped a quick series of rolls, like a car revving at the starting line: all of his fingers were taped.

Then Alba made a series of riveting thunders across the stage with her heels. Santiago answered with his own from the other side of the stage. The singer shouted "Olé!" The guitars banged a loud chord, the singer and the drummer clapped fast staccato, three dancers rippled castanets....

And they were off.

M ary Ann wasn't kidding: *Revelaciones* never stopped—not for 105 minutes; nor did you want it to. The basis of everything was flamenco—hard, dramatic, and tender—but which veered off into mixes with jazz, tango, even ballroom. It was easy to see why it had taken Sergio years to find the right combination of dancers: they had to change from flamenco to tango or tango to jazz. The *Gitanos,* a versatile crew indeed, kept up with all this, and without a scrap of score sheet among them. The singer occasionally chopped the air to cue them—that was all.

The dancers flew up and down the stage, either dancing, changing costumes behind the mirrors, toweling off, or gulping water—all the bottles replaced by Sergio, who moved behind the clothes racks and mirrors. And drink they did; the many nail-pounding flamenco numbers were incredibly demanding. The men, who often danced shirtless, finished their numbers as shiny as fish, the women with their hair stuck to their foreheads.

Their only break was during solos or duos—Alba, long hair flying, did a gut-sensuous tango with the African. Twice Sergio came on stage in his janitor's togs, pushing a six-foot wide mop of the kind they use in basketball games between periods. People shouted, "Sergio! Dance!" He only flapped a grumpy hand. The dancers, mock-angry, pointed to places on the floor he had missed. At one point, Alba snatched the mop and did one side of the stage, bitching at Sergio in Spanish. Then the *Gitanos* got into it, implying that cleaning was a woman's job to start with. Nobody could understand a word. It was hilarious.

The third time Sergio came out, he danced with the mop, or at least with its long, day-glow-pink pole. That's right: just as in Fred Astaire's famous scene with the coat rack. Sergio dodged and played and jigged around it while the *Gitanos* played the same tune as in Astaire's routine. And Sergio carried it off with real art. The idea was simple: the universality of music and dance. If a Gypsy band and Sergio Adán could do this same routine a half-century later, the possibilities for mixing and matching styles and music were endless.

And then there was Mary Ann's part. I had wondered often, since my conversation with Sergio in his studio, what he had meant by "court jester." But that's just what she was. She was the single thread running through the entire eclectic production. Once, she came out "late" for a new number, and the Gitano singer-leader stopped the band. He gestured to the audience—"I'm sorry"—strode over to her, where she was changing behind the clothes racks, griping at "Mariana" in Spanish and pointing at his watch. When he reached the clothes racks—two were pulled together for her and another dancer to change clothes—she screamed in alarm, making him jump back. Then she darted out, pulling on a blouse and bitching right back at the amazed man in Spanish. Then she walked right down center stage and said to the audience, "I told the man, 'I'm *comin'*, and I meant I am *comin'!*"

On two occasions, three couples began to dance, and Mary Ann was left grasping the air for a partner. So she danced through the couples, pounding nails faster and harder than any of them, and so well that the *Gitanos* roared their approval—quite out of the script.

The sparks of humor, rare for dance, provided the perfect accent for the otherwise artistic program. Just ask Raymond Radow, whose show closed after ten days.

And the heart of it, the *Revelación,* was Mary Ann. At the end of the program, the *Gitanos* clapping in staccato and strumming and singing for all they were worth, the stage faded to dark, with one spotlight each on Mary Ann and Santiago—clearly the male lead. It was their only number together, though as with a romance movie, you had anticipated this for most of the show. They did a furious, heel-pounding flamenco, challenging and answering one another by turns, and so long and hard and loud that their sudden STOP made you jump. In the silence, a guitar strummed a single chord, Santiago pivoted—and disappeared. It took you a moment to realize that he had slid behind a black screen rolled out from the wings.

Now it was just Mary Ann and one guitarist visible on the pitch-dark stage, a single beam of light on each. The guitar strummed warm, reflective chords, like waves lapping a shore, and Mary Ann floated in the dark, swaying, spinning, sliding, skimming, her big smile like a diamond floating in the air. With a flick, she sent her long blue dress flying up and over a black screen into oblivion, and now you could enjoy her wonderful body, displayed in a white gymnast's leotard with a rainbow of sequins down the sides. In casual violation of Sergio's rules, she rose to her tiptoes like a ship reaching the very crest of a wave, now slipped down the trough. She pirouetted, and sweat burst from her hair like sparks.

Finally, the chords falling from tension to final resolution, Mary Ann slid back and back, shoulders now hunched in pleasure, now released in a sigh. She might have been hanging from stage wires, so light was her contact with earth. Now she swept one way, then the other, one way, then the other, one way, then wiped herself away behind a black screen. The guitarist strummed a final chord, and the light on him blinked out. The other remained a moment longer, and her floating hand appeared, waving good-night. Perfect.

The ovation lasted twenty minutes and ended with Sergio and Santiago pushing a reluctant Mary Ann, towel around her neck and soaked in sweat to the waist, out to the very front of the stage for a last solo bow. The audience roared, and Mary Ann smiled and curtseyed with a startled dubiety; this only engaged her more with the audience. It was fabulous. More than that, it occurred to me, here was one of life's rare strokes of justice. After her cruel childhood, the sexual abuse, the endless embarrassments, the scary blur that was life outside the studio, the thousands of hours training, training, training, training—for once, redemption.

All it had taken was a half-delirious nuclear engineer to point out the green light at the end of the dock. That was the goal. And Mary Ann had jumped right into the water and swum for it against cold, wind, tide and current. She had taken all my overwrought, jet-lagged platitudes to heart, and now stood, wringing wet, at the goal.

Mary Ann, too, felt the poignancy of that historic moment: in her dressing room ten minutes later, I would find her in the middle of a hurricane of sobbing, Bertie the business manager standing over her, stroking her hair. "I'm not sad, Hal, I'm not. I'm real happy. But, but, but I just can't stop. Don't tell nobody, okay? Not even Alba."

Three weeks later, as the Bellevedere sold out night after night and *Revelaciones* rode a tidal wave of reviews and news reports, she appeared alone on the covers of *Time* and, posed with Santiago, *Newsweek*. But it is the *Time* cover that I like so much: Mary Ann during her solo, silhouetted in sequins and crowned by that gorgeous red hair, body raised effortlessly on one toe, left leg dead-level wrapped around an invisible lover, right arm around his shoulders, one grateful hand extended to the sky, her head cambered delicately, eyes closed, smiling like a baby just reaching sleep. I literally gasped when I saw it; Michelangelo could have done no better.

Everyone deserves their defining picture for the history books—Ali taunting the fallen Liston, Satchmo with his sweat and handkerchief and trumpet, Philippe Petit strolling his wire between the Twin Towers. Let that be Mary Ann's.

18

"*Hal!* Oh, I'm so glad you answered. I tried to get Sergio on the phone, but his phone was busy and so was Bertie's and I remembered you're arrivin' today. I'm so scared, Hal. I'm in the *police* station! They *arrested* me, Hal! And they took my fingerprints and read me my rights just like on TV 'cept I didn't do nothin' wrong. Just a man I met in a department store he handed me a bag of this powder and said it was good for my plants and that he liked the show so much and he just wanted to give me this stuff and said I should smell it, but I sneezed, and then the police stopped me when I was walkin' out 'cause I was buyin' this black sweater for Alba for her birthday and they said I was carryin' cocaine, Hal! *Cocaine!* They said it said so right on the bag, I just didn't notice, really honest, I didn't!"

It was about two weeks after opening night. I was in JFK, having just arrived from Mexico, and was planning to spend the weekend in New York. I tried to get in a word, but no good.

"And I said no, no, no, I never touch that stuff 'cause Sergio told me it's really bad for ya and it'll throw off your timin' like Sheena, and then I came here and the police let me call someone, anybody I like, and they let me use my cell phone, they were really nice about it, especially 'cause my hands are shakin' so hard I can't press the buttons right, so he even dialed it for me, this policeman, Mr. Arkus, 'cept he doesn't wear a uniform like those other guys, he was real nice but he's pretty serious too...."

I needed to shout to bring her to earth. I told her to give the phone to someone and asked where Mary Ann was.

Fifty minutes later, and barely ninety before Mary Ann was due on stage, I dragged my briefcase and suitcase through the precinct door. By this time, I had reached Bertie at the studio, who told me to keep her informed and that she would move heaven and earth, and I knew that where Mary Ann was concerned, heaven and earth were nothing for her.

"And you tell those fat mothuhfuckuhs down at the precinct that if they so much as touch a hair on that angel's head that I will shove a lawsuit so far up their ass they puke."

From the taxi, I also called my brother Henry, the lawyer. I told him to shut up and listen, and he did, first having walked straight out of a movie negotiation worth, he later told me, seven million bucks. He reduced the matter to size with four careful questions. I had intended to ask if he knew of any decent lawyers in New York; his reply was advice that I hadn't expected.

"Wrong, wrong, wrong. You're still in the heart-strings phase, buddy. Find 'em and pull 'em. Remind the investigating detective that it could be his/her daughter, his/her girlfriend. Like it's someone who played a dirty trick on your babe, it's someone trying to derail her career, besmirch her rep. You said she's got a rep there in the Apple, right?"

"She does now." The first earthquakes had been shaking the airwaves for more than a week by then. Serious critics were calling *Revelaciones* the best show since *A Chorus Line.*

"Perfect. Go the whole nine yards. Cry. Pull lapels. But not a word of negativity, got it? No threats, no taking his/her name down, no cheap shots about taxpayer dollars or haven't-you-got-anything-better-to-dos. Now if they say they're going to take her down on distribution, which they probably will if there's an actual bagful at stake, don't—"

"Distribution?"

"Possession with intent to distribute to third parties—like the other dancers, for example. If they go that way, then you talk up the money. Someone just walked up and gave this stuff to her in a department store, right? Therefore no exchange of money, therefore *very* suspect—whole thing. You play that up big time. There's your ace: she didn't *ask* for the shit, she didn't *pay* for it. If push comes to shove, call in—"

"Henry, what about a *lawyer?*"

"No lawyers, not yet. Everybody hates lawyers. Besides, it sounds to me like your babe's spilled every bean she ever had."

"You can say that again," I murmured.

"Now: if it comes to shove, call in the department store and ask them for video of your babe with the pusher. Still, personally, lawyer's instinct here, I don't think it'll get that far."

"No?" I said hopefully.

"First place, your babe's got a rep—in the *entertainment* world, in *New York.* You play that up: cops *love* stars. Cops fall all over each other here just to escort Dustin to the Oscars. Second place: Hal buddy, do you know how much space one single, simple, easy, open-and-shut-it coke bust uses up? Think megas, gigas. If those cops can avoid a write-fest and feel good doin' it, they will."

After all manner of argument with a police warden, I was allowed into the interrogation room. Nothing odd: a two-way mirror and a stink of antiseptic that could put you in a coma. There I found an ut-terly, utterly discomposed Mary Ann, whose ice-cold hands shook so hard that I had to put them under my shirt. She had been in a holding cell till then, and the hoods and junkies and hookers had scared the living shit out of her. In fact, the warden only allowed me in to calm her down; the detectives needed to get a "courtable" confession out of her. And if I couldn't do it, Mary Ann had to take a shot and spend the night in "the can."

Once I got Mary Ann to listen to me, I reminded her to count to one hundred, and then it would all be over. Mary Ann nodded, still trembling, and said, "Okay. Yeah. That's right. That's what I'm gonna do here: just close my eyes and count to a hundred. Just count, nice and slow and steady. Then it's all gonna be over."

I wondered.

At my insistence—I employed Henry's fillip that it could be *your* daughter in there—the warden then led me into a messy, roiled general office for detectives, pointed vaguely to the far wall, and said, "There's your detectives, Arkus and Pill." I wove across a junkyard of desks to them, dodging men with coffee cups and tripping on computer cables steeped in dust. Faded *Wanted* posters were the only decoration, and the windows, high up near the ceiling, were mud-streaked safety-glass.

Other pertinent facts of the case—I heard one of them recording their joint report—were these: the man who had approached Mary Ann was blond and thirtyish and round-faced. He told her he had seen her in the show. Then he presented her with a bag of cocaine. It was a big load, as those things go: 112 grams, the weight of a hamburger patty. He told her it was good for plants—she had plants in her apartment, didn't she? Well, yes, she did—a whole windowsill full of them that she and Alba were quite proud of. He invited her to smell the powder. She did, as the man quickly wiggled the bag under her nose—obviously trying to get some to hit home—but Mary Ann, by a miracle, sneezed violently three or four times, and saved herself. He and Mary Ann had a good laugh over that.

Then the man kindly re-tied the little sandwich bag, showed her where he had written "good for plants" on a bit of masking tape on the outside—"just so that you won't confuse it with flour!" he said with a chuckle. He wished her good luck and went on his way. Oh, and don't stick it in your purse till your outside, the man advised, or they'll think you're robbing the store. The NYPD detectives, alerted by the store's floor security that a woman was carrying a bag of cocaine, picked up Mary Ann as she was leaving. They knew it was cocaine because the lettering on the masking tape did not say "good for plants," but "PURE COCAINE FOR YOU"—just like that, in big capitals.

"All right, so somebody's trying to give her a bad reputation," I said to the detectives, having introduced myself.

"With *112 grams* of powduh? You could do the job plenty with ten," said Lieutenant William Arkus. He was chunky, dully dressed in a suit and pulled-down tie, and had a slightly bloated, alcoholic face that had been handsome ten years before.

"And save yourself, call it, what would you say, Bill? The cost of a trip to Vegas?" added Lieutenant Zynanna Pill.

"Just a weekend package deal, but that'd do it," Arkus deadpanned.

"Damn, I could use a trip to Vegas myself," said Pill, and I didn't doubt it. She was about 32, and I guessed that her long, pointed African face displayed many roles before she could sleep at night: those of cop, mother, and for some other equally exhausted face, girlfriend.

Arkus signed a form, the pen moving weightlessly in his brick-like hand. The two sat back-to-back at their desks and spoke to me sideways. "'Good for her plants'—duh fuck—now do you really believe that?" griped Arkus. "It's white, it's powdery, and she had a good sniff of it. Hell'd she think it was? Sugah?"

"Sure wasn't plant fertilizer," muttered Pill.

"Well, she went from talking with the man to buying a sweater. Doesn't that speak for her innocence?" I said.

"Hey, I'm not gonna be unreasonable here," said Pill, and I braced myself, for that very expression is used most often by the narrow-minded. "Look, if she had walked straight to store security and turned it in, dat would be one thing. We'd come, take a name and statement, and have a good day. But there she was, walking around the store so long that security got called in."

"But doesn't that prove my point?" I said gently, as if this were a merely intriguing, academic idea. "Who would walk around a department store with a bag of cocaine?"

"I've heard dumber stories," said Arkus. He was checking a written list of half-a-dozen addresses, though I couldn't see why. "One guy swore up and down to me he thought it was bakin' powduh he'd got by mistake from his neighbor. Told me such a good story that I actually went back the next day and talked to the neighbor."

Pill's head whipped round from her computer. "That guy in Queens? You didn't!" she gasped.

"Hadda get through a fuckin' 45-minute traffic jam and everything. Stood there in his doorway like the dumbest piece of shit you ever saw."

Pill laughed so shrilly I wanted to block my ears.

"What about the store's security vid?" I asked. "No money was exchanged, that part's verifiable, so this isn't exactly like the playground pusher getting a shipment to sell to others, is it? I mean, Ms. Jaalkov mentioned that she didn't actually pay for that stuff, right?"

"Already talked to Security. They're advised, it'll all get checked

157

tomorruh," said Arkus and banged a couple of keys on his computer.

"Tomorrow?" I blurted. "For the love of god, she has a performance at eight!"

"Eight?" Pill checked her watch, a large, manly thing: it was after seven. "Well, I got news for you: she's gonna miss it. Just arraignment is gonna take hours."

Arkus reached for a pack of mint gum, offered Pill a stick over his shoulder, took one for himself, and said, *"What* puhformance? She sing in the church choir?"

"She didn't tell you?"

"Tell us what?"

"Jesus!" I snatched my briefcase off the floor. "Mary Ann, you see, has no sense of, of, of...."

"Of what, for Chrissakes?" said Arkus.

"Of what she does." I jerked out my entire copy of *The New York Times* and dropped everything except the Entertainment Section on the floor; I had bought it in an airport in Buenos Aires the day before. "This is the woman you arrested. She's on in an hour in the Bellevedere."

Silence. Both detectives swiveled their chairs, staring at the foot-wide color photo, a PR shot that showed Mary Ann and Santiago leaning together, shoulder to shoulder, the pink mop handle between them. In front, Sergio sat on the floor, head in hand, looking like the janitor. "Can Arkansas dance flamenco?" read the caption. "Sergio Adán and principal dancers Mary Ann Jaalkov and Santiago San Juan."

"Fuckin' look at dat," Arkus muttered and glanced up at the date on the header.

"Oh yeah: *Revelaciones,"* murmured Pill. "Friend o' mine saw that last week. Said it was great."

"She the stah?" Arkus asked me.

"Yeah, one of two," I said.

They read a few lines and stared at the face.

"Motive?" said Pill aridly, looking up. She wore a leather jacket and pants and a stretchy top over a good bosom, though they did nothing for that storied face. "And I am talkin' *motive,* mister. I'm talkin' weekend-in-Vegas motive. So don't tell me it's some sensationalist rag that wants to raise readership for a couple o' days. You tell me who set her up and why."

Now, I thought. *Carefully. Use the momentum.*

I flipped out another of Henry's cards. "Easy. Someone doesn't like seeing little Miss Arkansas hit the big time, and that someone set her up. That someone wants her name in the papers beside the word 'cocaine.' And that someone would do it just to trip up the dance company because Mary Ann is—"

"Someone like *who?*" snapped Pill.

"How about Raymond Radow? More specifically how about his big star, Sheena Biggs? Sheena got fired in March and Mary Ann took her place. Ask *Sheena* about motive. Ask *Radow* about the millions his show has lost because it closed this week because *Revelaciones* is the hottest ticket in town."

"A *revenge* motive? Over a Broadway musical? Go fish," said Arkus.

Pill saved me. "Oh, you don't know those entertainment types, Bill. That's blood sport these days, what with fallin' revenues."

Arkus looked at the newspaper again. "Yeah, maybe."

They tipped, they tipped....

"Yeah, but how's this gonna wash?" said Arkus. "Okay, guy walks up to duh girl in the middle of Macy's and hands her a bag that says "pure coke for you" on it. Suspect takes said bag? Says thank you? Walks happily away? No no no no, fuck dat." He said, turning away.

"All right, you want an explanation? Here it is," I said. I took a breath and jumped off the deep end. "She can't read the bag. She's dyslexic. She can't even read that review in the paper. Not even the headlines."

Arkus puffed out his cheeks and blew. "Oh, su-u-u-u-re."

"Dyslexic—sees everything bassackward," said Pill doubtfully.

"That's right. It's really embarrassing for her—she tells everyone that she forgot her glasses, even me." Then it hit me: "Of course! That's the whole point: to get Mary hauled up in front of a judge and have to admit to the whole world that she can't read!"

Pill, who was still facing me at least partially, nodded. "Like 'specially if she's top bill in this show, you mean."

"That's it."

Arkus made a fussy gesture with his computer mouse. "Duh fuck. Dis is America. Everyone can read."

"Yeah, what is this? Dyslexics can learn to read," said Pill.

"Dis is America," Arkus repeated. "They got special programs—"

"Sure, but Mary Ann Jaalkov is from a small town in Arkansas. She—"

"Yeah, and she got special education, just like everybody else. It's *impossible* dat—"

"Hold on, Bill. Hold on. I've told you ten million times: you can go two miles from here—"

"And find kids where they don't have special ed. and runnin' water and they have to do their homework on the back of a fuckin' shovel," Arkus said tiredly.

"That's right. Man says she can't read, she's dyslexic, never got cured, you believe him. See what I mean about you bein' from Burb-land?" To me: "We have this kind of runnin' argument, y'see."

Arkus looked at her, swung his head through 270 degrees and looked at me. Then his fat hand darted forward and snatched his sheet of paper with the addresses. "Fine and fuckin' dandy: let's check it out." He creased the paper in half, fastidiously placed the crease on the edge of the table, and tore it off. On the clean half-sheet, he wrote with a black, felt-tip pen in letters an inch high: *I SUCK AS A DANCER*. He shoved it at me. "Here ya go, slugguh. She puts her autograph on dat, she walks." He launched his bulk out of the chair and brushed past me. "Let's go."

"Wait," said Pill. "She can't write, can she?"

"She can sign her name. It's just a scribble to her."

Arkus swung around: "One more thing, mistuh, and watch the lips heah: you whispuh to her, make any kind of hand sign, and it's all ovuh: she gets duh can, and she can slit her fuckin' wrists for all I care."

He stalked off, Pill followed, and I left my *Times* splayed on the floor and walked after them, praying I was right. Had she really memorized all those pages of *Gatsby*? If she hadn't, I was putting her in jail.

In the interrogation room, Mary Ann sat hunched over the table, her fists balled up over her chest, counting: "seventy-eight, seventy-nine." She was concentrating so deeply that she didn't hear me come in, and I was three steps across the room when she jumped up. "*Hal!*

160

Hal, is it gonna be okay? Am I gonna be all right?" she cried. "Hal, I'm gonna be late for the show tonight! Sergio's gonna be mad at me! They'll have ta put in Cindy for me and change ever'thing around, and the audience's gonna get mad at Sergio. He told us to take real good care of ourselves 'cause he can't afford more understudies yet, and 'specially for my part, it's just too doggone—"

I grabbed her shoulders and gave her a hard shake. That got her attention.

"Mary Ann, *listen up!* Now calm down. I think we're making some progress here. It looks like someone played a bad practical joke on you."

"Yeah, bad. *Real* bad," Mary Ann panted.

"These detectives have finally figured that out, and I think that everything is going to be okay."

"Oh, good, oh, thank you both so much. I'm just so real sorry to be a bother to ever'body."

I released her gently and led her over to the table. "But you know, Mary Ann, I think it might help things a little if you signed an autograph for Lieutenant Arkus's wife. She—"

"My sister Louise, actually," cracked Arkus. "I'm divorced. She went to your show last week."

"Well, yeah, sure! Hey, I used to have a friend Louise. She used to dance with me back in Vegas."

I laid Arkus's paper on the table. "See here? I wrote out for you, 'Best wishes, Louise, from Mary Ann.' I thought you might be too nervous. All you have to do is sign."

"Yeah, that was probably a good idea. I *am* kinda, like, awful, y'know, squished up here."

"I wrote it nice and big so you can read it without your glasses," I said, pulling a pen out of my jacket pocket.

She looked at the page. "Yeah. Yeah, that looks fine." Her fingers bunched around the pen's tip, which she wiggled over the paper, making a signature that looked like a first-grader's drawing of his pet dog.

Why didn't I figure this out before? Why didn't anyone else? And I cursed the school systems of Arkansas and Nevada for having failed her so miserably.

Mary Ann got up and carried the paper over to Arkus. "There y'are, Mister Arkus. Say, y'all want to come to the show? I mean, not tonight, but how about if I send you a couple o' comp'mentary tickets that I still got? Sergio says you can't get a ticket for love or money anymore, on account of the show bein' a big hit and all, but I'd be real honored to invite you. And you too, Ms. Pill."

"That would be very nice, Ms. Jaalkov, but I'm afraid that might look like bribery, and we have strict rules about that," said Pill, poker-faced.

"Oh. Yeah. Bribery," Mary Ann said blankly. She didn't know what that was, and the detectives could see it. Whatever doubt Arkus still had melted away in that chubby face of his.

They accompanied her to the front desk, where a desk sergeant returned her personal items, Mary Ann apologizing left and right for "bein' such a crybaby, but it's just such a shock, what with the hand-cuffs and the bars in that jail, and that woman with that perfume takin' my fingerprints. Oh, gosh, Hal, what time is it? It must be gettin' real close to stage time. Sergio's gonna just have a fit. He says we all gotta be there 45 minutes before show time, and anybody who's not is gon-na lose a week o' pay. And that goes for the band, too."

"It's seven-thirty," said Arkus.

"Oh, is that too much? Sergio's gonna—"

"Don't worry, I've called Bertie, and—"

"You really gonna perform *now?*" blurted Pill, amazed. "I mean, af-ter what you been through—"

Mary Ann smiled. "Oh no, oh golly, dancin's the best thing in the world for a bad swallow. Just get out there and dance your head off."

Which must have moved Arkus, for he handsomely snagged a couple of cops to take Ms. Jaalkov and "her friend" directly to the Bellevedere, which they did, lights flashing. We got into the dressing room right at eight o'clock—the whole company had to hug her first, even Jake, the hippy lights-and-sound guy—just in time to hear Sergio announcing to the audience:

"Good evening, ladies and gentlemen." Light applause. "Ladies and gentlemen, we've had a slight technical proh-blem tonight. Our ohp-tions are as follows: we can bring ohn an understudy for Mary Ann

Jaalkov...." Groans—just what he was looking for, the shyster. "Or start our program *with* Mary Ann in about twenty minutes." Applause—a lot of it. "Okay, fine, we won't put it to a vote. So we would like to invite everyone to a drink and a snack out in the lohbby, ohn us—or actually, ohn Mary Ann, since I'm gonna to take it outta her pay." Laughter. "No, there was just a little slip-up, nohthing serious. We'll ring the bell for curtain call in about twenty minutes."

No doubt the steely Bertie had twisted a caterer's arm to whip up the treat on short notice.

"Ya hear that, Hal? They're gonna wait for me. All those people. Isn't that nice of 'em?"

"Maybe they just want to see the best dancer in New York."

"Oh, go on! We just got a great company—best company an audience ever saw." Bertie had also left sandwiches and bottles of water for Mary Ann in her dressing room, and now she wolfed them down. "I'm gonna jump higher 'n the sky tonight, Hal, I really am!" She looked at me suddenly and put down the water bottle. "Hal, I was a big crybaby today, wasn't I?"

"Police and criminal charges are a pretty big crisis, Mary Ann. I don't know if *I* would have done any better."

She shook her head; she wouldn't be fooled. "You woulda." She was taking off her shoes and now set them down without a sound. "You woulda just talked to 'em straight, explained everything, and you woulda been out o' that police station in two shakes." She bit off more sandwich. "It's the truth—me, I mean. Just plain as day. Alba must be kind of fed up too—always doin' stuff for me, explainin' stuff."

"Mary Ann, c'mon! That's—"

"Don't say anything, Hal. Just don't say anything, okay?" she snapped. "I'm mad—I'm mad at myself just like this one time I was practicin' this one jump in Vegas and every time I did it just right, I had my right knee out like this." She showed me a knee bent at a right angle. "I just couldn't help it. Every time I did the jump right, I had my knee out. Musta taken me a month to get my stupid ol' knee where it was s'posed to."

Stupid—that bitterest of words for her.

She was rubbing her hands together, brow furrowed over them.

"Well, I'm not gonna cry no more, okay? I'm not gonna call you up ever again wailin' like a hurt dog."

"Well, if you're in trouble," I began.

"No. No more. If I got a problem and I gotta call you, I'm gonna do it, y'know, like, like a lady. No more crybaby—no more!"

She huffed resolutely and stood up. "Okay, now we got a show to put on. Why don't you get out of here and let a lady get dressed? Instead o' standin' there like a dirty old man."

"I was hoping you wouldn't notice." I kissed her and headed for the door.

"Hey, y'know somethin'?" she said. I turned, my hand on the door-knob. "I was just thinkin' the other day, I never do anything for good ol' Hal, and I really gotta."

I looked into those bottomless dark eyes. Outside, someone was shouting for a new lamp, and someone ran past down the corridor. I went over to her and held her face in my hands. "Mary Ann, your gift has always been given. Always."

Tears welled up in her eyes. "Oh, Hal. That is the nicest thing that anyone ever said to me—ever, ever." She laid her forehead against my chest and gripped my belt. "Ever, ever. Ever, ever."

I watched the show from the wings that night. And she was right: she jumped higher than the sky.

19 So who had done it? Raymond Radow, inspired by a vengeful Sheena?

Of course not. Sheena was a bitch, but neither she nor Radow could have pulled off an operation like that. And an operation it had been, well-researched, well-considered, winnowed from many other ideas, and executed perfectly—or, I should say, professionally: the timing of the man handing her the bag of cocaine, the writing on it, the busy phones of both Sergio and Bertie, me arriving at JFK. And lest you have any doubts, when I got back to Chicago late Sunday night, I found in my mailbox a six-inch nail, a red ribbon tied to it.

You want cooperation? Put his comrade on the rack. Or his brother. Or his girl, Salk had said. And for an hour that night, I lay awake in my bed, figuring that my only option was to give in. This time, Mary Ann had had a miraculous escape, but Salk and company would try again, and Mary Ann would never live down a huge public embarrassment. I couldn't put her through the ordeal. Ralph and Jean-Jacques would understand. I did, however, decide to talk with AllPoint's contact at the FBI before making any move.

Which turned out to be a good idea. From a pay phone, I told Special Agent Fred Wapping what had happened, and he told me to stay cool and keep Chintsy guessing. A couple of good breaks had come up in the case; their investigation was proceeding much faster than they had expected: "We're not talking months, but weeks, so hang on."

I said I would—though I called Bertie and Sergio, and let them know the score. They said that they would make sure Mary Ann had constant company outside the studio. That was easy: workouts now were limited to morning sessions, and nearly every afternoon was scheduled for interviews with all possible manifestations of the news media, Mary Ann being the most in demand along with Sergio and Santiago.

I went to New York the following weekend, Mary Ann's *Time* cover now the talk of the town. It was Sunday, and we were having a late breakfast—past noon, and Alba wasn't even up yet, though the company had a three o'clock performance on Sundays. The previous night, the *Gitanos*—the word all the musicians used to describe their Roma, or Gypsy, blood—had improvised yet another post-performance party, this to celebrate their discovery of a Spanish bar in the neighborhood. One of the guitarists brought his instrument, the drinks went round, and the flamenco lasted long into the night. Mary Ann danced every number; she single-handedly wore out the entire company—*Gitanos*, dancers, and techies.

"C'mon, ya bunch of ol' ragbags!" she taunted everyone. Your correspondent did what he could to defend Chicago's reputation.

At any rate, the next morning Mary Ann was calm and cheerful. It seemed to me time to get down to her reading problem. I had thought to go out quickly and get a newspaper, open it, and tell Mary Ann that there was a review of last night's show. Her glasses were three steps from the counter where we were having breakfast; she wouldn't be able to pull the old no-glasses dodge on me.

Then I thought the better of that. There was no use humiliating her.

"Mary Ann, can I ask you something that's maybe a little embarrassing?"

She shrugged. "Yeah, sure."

I took a breath. "Tell me about your reading problem. It's time we get this squared away."

She licked her lips. "What reading problem?"

"That you can't read."

"Why, I can read." She looked around for her glasses and book, but I cut in.

"Mary Ann, I know for a fact that you can't read."

"But I read for you that one time—"

"That was an audio book, and you memorized the recording, right?"

She looked at me a long moment. Then she lied, straight away: "I don't have a CD of that book."

"I found it in your drawer." I raised a hand before she could object. "Mary Ann, it's nothing terrible. I only want to help you."

Mary Ann's face hardened, and she got to her feet with a momentousness that frightened me. "You just keep kickin' me where it hurts, don't ya?" she began. "It's just that lots of times I don't have my glasses, that's all. So I take a picture o' somethin' and send it to you. Sounds like I gotta find me somebody else, though, 'cause I can't get two minutes without you throwin' all this shit in my face and makin' me *miz'ble!*"

"But that bag of cocaine had—"

"I don't care about no bag o' cocaine. Why don't you just go back to Chicago and forget me, 'cause I'm not gonna, I'm not gonna...." Then she burst out, her speech pure Arkansas: "And if you go 'round tellin' people I can't read, I'm gonna get a flat rock and bust your fuckin' head wide open!"

My god, who is this? I thought. "Mary Ann, I would never do that," I said. "I'm only trying to help you."

166

"Yeah, right. Just like ol' Frank. Just like everybody who wants a good laugh. 'Yeah, let's get ol' Mary Ann up here and make her read somethin'.'"

"Look, if you have dyslexia or something, we can get you a special teacher, and—"

"I don't got no dyslexia!" she shouted. "And I don't want no special teacher, and I don't want anybody hangin' around me kickin' me 'cause I don't have much education. I go out and dance every night, and everybody's happy with me just like that, so *you just LEAVE ME BE!*"

Alba flew out of her room, tying her bathrobe. "What's happening here?"

"Get back in your room!" Mary Ann snarled. "This is between me and Hal, but he's leavin' soon, 'cause I can't stand him no more."

Alba looked at me and went back in.

Mary Ann burst into tears. "'Cept now she's listenin' at the door to see what's goin' wrong, and she's gonna think I'm some kind of stupeface from Arkansas, just when everything was goin' so good!" Mary Ann kicked my leg, and the bruise would last a fortnight. "You get outta here. I'm through with you! You and your fuckin' education and knowin' ever'thing and all that shit! Get out! *Get out!*"

Her profanity amazed me. I got my suitcase and pottered around the bedroom, picking up odds and ends and putting them in. I hoped that Mary Ann might calm down, but she watched me from the doorway, hands on hips, eyes bulging wildly. I wondered if she was denying the matter to me or to herself.

I closed the case and got my jacket. "Mary Ann—one last time: I only want to help. The fact that you can't read makes no difference—"

"Oh yes, it does. You just wanna prove you're smarter 'n I am. You just wanna take care o' me 'cause it makes you feel good—like a big, big man, huh? And I gotta sit here an' take it, just as usual, right? Well, I'm not stupid, y'understand, Hal? I am *not* stupid. I'm just as smart as anybody, an' everybody stands up and applauds for me every night. Anybody do that for you? Huh? *Huh?*"

"Christ, you're starting to sound like Sheena."

"And you're startin' to sound like, like—"

I walked up to her in the doorway, and she didn't move. "You wanted to be grown-up, didn't you? So face your problems," I snapped.

Mary Ann's answer was to snatch my suitcase, walk into the living room and throw it ten feet across the room, where it hit the door, cracking it. I took a step after it, and she shoved me so hard from behind I had whiplash the next day. "Faster! Move it! *Get out!*"

I did what she said, to the letter, and without a word.

Yet as I walked down the two flights to the street—is anything stranger than love?—I found it was not regret or bitterness or anger that bubbled in my stomach; it was relief. I had discovered her dark side—just like my ex's. And for once I would avoid making the same mistake twice.

Besides, Mary Ann was right: I felt superior. I had fallen in love at least partly because I felt sorry for her, because I'd wanted to help her. Perhaps her own sense of inferiority had given me the upper hand in the relationship. It wasn't just love, it was the bracing superiority of raising up someone in need, of steering a life, of "being an influence." When I had studied at Oxford I often heard the phrase, "Cool as charity." Now I understood it. I had been a fool to make love with Mary Ann. As always, sex had muddied everything.

I swatted open the street door and with satisfaction heard it clang shut behind me.

20

I had a bad couple of weeks, in which I felt as if I were walking around under a desert sun. Everywhere I went I was sweating, even when I was cold. And I wasn't pleasant company.

I had work in South Korea, South Africa, and Sao Paulo. The projects from which Salk's threats had banned me required me to spend nights on my PC, checking in with Perry on the other side of the planet. He was doing a great job, but it was his first one, and he needed to be talked through it.

In Seoul, I found that the Koreans hadn't done a thorough documentation of their water-flow monitors, and I had to work through

1,547 pages of their turgid, poorly-translated crap in order to figure out exactly how they were getting around the regulations. Documentation is the coinage of the nuclear realm, and you cannot skimp on it.

All of which I explained to them—caustically, pointedly, and loudly—through a beautiful young woman who interpreted for me and whom I suspected of softening my remarks. I told her this, and her face went bright as sunburn. So I said I was going to make a recording, made everyone wait till while I set up my cell phone, and told her I was going to check her work when I got back to Chicago, and her pretty head would roll if my remarks were not translated exactly.

But from that point on, I think they were: the room went dead silent. As I packed up my briefcase, I threatened quite seriously to report them to the IAEA if they kept cutting corners. "This is a nuclear-power plant we're working on, gentlemen, *not a goddamn birthday cake!*" And I headed for my taxi, for by then the interpreter was in tears and the guys were looking protective.

In Sao Paulo, the political attaché to the Argentine Embassy in Brazil served me twenty-five minutes of grandiloquence in the bar of my hotel, letting me know that his government disliked the location of any nuclear power plant in Chile near the border with his country. He ludicrously suggested that I give the lead contractor a headache by pulling AllPoint out of the project, and offered to pay me for my trouble. I pointed out that any single place in Chile, the world's thinnest country, was near the border with Argentina: "Unless they move the plant to the Easter Islands," I said. He didn't see the humor.

I gave myself a night with Marisa, my favorite hooker in Sao Paulo, and enjoyed myself so much that, with her assistance, I worked my way in four successive nights through the entire staff of the brothel.

Then, back in Chicago, my kinda town, Telma punched the lights out of our expert in cooling circuitry maintenance panels, and though Larry really deserved most of what he got—*most,* for Telma, not greatly sensitive, flirts pretty heavily—I took him to lunch and cooled his circuitry, while Jean-Jacques did his best by Telma, and got her into a downtown hotel bed for "a full-throttle whack," which he reported to me with Gallic zest that evening over drinks in Stubb's, since it was Friday. Then he asked, "Zee sings are going bad with your dancer girlfriend, I sink?"

"Things certainly are. They're finished."

"Ah. *Tant pis.* I am sorry. You know, I have always wanted to have a relationship wiss a performair—actor, dansair, singair; I don't care. You and I, Hal, we are people of sought. Action is not our sing. But a performair has a soughtlessness, a coldness, a sort of, ah, *chute*—'flight' is the best translation. A performair can step out in front of a sousand people and do somesing wonderful. I have always wanted to explore such a person. Sex, you know, what is it? It is a private performance. It is an exploration of character, maybe the soul, too, if she is good."

Well, zat gave me much food for sought—and to get drunk over.

I also got a call from Edgerton Salk. Chintsy had received AllPoint's lawsuit. "Legal has it right now, but the prelim studies look very good for you. Must have cost a good chunk of change to put together a case like that." I heard a horn honk in the background, and I assumed he was in his company limo, on his way to wherever stainless-steel executives like him drink and moan about their greedy suppliers with each other.

"We'll get it back when you pay us the court costs," I said. "You know, Edgerton, there's still a chance to avoid all this: full payment, right now, and we'll waive the late-payment fees. But once the gears of the court begin to grind, that's it. It's all off."

"Well, we're about to cut the supplier pies on those plants in Scottsdale and Mexico. I'm sure we'll get this solved by then."

If he expected me to beg, he was talking to the wrong man. I was in no mood for conciliation. "Frankly, I doubt it," I said sourly.

Salk changed the subject, and his voice had a harder edge. "Saw a picture of your girl in *Time Magazine*. Great legs," he said.

"Least part of her." It occurred to me to tell him that we were no longer together, but then I doubted he would believe me.

"Tell me something, Hal—I mean, just between us."

Suddenly I knew what was coming. *You bastard. You motherfucking bastard.*

"She read any good books lately?" he asked, and hung up.

here was also news about *Holy Tent of God,* which I caught on an international newscast in Jo'burg. Reverend Richard T. Jaalkov was in fine form, hurling broadsides left and right. His traveling show had been in Boston the week before, and I don't know if Bostonians are inhospitable people or if Jaalkov had simply shot one broadside too many, but they gave him one hell of a welcome. About six hundred people—most of them gays and lesbians—turned out on Sunday morning to protest against him, and another hundred to support him.

One of the hundred—there's always one asshole in a hundred—a thick, gopher-faced guy with huge buck teeth, took offense at the chants of the anti-Jaalkov group, pulled a crowbar out of his pant leg, and reduced their numbers by ten before he could be gang-tackled. The odd thing was, he got away with it. Before the Boston police could burrow through the melee, a few of the Reverend's fans bundled the assailant into a stationwagon and drove him away at top speed. The police were hopping mad: nobody got the license plate, since the front one was missing and the rear one hidden under an open tailgate. Even the crowbar disappeared.

To make matters even worse, the Reverend had, well, a *quaint* take on the matter. In his sermon, he commented on the "sad events o' this mornin', right here on our premises, may the Lord help us." He made the standard bow to non-violence, then said that he "understood the anger" of the crowbar-swinger when faced with "satanic homos." And that wasn't all:

"We'll never know this man's name, never know what was in his heart or what sense, earthly or divine, directed his steps. But y'know"—now ambling out from behind his pulpit, real earthy and frank, smacking his ragged mop of a Bible against his thigh—"I got to thinkin': was he a man at all?"

A general gasp from the choir behind him.

"Now *there's* a question for our prayers and meditations. *Was he, good friends, a man?* Jumped on, folded, spindled and mutilated by a dozen homos—yes—but did anybody see him bleedin'? Anybody? C'mon, you were all there—speak up if you did. Did anybody see him bleedin'?"

You guessed it: no one had.

Jaalkov nodded and, putting down the Bible, ran a handkerchief over his sweaty mug.

"Just like I thought, good friends, just like I thought. Know why? *'Cause praise the Lord I believe that young man was nothin' less than an agent o' God Almighty!*" the Reverend thundered. "An *angel* has walked in our midst, good friends! We have had a sign from God Almighty today on *Holy Tent of God*! Can I have an Amen?" And an Amen he got, so loud that the needles must have popped off the sound gauges.

I heard nothing from Mary Ann, though Alba called once to tell me that Mary Ann had been either snappish or silent. I asked if her performance was affected, and she said no, though she was like a light that snapped on for dance and went out as soon as she walked off stage. She went to none of the post-performance *juergas*.

And I got a call from Bertie, of all people. It was Friday—when I was still sitting in the bar with Jean-Jacques, actually. She said that she was going to be in Chicago visiting an uncle. Could she drop by on Sunday at around seven?

"To talk about Mary Ann, no," I said.

"I won't even mention her—it's to do with Sergio. He needs a favuh."

T he Friday drinks with Jean-Jacques lowered my mental state to mellow and then to mush. I called my brother Henry and listened to him blab for a while. He'd seen Mary Ann on the cover of *Time*. "Like wow and double-wow, man," he purred. I enjoyed his jealousy, though I didn't tell him about our breakup, unwilling to go into the ups and downs of love.

Then suddenly I very much wanted to go into them and called my sister Beth. Henry's big shoulder is fine for flattening halfbacks, but not for crying on.

It was a call that changed Mary Ann's life.

Beth is a professor of Journalism and Media Studies at Washington State and a very brainy, tenacious woman. Our parents, you may have noticed, did not raise any deadbeats. She listened to me for a while, made the requisite squawks and squeaks, and then got interested in my story about Mary Ann's dyslexia.

"*How old* did you say she was?" she asked.

"Twenty, maybe twenty-one. Mary Ann was born on a farm in rural Arkansas, and I have a feeling that it's not a coincidence that her birthday is Christmas Day."

"Twenty—now that *is* strange."

"Why?"

"Because dyslexia has to be treated in its early stages; I've read a few things about it. If not, it gets progressively worse."

"Progressive?" I said in alarm.

"Sure. By the time a dyslexic is twenty, he or she often has real psychological problems. Just making a bed in the right order becomes a challenge."

"Well, she doesn't—"

"And she's a dancer! That's right! How can she keep everything in order—all those steps and different parts of the program? Dyslexics are challenged just keeping things in their places."

"Well, she has a terrific memory. She can quote whole conversations, word for word from years ago." I wondered why I was bragging for her.

"Uh-*huh!*" Beth said, and I could hear those professorial gears turning over two thousand miles of telephone line. "Mom told me something... she speaks Spanish? And she's not a native?"

"And Vietnamese—she learned from the cleaning lady."

Silence—of the gnawing kind that I fear.

"Well, I've got news for you, dear: the last thing a dyslexic can learn is foreign languages. They have trouble enough with their own."

"Is that so?"

"Let's get this down to basics: how does she *know* that she's dyslexic? Who told her? She's had testing, special ed.?"

"Actually, I don't know," I said, now feeling like a fool, which I often do around Beth. "All I know is that someone else jerked her chain on the reading thing, and Mary Ann told her she had dyslexia."

Beth had an odd habit of pursing her lips and kissing the air when she was thinking, and she now treated me to a little smooching music. "No. No, this is a hoax, this is a pose—I'd stake my job on it."

"Beth: *she can't read*—that one goes to the bank."

"Oh, I don't doubt that. But this is the classic dodge. She has a fantastic oral memory, speaks languages, and I'll bet she's super-sensitive and has a finely-tuned intuition, too, right?"

"Yeah. How did you know?"

"All right, then: case closed. Dyslexia is not the problem."

"Glad to hear it. What is?"

Beth chuckled. "Hal, don't you see it? It's obvious."

"I guess not."

"Illiteracy, dear, illiteracy—plain and simple. In fact, this all sounds to me like the classic case of a child who, for whatever reason, starts school late in life, feels ridiculous because all her friends are way ahead of her, and stops going. One fine day she's watching the *Discovery Channel* and she hears about something called dyslexia. Dyslexia means you can't read. Eureka! Problem solved: some people have diabetes, I have dyslexia."

Of course—just the glasses without correction should have told me, and all the questions about the most normal things in the world.

"If you ever see her again," Beth said at the end of our conversation, "tell her that if she'll buckle down to it, in six months she can be reading *The New York Times* on the subway on her way to the dance studio."

A t that point I very nearly called Mary Ann—I fought a war with my finger poised over the button of my speed-dialer—at least to tell her Beth's good news. But it wasn't the type of thing I wanted to discuss drunk, and she would probably have hung up on me, anyway.

Sunday. I had no doubt that by "around seven," Bertie had meant "seven," so I had myself in viewable condition by that time. And on the stroke of seven, the security man downstairs called to announce "Bertie Langfeldt." I hung out the doorway and waited for the elevator.

Bertie stepped out, pulling Mary Ann after her.

"Hiya, hon'. We got here as early as we could after the matinee show. By the way, I got everything squared away on that favuh fuh Sergio, so don't you worry." And she sped Mary Ann on her way down the hall with a two-handed thrust, and when Mary Ann turned around, Bertie was already in the elevator. "You two probably wanna talk, so I'll leave you alone."

"Bertie!" Mary Ann shouted, rushing back. "Don't just go and leave me! You gotta help me explain the—"

But the doors slid shut. Mary Ann stood in front of them, head down, fingertips of her far hand touching the smooth metal as if they conveyed a message or electrical current to her. She was wearing gym shoes and good jeans, and a light-blue blouse that looked fine with that lovely red hair. Finally she turned just her head to me, fear and shame rising and falling in her face like two kids on a teeter-totter.

"Hi," she muttered.

I said something, probably in English.

Whatever she saw in my face, it swatted away her fears, and her face burst into a smile. She ran down the hall to me and jumped into my arms—so hard that we fell down on the carpet, rolling and kissing like a couple of squirrels over an acorn. I didn't give a damn about her lack of education, my feeling of superiority, or her dark side. None of that reached even the base of the mountain of love I felt for her. We rolled over and over down the hall, and it was the happiest moment of my life. *The* happiest—nothing else even comes close. To this day, I still feel guilty to have had all that joy to myself.

21 Late that evening, we sat on some fat cushions on my twenty-fourth-floor balcony overlooking a sparkling Chicago July skyline. Between us on the floor sat a bowl of fruit, a plate of sandwiches and a bottle of red wine. The rituals of making-up had been observed; now came the words.

"See, I just get so doggone tired o' people explainin' stuff to me," Mary Ann said finally. She was looking away at the skyline, knees bunched up to her chin. "I know they mean well—I know that—and I know they don't mean to, y'know, like, give me a bad swallow, but it, y'know, just happens. Hal, all I'm ever doin' is takin' direction! And if it's like Sergio, that's okay, 'cause he's tryin' to get the steps right, and with the music and everything like that. And I was thinkin' these last few weeks—I mean, before we had our, y'know, our problem—that for once in my life I was gettin' past that."

I tried to squeeze her hand, but she drew it away and wiped a tear out of her eye.

"I know how to get around New York on the subway real good—I even helped a couple o' tourists get the airport subway once! And Sergio's happy with my performance, and the show's goin' well, and, and, like the applause and pictures and interviews and all. And I know some really super shops on Fifth Avenue, and I got a credit card, and I don't need Alba to take me there or nothin', and, and, and, and then when you asked me—'bout the readin'...."

She began to cry; I put my hand on her shoulder, but she only gave it a squeeze and pushed it away. "I just went crazy. Here I am again, the last one in line, still just ol' Stupe-face and nothin' but."

"I can imagine."

She sipped the wine. "And all the time I'm afraid o' losin' you, too. 'Cause I know that education and a good, supple, open mind is important to you. You told me that on the plane: 'education and a good supple, open mind'—that's what you appreciate most in people. And 'intelligence is the right attitude.' That's the one I like best: 'intelligence is the right attitude.'"

"That's what I said, all right. A basketball coach told me that once."

"'Cept, y'know, I gotta go around with you, and what if, like, you told your mother I can't read? She'd tell you to find yourself another girlfriend—and before you catch something, too."

"Catch something?"

Mary Ann swallowed. "Yeah, like my dyslexia. I got it real bad, Hal. I can't read to save my life—'cept maybe my name a little, dependin'. I can do stuff with numbers okay, but that's about it. That's why I carry those glasses around—'cause then I tell people I forgot 'em, and they can tell me what the menu says or somethin'."

"You can't catch dyslexia," I said.

"Are you sure? 'Cause one time in Vegas, there was this guy who was my dance partner for a few months—it was a course on ballroom, y'know—and then later on he told me he had dyslexia. I didn't say nothing, but gosh, I felt awful."

"No, you didn't give it to him. Impossible."

"Good. I mean, I never wanted to ask anyone about it, not even Alba, 'cause then people start to think you got it."

"Dyslexia isn't a disease, Mary Ann. It's a sort of"—I tried to choose my words carefully, picking from the articles on the Internet I had read the day before—"it's a kind of problem of the brain. From birth. And even people who have it, most of them can learn to read. It just takes more time and effort."

Mary Ann's head whipped around to me. *"They can learn to read?"*

She was so surprised that for a moment I wondered if we were talking about the same thing. "Yeah, sure, of course," I sputtered. "With special programs, in school."

Her brow wrinkled deeply. "Well, now, then…what the…? I thought that's what dyslexia was, y'know, like, just that: ya can't read."

"Mary Ann, where exactly did you hear about dyslexia?"

"Oh, some girls talkin' in the studio in Little Rock. One girl, her brother had dyslexia, and she was talkin' about it with another girl."

My eyes grew wide. "That's it? You never went to a specialist or, or a doctor—nothing?"

"Yeah, I guess that wasn't too smart, huh?" She looked sideways at me. "Hal, you're not gonna think I'm—"

"I'm not going to think your stupid. Ever. I promise. Because you're not." I pulled her to me and covered her face with kisses. "You're the greatest woman ever born. You make the whole world a better place."

There followed a period of, not to put too fine a point on it, a rugby scrum but without the ball. But you wouldn't be interested in that.

When that had run its course, Mary Ann made me a pot of soup. She took my little-used spices out and sniffed each one, and then dabbed in a few flakes from high up—above her head—and seemed to listen to them as they fell into the soup. When it was simmering—it would turn out a veritable bouquet of flavors, better than in the best restaurant—we sat on the sofa, at opposite ends, and I told Mary Ann about reading classes in school and different levels of readers, and generally how kids are taught to read.

This, too, was news to Broadway's hottest star. Her mouth turned into an O again, and she had that left-the-tap-running look. "Now just hold on. Wait. So, it's like, you mean—okay, like *everybody*, like, people, um, like I mean, a *normal* person, he has to *learn* to read? Like in school and all?"

"Sure. Where else?"

Mary Ann leaned forward and seized my left foreleg. "No, no, Hal. That ain't it, that ain't it. Listen to me. You mean people have to *learn* to read? Ever'body? Even Alba? Like, like, you're not *born* with it?"

"*Born with it?* No. No, not at all. Everybody learns to read in school."

"Oh, wow," Mary Ann said softly, falling back against the armrest. "Oh golly-gosh, what a, what a...." And she ran a hand scratchingly through her hair—and once again, I had a privileged glimpse down the long, aguish hallway of ignorance.

"You thought reading was just a, a natural ability?"

"Well. Heck. Yeah." Mary Ann swallowed hard and cleared her throat. "I mean, not little kids and all, but I just figured that ever'body figured it out by the time they were eight or nine or something like that. I mean, people learn ta *talk,* don't they, and nobody teaches 'em *that.*"

I was trying not to stare. "I never thought of it that way. That's really a good point." And I helped this point down with a big slug of Ribera del Duero, a present from Alba's boyfriend weeks earlier.

"Well, heck, why not? If people can talk, they can read. I never met nobody 'cept me who can't read."

When we'd finished the soup, I took one of her feet and began massaging it. It was as solid as smoked ham; the calluses on the heel and ball would have withstood a bed of nails

"Oh, Hal, that is so nice. My poor ol' feet, one o' these days they're just gonna walk off the job and tell me to go soak my head."

I rubbed a good while—before I got to the big question. "Mary Ann, just so that I understand everything, okay? Tell me: have you ever, ever in your life been in a school?"

You're expecting a simple yes or no, right? So was I. How little we knew our girl.

The candles I'd lit waggled for a while, and I changed feet.

"Now, when I was in Vegas," she murmured, "the dance schools, y'know, they always wanted to get new members—y'know, 'cause they can make more money with more students? So now and then we used to give recitals in schools, to get students to sign up, y'know?"

"Yeah."

"Okay. Well, like... Usually we hadda change in the girls bathroom. And this one time, like, b'fore the program? I ran down the hallway and up some stairs and looked into the classrooms. And I went in one. And I sat down in one o' them seats with the little desk, and I just looked around, all over, and I tried as hard as I could to think of what they did there. I mean, all those desks and chairs in nice little rows, all lookin' the same way, to the blackboards—blackboards with a lot o' numbers on 'em. I can read numbers, y'know. And I remember seein' like, drawings and colored paper on the walls and pictures of big ol' bugs and fish and a astronaut and picture of a naked man and a woman, but, like, nothin' harloty: all the veins were showin'—kinda gross, y'know. And on the shelf by the window, there was a bunch o' little plastic airplanes.

"And there was this kinda, y'know, *smell.* All the schools had it. I mean, maybe not a good smell, like perfume, but I always thought, well, maybe that's what all this learnin' smells like. When some o' the girls came to the studio from school in the afternoon, that was just the smell they had on 'em. But y'see, Hal, I couldn't figure it out, when I was sittin' there, I mean. I tried and tried but I couldn't. I mean, what kids *do* in a school? I mean, here ya got bugs and there ya got little plastic airplanes, and over there's the numbers. I mean, what's that all about?"

She might have found out from the other girls, she told me, but didn't dare ask, and kept to herself. Just her accent seemed to invite ridicule. During one full week, she remembered, the other girls tittered at her, "Mary Ann, your epidermis is showing! Your *epidermis* is showing!" until Mary Ann was nearly insane with anxiety.

"And I'm so happy now, Hal. Every day I walk into Sergio's studio, and I drink some tea and talk with the others—just about nothin', just about the weather or how stupid ol' Sheena was—and I'm just so happy."

"Know what'll make you happier?" I said, sitting up. "If you learn to read."

Mary Ann licked her lips. "Oh, Hal, I don't know. That stuff, y'know...."

"Mary Ann, it's easy—it won't take you six months to learn."

"Oh, go soak your head! Six months? Those kids in school, I don't know, but they must study readin' for *years*."

"Sure, but they're younger, and you have a great memory."

"Really? Just six months? *Really, Hal?*"

"If that. Look, you're not dyslexic. It'll be like falling off a log."

"And write, too?"

"Sure—just takes practice. Let me get some paper and a pen."

In a flash I was back. I wrote the letters from A to D, both in capitals and lower-case. "Now this is how it works. Each letter has two versions: big and small."

"Oh, golly. Ya mean I gotta learn two for each letter?"

"Well, yeah, but they usually look the same—most of the time, the big letters are just taller."

"Okay. And what's that for, like? The big letters are more important?"

"Not exactly. We use the big letters to start off, for example, days of the week, or countries, or names. Or sentences. So that you know it's a new sentence and not part of the last one."

Mary Ann thought this over, brow wrinkled. "Oh. Yeah. Hey, that's a good idea, huh?"

22 Looking back on how events closed in on Mary Ann that summer, I am surprised that it took so long for someone to notice that America's new national Sunday-morning star, Reverend Richard T. Jaalkov, had the same unusual last name as a dancer in Sergio Adán's hit show, *Revelaciones*. Her name had appeared on the cover of *Time* and was mentioned most often in reviews.

But finally, it happened. Bertie received a call from a reporter who covered religion at the *Baltimore Sun*. He was looking into Jaalkov and his rising movement. The weekend before, he had seen *Revelaciones* and, in the program, Mary Ann's name. Was there any relation between her and the Reverend?

And Bertie, that worthy, whom I had briefed on the situation, had the answer ready. Yes, he was her father, there hadn't been much contact between the two over the last several years: blah-blah-blah in strict accordance with the wording approved by the Right Rev. himself, which Bertie delivered in a tone dull enough to put a baby to sleep. The *Sun* reporter thanked her and disappeared below the waterline, as did others.

The Reverend was also asked about Mary Ann, and he played it cool, too. I noticed, however, that he avoided mentioning Mary Ann's profession, telling a reporter that she was "one of a number of participants" in "a New York play." For a week or so, the connection between the Jaalkovs flickered in the People columns of newspapers and blogs. Then it flickered out.

Or almost did. *The Mike Davis Late and Live Show* called up Sergio Adán and asked if Mary Ann might come on—and turned the flickering into a national bonfire.

Sergio liked the idea of coast-to-coast publicity, because the show was getting more and more bookings outside the Big Apple; a full-scale national tour was programmed for autumn. And Mary Ann was excited about doing a national TV program. She had the show's producer call me, though, mainly to clarify matters regarding the Reverend.

The producer told me the basic idea of the interview: first some video footage of one her flamenco riffs and then a bit of her solo finale. The interview itself would be "pure softball." I told him that the Reverend was a touchy issue, and he answered, "No sweat—Teflon all the way. Mike'll have to ask about it, since it's out in the open, but we can play it any way you like."

The show was in Los Angeles; Mary Ann flew to Chicago after her Sunday matinee show, and we flew to the west coast the next morning, as Monday was the company's day off. I was glad to be going, and not only to share the experience. I had received a message from Special Agent Wapping: there was "unusual movement" at Chintsy Nuclear's contracted security agency, which, the Bureau suspected, was behind the cocaine prank. "Have somebody physically accompany Ms. Jaalkov at all times until further notice," he told me. "From what we can tell, it's going down in the next few days—a Force Ten scam that's supposed to turn her into mush." (I called Bertie, who put two discreet killers in the front row of the Bellevedere to keep an eye on Mary Ann during the pre-show chitchat with the audience.)

For the rest of it, *Davis Show* preparations had gone smoothly. Bertie had sent show footage, Mary Ann had been driven to a chichi boutique and lavishly outfitted for the interview—her outfit, shoes included, would have bought a small car. The *Davis* producer sent me a list of Mike Davis's questions. They dealt mainly with the daily life of a dancer, the training. Could she mention her personal life? Yes, she would say that she had a boyfriend. On the flight to L.A., Mary Ann and I went through the questions and answers, especially the one about the Reverend. She recited it perfectly.

We also had time to go over a few more letters of the alphabet.

A show limousine picked us up at LAX, and at the studio we met Davis, who quickly put her at ease, clowning and trying to dance flamenco with her. "Oh, I better not, Mike. I get all sweaty. Gosh, the buckets I sweat once I get goin'!" It was a good thing she said that. Davis's writers had considered going over some flamenco steps, especially when the other guest came on: no less than movie megastar Dixon Phelps. He and Mary Ann went through a dry run of the interview; all went well. He added that he might ask a question "off the cuff," but that everything looked good.

Then Davis went away for makeup and to retouch his monologue; Mary Ann got made up, too, and put on her Fifth Avenue rags: a tight-fitting white blouse tailored to that magnificent torso, and an ankle-length, flowered silk dress of Japanese design. In the sound-proofed lounge backstage, we were introduced to Dixon Phelps. He stepped back from Mary Ann, looked her over from top to bottom, and groaned a laugh. "Hell, with *you* sitting on the set, who's gonna listen to me promote my film?"

The show began. The four of us—Phelps's manager was there, too—sat sipping drinks from the bar and eating peanuts and chuckling over Davis's opening routine. Then came the commercials, and Mary Ann was called to be ready.

"Nervous?" Phelps asked. "'Cause if you are, I have a sure-fire way to—"

She smoothed down her dress. "Heck, no. Just real excited. That is somethin' that I never understand. Why's everybody nervous before a show? Heck, it's the best part of the day. Everybody's just out there, waitin' for ya and ready to clap." I gave her a good-luck peck on the cheek, and she whispered, "Payin' at the supermarket, with everybody waitin' behind ya—*that's* terrible."

A moment later, she stepped out on stage in front of six million people, smiling and cheerful as if there to see an old friend.

She was different now, I noticed, in show mode: the back straighter, the neck stiffer, the hands fluttering at the end of supple arms. She crossed to Davis with swift, fluid steps, feet coming down precisely on heels as thin as pencils. After kissing Davis, she flashed her long teeth at the audience and curtseyed artfully, right hand holding her dress, left drawing a treble clef. She moved to the interviewee's chair and sat, back not a point off vertical, on its front ten inches. During the entire interview, she sat with her perfect shoulders squared, legs crossed, fingers lazily locked over one knee. If you saw the interview and listened to that husky accent, you might have wondered where a girl from Blue Ball, Arkansas, had learned that kind of casual grace.

The film clip was run, the chitchat pattered along, Davis cracking one liners. People loved Mary Ann, if only because she was different, not the usual talk-show dolly plugging a movie. Her answer about me was especially good: "Oh, you know, Mike, my boyfriend Hal's just the sweetest thing ever born."

"Pretty sexy, is he?" asked Davis.

"Well, put it this way." Mary Ann replied by moving her hands in a graceful flamenco motion and doing a swift staccato with her heels. "Olé!"

The audience roared; she had them wrapped around her little finger. She had no pretensions, none whatever, and that spontaneous vivacity, clean as a shaft of sunlight, sparkled through the set. Dixon

Phelps watched with an entertainer's eye, and saw quite rightly that his movie plug was about to be upstaged. He leaned sideways to his manager and began a worried conversation. It ended this way:

"No. No, listen to me, Dix. Just listen the fuck up for once. What you do, Dix, is bring *her* into it. Forget Davis—*fuck* Davis—and talk to her. Get *her* to plug *you*. Get her to—*Hey!* I got it, I got it, I got it! After a minute or two, you get up, throw Davis out of his chair, sit him on the sofa, and start talking to the girl. Action, see? Christ alive, that's what the people want, isn't it?"

A production assistant came in. "Mr. Phelps, we're one minute to finale and commercials. Last chance for a bathroom break."

On the TV screen, Davis had glanced off-stage and taken the same signal. "Mary Ann, just one last thing—a serious matter, but something I've heard about and I'd just like to ask, if it's all right with you."

"My pleasure."

It wasn't mine, not at all. The list of questions had not been exhausted, but none of the remaining ones were even ballpark serious. I saw Davis put on a boyish smirk, and I remembered that he had a reputation for zinging guests with offbeat questions.

"Mary Ann, you're a wonderful dancer, but…isn't it true that you can't write?"

"Who told him that?" I shouted, leaping off the sofa. I jerked the producer's assistant to me. "Tell him to take back the question, or I'm going out there right now!"

"He doesn't have an earjack, sir!" the woman snapped, pulling away.

I grabbed the handle of the door, and she threw herself against it. Even Phelps had grabbed me. "C'mon, now, it's not worth all that," he said.

"Open that door, and you'll eat lawsuits for fifty years!" snarled his manager, snatching my tie.

I looked at the monitor. It was a six-foot wide monster, and as I remember it now, I am inside of it, running full tilt towards Mary Ann as if to knock her out of the way of a falling beam or an onrushing car.

I was already too late.

Mary Ann's lips come together in a pout, and she looks down at her polished nails over her knee, though clearly not checking them.

The broad shoulders rotate a few degrees like a clothing rod against a nasty wind, though they stay as level as water in a bowl. Her forehead wrinkles, which denotes great decision, and with dread I realize that this is all my fault:

Salk's people—they slipped it in under my radar. Somehow they got to Davis. And I knew that if Mary Ann cracked up here, I would never forgive myself.

The audience, which has been laughing with her up to now, has fallen silent. Mike Davis is just realizing that he's wandered into quicksand. But he's too late as well. Mary Ann opens her mouth, and steps into eternity.

"Well, now, that's, that's actually true, Mike," she said softly. "I, um, I *can't* write—or read. I never went to school."

Davis's head shot backwards as if punched. *"What?"*

The back a degree straighter—if possible—the shake of her head barely perceptible. "'Fraid not. I was always workin' or doin' chores on my family's farm—in Ark'nsas. And then I spent all my days at dance school, 'specially when I lived in Vegas. So, it's like, I never learned to read or, or anything."

Shock, anger and indecision scuffled for room in Davis's face. Whatever he had expected for an answer, it was not this. "Mary Ann, I'm sorry. I didn't mean to—"

Mary Ann waved this away. "No, that's fine, Mike. I *am* learnin' now, though, 'cause, y'know, that stuff's important. It sort of... it makes you *complete,* y'know, and, and, and grown-up."

"Ah, so, like in a *program* is that, Mary Ann, or...?" He was flailing around for a funny line and not finding one.

So Mary Ann provided it for him. "No. Some friends are helpin' me—I got the greatest friends in the world, y'know. And Hal, too. This mornin' on the plane, we were workin' on the big R and the little R." A thoughtful scowl. "They're pretty ugly lookin', doncha think?"

Tension exploded into laughter and applause, and Mary Ann, feeling the audience with her, flashed a grin at them.

Davis, mock-dumb: "Well, Mary Ann, heck, now that I think of it...."

"I mean, jeepers, all those little parts jus' for a dumb li'l ol' R?

Who ever thought that up? Or the G—that's another one. Somebody oughta do somethin' 'bout Gs. They're ugly as a busted-off stick." She giggled and looked at the audience. "Well, aren't they?"

More applause.

Davis: "Absolutely right. Damn right. Let's hear it for her, folks. That's terrific, Mary Ann. And best of luck to you. Can you stay and say hello to Dixon Phelps?"

But Mary Ann didn't hear as, reacting to the applause, she stood and smiled gratefully and performed her theater bow.

"We'll be right back after this with...."

By now, though, the ovation for her was drowning everything out. The camera panned the audience, and it was rising to its feet to the very back of the auditorium. Even a chubby Mexican security guard standing in the aisle was clapping his big paws like mad, his utility belt shaking all around him. In a moment, the segment was over, though the applause never stopped right through the commercial break.

In the lounge, Dixon Phelps laughed, smoothed back his hair, and walked out. "Well, here goes nothin'!"

D ixon Phelps took his manager's advice, every word of it. After two minutes of chatting with Davis and trying to talk, on his other side, to Mary Ann, he got up, jerked Davis out of his chair, and started interviewing Mary Ann:

"So Mary Ann, how do you like living in New York?"

"What's up next in your career?"

"Would you come see my new film, a re-make of *Bullitt*, if I gave you a free ticket, a big box of popcorn, and a million dollars?"

All the while, Davis ran around, trying to get their attention: "Hello! Hello! Hey, this is *my* show! *I* do the interviews! Angus, give me some music—anything! Save me! *He-e-e-lp!*" At one point, Mary Ann broke down laughing, head in arms on the edge of the desk, and had to wipe the tears away from her eyes.

Davis, calling from the band section: "Ah, Dix, what about your film clip? Aren't you going to –"

Phelps jumped out of the chair and ran around in front of the desk. *"Blam! Boom! Rat-tat-tat-tat! Oh my god, we're all gonna die!* Okay, everybody get the idea?" He ran back around the desk. "So tell me, Mary Ann, what famous people have come to see *Revelaciones* in New York?"

"This is the craziest guy I've ever seen in my life!" Mary Ann shrieked, doubled up with laughter.

After the next commercial break, Davis threw Phelps out of the host's chair and put Mary Ann in it:

"Okay, now *I'm* givin' the interview, and you two are gonna listen up and answer!" she snapped.

Phelps and Davis fought for the interviewee's chair, and Mary Ann had to establish order: "Mike, now you sit over there on the sofa, and Dixon, you're the guest, you sit in the good chair. Now behave yourselves! And Mike, take that shoe offa the coffee table! What did your mother teach you?"

Mock-chastised, he did. Again, Mary Ann broke down laughing.

"All right, now let's get some answers here. Ah, Dixon, ah, I saw on *Entertainment Planet* that you got a girlfriend, Gina Pindel? Big supermodel and all. You gonna marry her or what?"

Davis, from the other side: "Yeah, Dix. You gonna marry her or what?"

"Mike! Now you just sit tight and keep your pants on."

Phelps stuck out his tongue at him, and Mary Ann burst out laughing again.

This for a few minutes. Then someone signaled Davis for commercials.

"Ah, Mary Ann, we've got a commercial break coming up," he suggested, raising a timid hand.

"Oh, golly. I was just gettin' warmed up. Can we skip it?"

Laughter. Actually, it never completely stopped from the moment Dixon Phelps pulled his coup d'état.

Davis: "Well, if I did that, I'd lose my job."

"Oh, wow. You hard-up for money, Mike? You don't look it." And a grin and a wink at the audience, who ate it up.

"No, but I just like to have something to do in the afternoon, Mary Ann. Otherwise, my wife gets nervous, seeing me around the house all the time."

"Ah. Well, okay. Let's just do a commercial for poor ol' Mrs. Davis, then. So, like, like, just what you did the other times, right? Don't go away and don't change channels and stuff like that, right?"

"Give or take—yeah, that'll do it."

Mary Ann looked around the studio. "Zit matter what camera?"

Someone off-stage yelled, "Mary Ann! Over here!"

"Ah, okay. Great." She looked into the camera and grinned. "Okay, well, ever'body listen up. We're gonna show some commercials here. So, um, anybody changes the channel, you're a big ol' rat and a creep ta boot, got it?"

23

As I said before, the Davis program with Mary Ann ran on Monday night. On Tuesday, the segment with Davis's writing question appeared on every news program in the English-speaking world and most of the rest in translation. On Wednesday, two things happened. First, Bertie was flooded—overwhelmed, inundated, buried, swamped—with requests for interviews with Mary Ann. All the Moby Dick daytime-blab stars wanted to talk to her, as did *The New York Times, 60 Minutes,* and CNN.

Second, reporters surrounded *Holy Tent of God* like an army laying siege, all wanting to ask Reverend Richard T. Jaalkov why such a fine Christian had never seen to his daughter's education. Here, however, the Reverend had a good break: *Holy Tent* was setting up for the week in Amarillo, Texas, where the show's support was strong. *Holy Tent* flacks rushed to the ramparts and kept the media at bay, so Jaalkov had until his big Sunday show to weigh his options. On Wednesday night, he called me; I was ready.

As usual, I'll just give you the highlights; there's no use making everybody suffer the Reverend's blather. That so many people willingly do on Sunday mornings must be as a form of penitence.

I was making a spaghetti dinner, and by the time I got a word in, the spaghetti was cooked. I was desperately hungry, having arrived from Vancouver at noon and been in meetings all afternoon. I hadn't eaten more than a Reese's Cup for twelve hours. I was bent over my stove and with a lot of spices was trying to remember what Mary Ann had done with that soup. But when the Reverend started comparing Mary Ann to Judas, it was time to reel him in. I reminded him that Judas had not suffered sexual abuse as a child.

"So this means you're going to drag a good man's name through the mud and bring down his min'stry—all for a stroke o' his sons' poor judgment more than ten years ago?"

"It wasn't a stroke. It happened often. And *you* didn't stop it."

"I didn't know about it till shortly b'fore the girl ran away. And I was as angry as Jesus in the temple, lemme tell ya. I gave those boys a good talkin'-to—you just ask 'em."

"Actually, the *boys'* conduct is not what most concerns me, Reverend."

A dramatic silence. "And just what do you mean by that, sir?"

"I mean your own practices left something to be desired."

"*Me?* How dare you make that kind of accusation, sir?" And more blather—again, not worth wasting your eyes on.

The interesting point here was the strategy: denial. He would throw all the blame on the boys, the older of whom, Ham, news reports would later inform me, had died of Hepatitis C two years before. "When I said that Mary Ann was a poor lamb who needed serious professional help, I wasn't makin' nothin' up. She does. She'll tell you I had satanic ritu'ls, too, just to get back at me."

"Well, if you really *were* a kind, loving father, what possible motive would she have for doing that?" I asked, trying more rosemary on the sauce.

More blather—much more. I knew where it was leading and could have cut it off, but I wanted him to abuse me plenty so that later on he might feel inclined to listen to me. I showered the sauce with white pepper, tested the result, accepted fate like a man, set the phone on top of the kitchen counter, and started making a salad.

When I thought—foolishly—that the Reverend had run out of gas, I set about mending fences:

"Let's get down to business, Reverend. Mary Ann isn't eager to talk about it. She would never have admitted it to *me* if I hadn't asked about her virginity—or lack thereof."

"Oh, so you're havin' relations, are you?" the Reverend chuckled. "It figgers. That girl is the biggest harlot under God Almighty's sun—always was."

"Go fuck yourself, Reverend."

He didn't, too busy talking. "The boys told me she didn't mind a good ruttin'. Soon as they got in from the fields, there she was, naked as God gave her to us, pullin' at the boys' flies."

"Guys in their twenties seduced by their ten-year-old sister—imagine that."

This hit a nerve. "My boys worked like niggers every day o' their lives and don't you forget it!" the Reverend bellowed. "You try comin' home with your tongue hanging' down to their knees and then some girl is waitin' there naked for ya. They ran that farm at a profit with no more than their blood, sweat and tears, and no man could ever...."

On and on. I dripped olive oil and vinegar on the salad, something I'd learned from Alba. Finally, he ran out of words or ideas and stopped.

"Look, Reverend—cutting to the chase here—I just want to let you know that our original deal still stands. You stay away from Mary Ann, and she has nothing to say about you."

The Reverend roared with laughter. "Listen to this boy talk outta both sides o' his sinnin' mouth! What the hell do you mean, 'not a word'? That little harlot goes tellin' the whole world I never sent her to school, and you call that not sayin' a word about me?"

"As I told you years ago at the beginning of this conversation, that was in response to a question *that she didn't expect*. It was *never* discussed in the pre-show interview. The part about you I wrote out *myself* and that is *exactly* what she said."

"You 'spect me to believe that? I'm a Christian, sir, but not a damn—"

"Didn't you see a clip of the interview?"

"Sure I saw it. I couldn't *believe* that she was flaunting our agreement like—"

"Then watch again. The question hit her like a lead pipe. Davis was shocked, too."

More laughter. "And where did that Davis guy find out so's he could ask her, huh? Wouldn't 'a' been good ol' Mr. Yankee Slick, would it?"

"Funny story, that one. Seems some guy in the studio cafeteria came up to Davis's assistant producer during the pre-show and said that he—Davis—could zing Mary Ann with a crack about her problem with writing. He told the guy that Mary Ann has small-motor problems, and that—"

"Small *what?*"

"Small-motor problems, which means she has difficulty using her hands for small tasks, like writing." I didn't add that the man who talked to the assistant producer turned out to be the same guy—pasty face and wide snake eyes—that had handed Mary Ann the bag of cocaine in the New York department store. With just one look at the security photo sent by the Bureau, the *Davis* AP confirmed that it was him.

"That's so much cock and bull."

"Well, it's the truth. The guy told the *Davis* AP he was one of the managers in Adán's company, and that they all kidded her about how hard it is for her to sign an autograph. See how it works, Reverend? They laugh at her one little physical disability, but they *marvel* at her dancing. Davis slipped it in, hoping for a little surprise, had a good one-liner ready. Perfect way to end the interview."

"Yeah, sure. You heathens got so many ways to—"

My stomach rumbled. "*For Christ's sake, Reverend!* You think she *likes* to talk about her lack of education? Davis had expected her *to laugh.* Instead, he'd stumbled into a major embarrassment, maybe even a lawsuit. And by the way, he was sorry as hell. Just before the next guest came on—during the commercials?—he wanted to apologize right then and there on the air to Mary Ann. She told him to forget about it, let it slide. She didn't want any waves made—and she didn't want to cause *you* more embarrassment." The last part was a lie, a stab at placating the Reverend, which did no good.

"Yeah, but who told this guy who talked to Davis's producer?"

"Well now, I was hoping *you* could tell *me,*" I said. "You have enough enemies to fill an army. I didn't say anything to the *Davis* people, but it sounds to me like somebody did some research on you and slipped Davis's assistant the information, thinking it would reflect on *you.*"

As I'd hoped, this gave the Reverend food for thought. "All right.

Coulda happened that way. Not sayin' it was, though. Boy, you got less cred'bility than—"

"Shut up," I snapped tiredly. "You don't believe me, fine. Check out the *Davis Show's* website and look at the statement they put out. Davis regrets the incident, admires how Mary Ann handled the question, supports her drive to get an education, and so on and so forth. *And* he's offered to have the whole dance company put on a segment during their national tour later this year."

The Reverend grunted. "I'll take a look."

"You do that. Just read between the lines: Does it sound like they knew about Mary Ann's problem? No, it does not. More like, the producer's *desperate* to stave off a lawsuit."

A petulant sigh. "All right, all right. Let's say I look up the website and see it for m'self. Let's say I figure that one way or another some beans got spilled and no harm was intended. Fine and well." He banged a fist on something that broke. *"So what do I tell these damn heathens in the media who're outside my front door askin' about my p'rental duties as a father?"* he bellowed. "Why'd she have to say that stuff about how she was workin' on the farm? Made me sound like an Egyptian slave-driver!"

If the shoe fits, wear it, I thought dryly. Still, this *was* the sticking point, and I had given it much thought. The Reverend was quite right: he was cornered. "Look, why don't you just tell the truth?"

"The truth?" the Reverend cried as if it were a pestilence.

"That's right. Tell the truth, but tell it *your* way. Back then, the farm wasn't doing well. You needed Mary Ann there to cook and clean. You now know that it wasn't right and ask her forgiveness. Done."

"That's it?"

"That's it. I've already talked to Mary Ann and she has no trouble with publicly accepting your apology—cameras rolling, the whole bit. And if she does any more interviews, the standard condition is she won't take any questions about family. Okay, you'll take a few lumps. But it'll pass. *And* the matter of Bolts and the family sex romps will stay buried."

"But that's, that's... Lumps—boy, you don't know what lumps are. Why, in my org'nization... I don't know... That, and when things were goin' so well, too, doggonnit! Word is I'm gonna be givin' the bene-diction in the next pres'dential inauguration. And now I got these unholy Pharisees tearin' away at me left and right, top people in our org'nization bangin' on my door...."

I wondered about his bosses Besby and White. Who could tell? Maybe they were standing right beside him turning the screws on his thumbs.

"It's a day in the news, Reverend. We all handle it low-key, and in a week, everyone will have forgotten."

The Reverend floated back to earth. "All right. We'll have to... I guess that's about the only, the only way." I could hear him panting. "I'd still like to know who the filthy Pharisee was that tipped off that Davis guy. There's a son-of-a-harlot if there ever was one."

I haven't told you Mary Ann's reaction to Davis's question. That was a moment for the history books, too, though a more per-sonal history.

A limousine carried us to LAX, where I would spend the night before a flight to Vancouver; Mary Ann would take a night flight for New York. She had to be in the studio the next day to work out, since she had done nothing all Monday. She had changed into normal clothes, her Fifth Avenue outfit hanging on a hook by the door, and her Manolo Blahniks sitting in their box beside her on the jump seat like a sleeping puppy.

"Well, I guess if I'd hadda choose, I wouldn't 'a' talked about it," she said with a shrug. "But when he asked, I just thought, 'Now don't start bawlin' like a big ol' crybaby. Just talk clean and straight—like Hal.'" She took up my hand and kissed me on the knuckle. "Hey, what were you talkin' about with the producer when I came out? Sounded pretty serious."

I explained to her about Chintsy Nuclear and the attempt to black-mail me; it was time she knew. I said that Sheena Biggs had probably tipped them to Mary Ann's reading problem, and that Chintsy was be-hind the bag of cocaine in Macy's and the trick question on the *Davis* program tonight. I had received a letter by messenger towards the end of the show, and I showed it to her. It was a single computer-printed line that read, *What's between a hammer and a piece of wood?* The answer was, of course, a nail.

"You see what I mean? They're trying to force me to accept their conditions by doing things to you."

Mary Ann's brow wrinkled, and she nodded slowly. "They owe your company a million dollars, huh? Yeah, there are some real big ol' rats that'll do anything for a few bucks. You know, last week, walkin' to the theater with Alba? There was this nice couple o' girls from Argentina—they spoke Spanish kinda funny—and they were cryin' and I asked 'em what's wrong, and they said that someone sold 'em false tickets to the show. False tickets! I saw 'em, Hal, and they looked just perfect, too, same cardboard 'n' ever'thing. I called up Bertie, and she got 'em some comp'mentaries—'cept they couldn't sit together. But yeah, there's a rat under every rock, you can bet on that."

"Anyway, until I get this thing with the company resolved, you have to be careful—careful with strangers, with packages."

"Yeah, since the show got big, Sergio always gets a driver with a mini-bus for all the dancers after the show. And he told me to be careful if anyone asks me for an autograph or wants to take his picture with me."

"It's good advice. And remember the Reverend isn't going to be too happy, either."

This alarmed her. "The Reverent? Why?"

"Well, because you just said on national TV that you were working on the farm so much that you couldn't go to school."

"Oh, yeah." Her eyes got big. "Oh, golly! Hal, I didn't mean ta—"

"Don't worry, don't worry. I'll smooth it with him. But if anybody else asks—"

"Yeah. No comment—nothin' to say, no no no. Right." Then she jerked forward to me and grabbed my hands. "Okay, but y'know, right now we're together, and we're just hardly ever together, and I don't wanna talk about the ol' Reverent or anything... Look, I was thinkin'. When I learn the alphabet, do you think we could get into bed and read one o' these days? Alba does that when she goes to bed with Javier, and she looks so peaceful. Think we could?"

"Sure."

It was a simple thing to say, but she took it seriously. She nodded and tucked the tidbit away; it seemed to calm her. "Okay. Also 'cause you'd be right there, y'know, and if I had trouble with a word, you could tell me."

"I'd tell you not to bother me," I said with a grin.

"Rat. 'Course, when we got tired o' readin', we could do somethin' else, too," she whispered, straddling my legs and pulling my face to hers. I watched the streetlights tossing shrouds over her sweet face above me.

"My god, you've grown up so much," I blurted.

This pleased her. "Really, Hal? I'm older now—old enough for you?" she said, searching my eyes for any of the flattery that so often humiliated her.

She *was* older, I told her honestly, and pride bloomed in her face.

"Well, that's, that's just great." She traced my face with two fingertips. "Hal, doncha think we could, y'know, like, live together, or, or, or, like, y'know, get married or somethin'? 'Cause ya know what I want most in the whole world? It's just to, to go home and see you there— just sittin' there in a chair readin' one o' your books or a newspaper or gluin' together a busted dish—like you did the other day for Alba, y'know? Or whatever. And I'd make you a good soup and, and we'd just sit in the living room sewin' or playin' Parcheesi—and just wearin' old clothes, nothin' special. Just a tee-shirt and a pair o' shorts. And especially, like, y'know, doin' the wash. That's what I always"—a sheepish giggle—"I always kinda think about that."

I waited for her to go on, and she didn't. "The wash?" I prompted.

"Yeah, like, okay, maybe this sounds dumb, but, y'know, that's just what I think about sometimes: puttin' in a load, and I holler out the door and ask you if you have anything colored to put in the wash 'cause I'm gonna do a load o' colored. And you say, 'Hold on a sec', I got a pair o' jeans'—or, y'know, whatever." She stopped. "Uh-oh. Did I say something stupid?"

Stupid was not the word, and, throat tight, I shook my head. "Mary Ann, that's really, really... beautiful."

"Oh. Whew! Good. So, whaddaya think?"

I coughed a little, swallowed, found my voice. "Well, normally, you know, it's the *man* who asks the *woman* to marry him."

"*Oh!* Oh, right. Sorry." Mary Ann sat back on my legs and took my hands. "Okay. You go."

So I did.

24

The day after the *Davis* interview, I spoke again with Special Agent Wapping, this time to call off the whole thing: the investigation, Chintsy, their security service—everything. Twice Mary Ann had dodged Edgerton Salk's bullets, and that was enough. I wasn't going to wait for the third. (Which, incidentally, may have come from Sheena Biggs herself. Two days after the *Davis* appearance, Sheena called Mary Ann to invite her out for a drink and talk about taping a dance show together. Mary Ann hung up on her—she was indeed getting older.) I also told Wapping that I was going to call off the lawsuit against Chintsy, take what Salk offered, and count my blessings—first among them Mary Ann.

"Hold on, Hal. Would you just let me get a word in—*God!*" he snapped after listening to my diatribe. "There's no need for all that. I was just about to call *you*, actually. Everything is set. We're all ready. Call Salk and make an appointment with him in New York. Just swing by the Bureau's Manhattan HQ an hour before."

I did this, implying to Salk's secretary that I was willing to make concessions, and set the meet for Friday. It was just as well. This way I could make just one trip out to New York and spend the weekend there. It would also give me a chance to shop for an engagement ring.

On Friday, at three o'clock, I walked through the revolving doors of the Chintsy Building for the final showdown. The security guards put my briefcase and cell phone through a scanner and waved a metal-detecting wand over me. It squawked at my tie-clip. The guard, with laudable intuition, saw this as a weapon that might destroy a Chintsy executive, and asked me to take it off. I did, holding it high in my right hand, while the wand finished its work. Then they asked me all manner of dumb questions, and finally vouchsafed me a building pass.

A security guard escorted me into the elevator and all the way up to Salk's lair on the sixty-second floor. That procedure was new, too, he explained. I replied that the ways of God and Security were infinite; he took this as a compliment.

Edgerton Salk awaited me in his office, which was as big as a stadium and about as cozy, with all manner of sharp-cornered minimalist furniture and chrome decor. His view of the old Pan Am Building one way and the Empire State Building the other didn't do much for me, either; but maybe you had to see them when the leaves were on the turn. Salk stood up to offer me his hand, but didn't bother coming around his desk. Not a strand of his militarily parted silver hair had changed since our last meeting. And if he had changed his clothes, it didn't show: the same white shirt, the same macho-man blue tie with shadowy stripes. His desk was shiny, his shoes pointy; they were supple Italians with real-leather soles, and not much worn, as I could see for myself when he tilted back, crossing his legs and wedging the right sole between one knee and the edge of his desk, bending the toe back cruelly.

"We're very impressed with AllPoint's lawsuit, Hal. Very nicely done. Legal tells me it looks airtight—right down to the part about punitive costs. Don't worry, though. No offense taken. I thought it might take a while for you to come round, and I'm here to listen," he said. His lip-less smile shot for pleasantness and reached Halloweenness.

"There's nothing like dealing with a reasonable man, Edgerton. Makes business all the smoother. Yes, I think we can finish this today."

"How's that girl of yours? Hale, happy, still in one piece, all that sort of thing?"

Spoken like a true blackmailer.

"Mary Ann? Never better. See her on *Mike Davis*? Handled the interview like a champ. Standing ovation right through the commercial break. Cameraman told me he'd been doing *Davis* for eleven years and never seen anything like it."

Salk began to doubt that my mission was surrender. I shoveled in more shit:

"Now she's getting so many requests for interviews that she hardly has time to work out. *60 Minutes*'s producer called, saying if he didn't get her on, he was fired."

Salk's voice now came out as brittle as ice: "That right? *60 Minutes*?

Well, do let me know when she's on."

"No, no—not gonna happen: Sergio Adán and Mary Ann talked it over, and they just can't work it in. Not for the next few weeks, anyways. Guy couldn't believe it: someone refusing *60 Minutes*. Once the national tour gets going, they said they'll see what they can shake loose—*maybe*."

"Hal, Hal, you tell her to accept. *Carpe diem,* my advice. Girl in her position? My goodness."

I chuckled. I whacked a thigh. "You kidding? She's got more *diems* left than you and I put together!"

"Oh, I wouldn't count on that. Dangerous life, a dancer's." His voice was turning ugly. I could see why he'd ordered special precautions with the security check. He knew where this was heading, and so did I. "I mean, just throw a hip out of joint, tear a tendon, bang an ankle, and you're all finished. Say she's on the subway, someone trips, knocks against the side of her knee, takes it out—end of career."

I laughed openly. "Mary Ann? We should build our reactors that strong! Even with the show, she's in the studio every morning at eleven and works out for three hours. Sergio Adán said he—"

"I think you'd better focus on the matter at hand, don't you?" Salk barked.

"Fair enough—hell, what are a couple of nuclear engineers doing, anyways, gossiping about their girlfriends?" I laughed with my best chuckleheaded voice.

"I said 'focus'!" he shouted in his lieutenant's voice—so loudly I jumped.

I took a breath to get back my composure. "Fine. Focus ya want, focus ya get," I said, clapping my hands and sitting forward to his desk. "Edgerton," I announced cagily, like a used-car salesman, "we are prepared to give you a ten-percent discount."

His face dropped open; he couldn't believe it.

"That's our best offer for an old and respected client: we'll take ninety percent of invoice, *plus* what we've already spent on the lawsuit—all itemized for your inspection, no problem there. Late word from the lawyer is it'll run to a little under a sixty grand. No late-payment penalty, lawsuit dropped, no hard feelings, and not a word to anyone, least of all the business press, about that, ah, *slight cash-flow problem* you guys are having and how you're resolving it by stiffing your suppliers." I opened my hands invitingly as if to lay this basket of goodies on his desk and taunted him: "How's that for focus?"

"I'm focusing on something else that's going to drop, and it's not a lawsuit!" he snarled. He uncrossed his legs and sat square before his desk. "You're feeling pretty damn cocky, aren't you?"

"Oh, what are you going to tell me now?" I sneered. "That you chew out a dozen guys like me before breakfast? You're all wet, Salk. You, your lame threats, and your company that's looking more like Enron with each passing day. Mary Ann's dodged your two best bullets. She's a national story now. A national *success* story. You can't touch her."

"I never heard that she goes around with bodyguards. She can't stay lucky forever."

"That's—"

Salk rose and came round his desk to me. "Get this straight right now, Dormund. I'm an executive. I'm paid to execute. *Get it?* I'm paid to get things done. I'm paid to put results on the platter with no side dish of excuses—and that's what I plan to do."

"Great." I rose, too. "So we can count on an early transfer for around nine hundred Gs, and I'll send that lawyer's bill around next week, right?"

For that question I took a slug in the stomach that must have flattened my intestines against my backbone. I fell back in the chair doubled over, gasping for breath.

"You stupid bastard," came the voice from above me as fire raged through the middle of my body. "You fucking stupid proud son-of-a-bitch. You still don't think I'll go all the way, do you? Take us to court—go ahead—and I'll have her legs broken, and then I'll do yours, too, just for fun. I'll have that pretty red hair of hers jerked out in handfuls. Y'know, I just can't figure out why the hell I've been so patient with you. Respect, probably. Dumb idea. But if you think I can't ratchet up on you, you're dead wrong. I haven't even started."

I was trying to get a breath and not making any progress.

"You'll take your twenty percent and get the fuck out of my office. *Is that right?*"

I nodded.

"I said, *Is that right?*"

"Right, right," I whispered with what breath was left in my lungs.

"Good. I'll throw you part of the Scottsdale job next month—just out of pity for AllPoint's shithead manager who doesn't know how to do business in the big leagues. Now get the *fuck* out of my office. Bathroom's down the hall on the right. Have the decency not to puke in front of Melissa on the way."

I did spare Melissa a mess, though not the janitor. Ten minutes later, much the worse for wear, I came out of the bathroom, stepping over the bit of blood-laced vomit that had fallen short of the urinals, just as the Special Agent Fred Wapping and some of his buddies were entering Salk's office. My tie clip was a microphone, for which a judge had issued a warrant to aid the FBI's blackmail investigation.

At the same moment, other agents were invading the small "security" firm in Virginia that handled delicate matters for Chintsy. The Bureau boys had had their eye on it for some time—hence the fast progress on my case—in regard to matters related to the Chinese mafia and the Israeli Mossad. My tribulations gave the agents a wonderful excuse to rifle their files. They found Mary Ann's pasty-faced angel of cocaine right at his desk, as well as all of his expense sheets, these prepared with a thoroughness and detail that I wish AllPoint employees would emulate. They described his buying cocaine and slipping the *Davis Show* assistant producer a juicy bribe—five thousand bucks—for his cooperation. The whole company ended up cuffed and tossed in the police van.

So did Edgerton Salk, who now had two airtight cases to deal with.

I saw *Revelaciones* again that night and invited Mary Ann to a good restaurant afterwards. There I slipped a diamond on her finger and got us properly engaged. Mary Ann was so thrilled that she even showed the waiter.

The *Gitanos* threw another wing-ding after the show that Saturday night because the guy that played the *cajón*—the dresser drawer—was going back to Spain to play in another band there; his cousin would replace him in New York. It was another fantastic party, and Mary Ann and I staggered to bed at four in the morning.

When I got up on Sunday morning, I put the phone back on the hook, and it immediately started ringing. It was a reporter from a local news program. He wanted to ask Mary Ann about the Reverend's statements.

"What statements?"

"Hell, it's all over the place. Jaalkov's saying Mary Ann isn't his daughter."

"What?"

"Her real father is a son of his, I guess—does 'Frank' ring a bell?"

It did. I told him I'd get back to him and turned on a 24-hour news show.

After items about Israelis and Palestinians, a flood in Illinois, a plane crash in Oregon, and sundry miseries:

"Reverend Richard T. Jaalkov, spiritual leader of *Holy Tent of God,* the itinerant show of Christian evangelism seen on cable TV worldwide, responded today to the growing clamor of critics who accuse him of being a neglectful parent. After denouncing Broadway dance star Mary Ann Jaalkov as 'a Broadway harlot,' he went on to say that she is *not* his daughter, but his *grand*daughter. Rick Tenna has the story. Rick?"

The reporter, in a light shirt and trousers, spoke to the camera, the papers on his clipboard flapping in the Amarillo breeze. Over his shoulder appeared a huge circus tent with a cross stuck in the ground beside the entrance, held in place by guy wires on the arms. He was shaking his groomed head. "Burt, all I can say is that it was the mother of all sermons."

Cut to video. The Reverend is standing, tears rolling down his long cheeks, hands on the wooden pulpit in front of him, looking above the camera at his "flock" in the risers. Behind him stands the choir: perfect, white faces dressed in green robes. At least I *thought* they were the choir, but they turned out to be a Greek chorus, echoing the trials, triumphs and tribulations of God's firebrand.

"...Not long after the birth, my wife died, so we just told everyone that Mary Ann was my daughter. Yes, it was a lie, and I repent for it, but what were we to tell people? That Frank had lain with a woman at the age of fourteen? Think of that poor boy's reputation."

You shyster. You were thinking of your own.

The Reverend holds up a paper. "Here's a copy of the birth certificate, signed and sealed in Waldron, capital o' Scott County, Arkansas. The mother was a harlot, ran off not long after the baby was born, and so we raised her ourselves—Frank, me, and my other two sons, Ham and Ted. And let me tell you, friends, she was the joy of the household, praise the Lord."

The Greek chorus murmurs its joy, too.

"Now then: Little Mary Ann turned five, and I just naturally assumed that she was goin' to school. Then I got back from a long road trip of doin' the Lord's work, and Mary Ann was at home. I was consternated, friends, *consternated!* I took my son Frank aside, and I spoke seriously with him, but—" A fresh sob for emphasis. "He said poor Mary Ann wasn't right in the head. She heard voices. She couldn't distinguish between dreams and reality. Right then"—another sob— "Mary Ann herself ran in. She was laughin'. She said she'd seen me jaybird naked outside her window that night." Another sob. "She swore up and down. But, but I hadn't been home for more 'n a month, my friends. And it was one thing and another. She was as crazy as a bedbug."

The Greek chorus moans in sympathy.

"You bastard," I murmured. "You slimy bastard. I swear to God we'll have you hauled up on a libel charge."

"Me, at first, I thought it was the lack of a mother that did it. So me and Frank, we talked and we prayed, and we decided to keep Mary Ann back for a year. No harm in that: take her to a doctor, see if it clears up. Never did, though, and she was happy just bein' part of the house, like her mother—rest in peace—had always been. She took up cookin' and cleanin'. And for a while there, she was just the sunshine of the house. Except for those stories, those incredible, weird fantasies. And many of them sexual in nature. I was consternated—Frank, too. Where was *that* comin' from? She made continual references to the private parts of the human male. Why? *Why?* Something was wrong here, friends, very wrong. And finally…."

The Greek chorus holds its breath.

Another gush of tears. "Turns out my oldest son Ham was doing unspeakable things with her. Unspeakable things, may God have mercy on me. Sexual things, perversion on a scale that...."

The chorus' wailing drowns him out.

So *that* was the idea: if Mary Ann says anything, it's because she was crazy, and besides, it was *only* Ham.

Rick Tenna reappeared. "Confirmation of these events was impossible, however, because *Ham* Jaalkov died two years ago of Hepatitis C. Neither of Ham's younger brothers, Ted and Frank Jaalkov, were implicated in the events, as, according to the *Reverend* Jaalkov, Ham had threatened *the entire family* with violence if they talked to anyone about the situation."

Back to the video. The Reverend by now has managed to recover his voice: "There was just no way to stop Ham, and Mary Ann ran away when she was, I don't remember, ten or eleven. Twelve maybe. We searched high and low, of course—no good, no good." The Reverend, face wet, is standing beside his pulpit now, one chunky forearm braced wearily on it as if he has spent the day beating the bushes for her. Sadly he waves a crumpled handkerchief. "No sign of her. I accept the blame, friends—full blame. And many is the time I have knelt before the Lord to ask forgiveness, to ask him, 'Did I do everything in my power to save that poor child?'"

The Greek chorus, some crying now, nods as one: of course he tried everything.

"Now I'm not sayin'—let no man interpret—that Mary Ann today is either crazy or mentally disturbed or in any way, um, *out o' kilter.* I'm not sayin' that, now."

Not saying that for the lawsuit, I thought.

"But if that's so, there's no doubt in my mind that it was my prayers—every night for ten years, my friends, *every night!*—that cured her. That's the only thing I can think of, the Lord be praised. But for what? What's happened since to her?" The tears crash down. "She's, she's, she's turned into the harlot that the Devil had planned!" A wipe of the holy eyes as the Greek chorus gasps. "Imagine my shock, good friends, imagine my earth-shatterin' woe, my unspeakable shame, when one fine day a few weeks ago, I'm in my office preparin' my sermon, deep in meditative communion with the Lord, when one o' my assistants comes runnin' in and flops a slick magazine down on my desk. And there, right on the cover of a national publication, dressed in fancy underwear that don't leave a square inch to the imagination, is my granddaughter Mary Ann, once the sunshine o' my household, my own flesh and blood, now a Broadway harlot dancin' to foreign music and leadin 'em to the devil by the thousands!"

You low piece of dirt.

Here the Reverend breaks down, collapses to one knee with one elbow still hung on the podium. And Frank, the transportation manager, his long chain bouncing and jigging beneath his good suit jacket, runs out from the wings to grab him, lift him up, hug him. He'd shaven for the cameo, I noticed.

"Thank you, Frank." To the microphone: "My son Frank, ladies and gentlemen. The father."

"Throw it all on Ham and Frank, huh?" I muttered, turning off the TV. "Shrewd move—gets you out of direct responsibility for not sending Mary Ann to school."

I made some coffee and got Mary Ann out of bed. She had a performance at three o'clock, anyways. I told her briefly about the Reverend—she listened, lips working. By the time the next cycle of news came around, she had showered and watched the report carefully.

But to her, the news wasn't the Reverend, but Frank, whom I'd hardly mentioned. "Yeah, so *Frank's* my father! Frank! That's great!"

I said nothing. To trade a religious fanatic for a tobacco-stinking shit-for-brains seemed to me—let's use that great business phrase—a horizontal move.

"Hal, we gotta call Frank, or, or the Reverent, but Frank'd be better. We gotta get goin' on this right now!" She was so excited that she was hopping up and down.

"Hell, Mary Ann, it's not like you've wasted a lot of money on Father's Day presents all these years. What's the difference?"

Mary Ann stood back from me, her mouth tragic. "Oh, Hal! Why aren't you takin' this serious?"

"I *am,* for god's sake! I'm listening to every word. It's just that—"

"Hal, if Frank's my father, *who's my mother?* Not the Reverent's wife."

Sheepishly: "Oh. Right."

"Who knows? Maybe I can find her and, and, and talk to her."

"Yeah, that's right. Tell you what, why don't we—"

"You still have Frank's phone number?"

"Yeah, let me get my phone. I'll give it to you."

"No, no. Hal, please, you call him. I, I can't, that'd be... Oh, I just make a mess o' those things. Please, Hal."

I called Frank, but he didn't answer. I called the Reverend.

"What can I do for ya there, Mr. Yankee Slick?" he asked breezily.

I didn't trouble to answer the question. "Who's the mother, Reverend? Mary Ann wants to know, and she's got a right."

"Don't know. Ask Frank."

"I've tried that. He won't answer his phone."

"No need. He's right here." He called for Frank. "Haven't heard much outta Mary Ann."

"You will. Half of the country wants an interview with her. Tomorrow's her day off, so she'll probably talk then. Probably to something like *The New York Times*."

"Uh-huh. So it'll hit *Tuesday* morning, huh? Yeah, that's what we figured. Okay! Lookin' forward to it."

His confidence amazed me.

"Yeah?" said Frank.

"Hi, Frank. Mary Ann wants information about her mother."

"She's dead. Ran away and died—not long after Mary Ann was borned."

"You sure?"

"Sure enough."

"What'd she die of?"

"Wolves, probably. Ran off into the woods—no place to be if you know what's good for ya. Me and Ted, we were out huntin' a month later, come across her clothes, all tore up."

"What was her name? Who was she?"

"Don't remember. Just some—" He stopped, and I could have sworn I heard the Reverend say something. "Just some girl," he said at last.

"She must have been older than you. What was the attraction?"

Frank only laughed.

"Was Mary Ann born right there on the farm?"

"Yeah—midwife come over from Blue Ball."

"What's gonna happen if I send around a private dick to investigate, see what he can come up with?"

Frank laughed. "That was all twenty years ago! What's he gonna find now?"

"Maybe her. Maybe the real cause of death. Who knows?"

But my attempt to rattle Frank got nowhere:

"Tell 'im good luck," he laughed—and hung up.

A group of fundamentalist-Christian protesters—less than two dozen—milled around in front of the theater for the three o'clock show. Three held signs with, I think, Biblical quotes printed on light cardboard and tacked on sticks. I couldn't see because the cardboard curled up and, when it began to rain, hung on the sticks like toilet paper. Others swung Bibles around and prayed and tried to give leaflets to ticket holders entering the theater. They muttered with irritation and shuffled inside. Finally, a few cement-faced cops showed up and moved them down the sidewalk.

After the show—Spain's *Infanta,* which is a sort of royal princess, and her husband visited everyone backstage and shook hands—we returned to the apartment. It was evening. Mary Ann fried thin strips of veal and Alba made what she called a "country salad," with a lot of oil, vinegar, potatoes, tomatoes, and olives. A friendly reporter from the *Times,* cleared by Bertie, would interview Mary Ann the next morning. We sat at the lunch counter and talked over what Mary Ann ought to say about the Reverend's sermon.

Actually, Alba and I talked. Mary Ann barely listened. For Bertie had done something else: she had given Mary Ann a copy of her birth certificate. During Mary Ann's first months in the company, Bertie, in straightening out Mary Ann's legal situation, had obtained it from the authorities in Scott County, Arkansas. (Frank's name as father, of course, had made no impression on Bertie.) Now Mary Ann ate her dinner with one hand and held up the document with the other. She stared at the name of her mother: Henrietta Breem. She knew all the letters now.

"Henrietta Breem," she said for the hundredth time. "You think she has red hair, too?"

"You probably got that from Frank," I said dryly.

"Mary Ann, pay attention!" said Alba. "We're trying to help you about your interview. Hal asked if do you want to talk about that the Reverend forced you to have sex?"

Mary Ann shrugged and ate more veal. "Not really."

"I think you ought to, Mary Ann," I said. "He's trying to throw everything on Ham, and you shouldn't let him. It was the Reverend that started raping you. The boys basically followed his lead."

"Yeah, that's true." She sighed. "Maybe I could just say he didn't treat me too good. I don't really wanna, y'know, like, talk about the, y'know, the this 'n' that."

"If you are uncomfortable with that," said Alba, "you should at least do very clear that not to tell you who your real father is was a horrible thing."

This got a little more response. "Yeah, that's for sure."

"Do you want to mention that you had to run away to escape all that?" I asked.

"Maybe. Yeah, I s'pose so."

"Well, you'd better decide *now*, because—"

Alba put down her fork with a crack. "'I suppose so'? Mary Ann, this man wants to ruin your life, and now he is saying to everyone that you are more or less a prostitute! You cannot put up with this! It's against your dignity! You have a public reputation, and this—" To me: "Excuse me, Hal. I must to speak Spanish for one moment." And off she went, gesturing and trilling and spanking the table with her palm. Mary Ann listened and nodded. "Yeah, I s'pose so," she said at the end. And rumpled her hair and sat thinking, brow furrowed. I said nothing, watching her out of the corner of my eye and improving the cheap red wine I'd bought at the corner store by adding lemon soda to it—another of Alba's kitchen tricks. "Yeah," she murmured again.

Without a word, she put down the birth certificate, got off the stool and went into her bedroom. She came out holding her cell phone. It was no good using the normal phone: it started ringing the moment anyone hung it on the receiver. She punched out a phone number—an act that answered a puzzle that had always stumped me: if she couldn't read, how did she find names on her speed-dialer? Answer: she didn't; she simply memorized all the phone numbers.

"Hello, Cindy? This is Mary Ann Jaalkov...Yeah, that's what I wanted to talk to you about. Cindy, I've decided I'm not goin' to do the interview, if you don't mind... Oh no, no—not with anyone else, either. It's just that, y'know, ah, see, I really don't have nothin' to say about the Reverent. I just don't care about what he said, that's all...Yeah, that's about it: if he wants to say that I'm the worst person that ever walked on the earth, well, that's, I just don't care. I just don't. It's like he's talkin' 'bout the weather, far's I'm concerned... Uh-huh...'Quote'? What's that mean?... Oh! Like, in the newspaper? Yeah, sure, go ahead. Everything I just said."

After the usual good-byes, she closed her phone and put it down on the coffee table, which, by the way, was now a real, wooden coffee table and not two boxes with a tablecloth thrown over them: Sergio had strewn the bloated profits from *Revelaciones* joyfully among the cast and crew.

Alba and I stared at her.

Mary Ann picked up her glasses, put them on, and grinned at us. "Ya can't hit me—I'm wearin' glasses."

Silence.

"'Cept I don't know why you can't hit a guy with glasses. It's just like anybody—"

"Mary Ann! What are you doing?" Alba burst out. "You must to talk to this woman! You must to say to her that this, this man, your grandfather, is pervert and rapist!"

Mary Ann took off the glasses, laid them in the case and put the case soundlessly on the table. She walked over to us and put her arms around our necks. I braced to get my neck broken, but she didn't squeeze the way she had before. She did it delicately and lovingly.

"Please don't get mad at me, okay?" she said in a sweet, angelic voice. "I just don't wanna talk about the ol' Reverent and his, y'know, his dumb ol' hollerin'. Don't you understand? Huh?" She stood back a bit, her hands still on our necks.

"Look at me. Just take a good, long look. I'm not scared anymore.

I got the best friends in the world. And I got a good place to live and a good job in New York City. And I'm learnin' to read and I'm gonna get married with, with my dreamboat man, and if I'm lucky, maybe I'm gonna find my mother. What do I wanna mess around with the Reverent for? He can go soak his big ol' head." She stroked the back of our heads a moment. "Okay?"

And then she drew us to her again and kissed us: that ended the argument.

The lobby intercom buzzed: flowers for Mary Ann. She went downstairs, and Alba looked at me with a smile. "She was made for dance, not for, ah, to throw the mud."

I nodded. "I guess. Some people are just made for beauty, aren't they?"

And then the gunshots—the second fired after a careful interval for re-aiming the gun—and the throaty grunt: *"Harlot!"* I heard it as I dashed down the stairs, to find Mary Ann lying on her back covered in flowers. I heard running footsteps outside and raced out after the bastard. I didn't give a damn if he shot at me too; maybe that was what I was hoping for.

But the gunman had done his work for the day. He sprinted down the sidewalk through a roaring rain, amateurishly holding the heavy automatic up near his shoulder as if it were a brick. He cut into the street between two parked cars, and, looking down the street to his right, waved with his free hand. The car—a tall SUV with tinted window was the only description I could give—burst out of the darkness. At first I thought it would pick him up, as he did. But it was going too fast.

"Hey! Where you going?" the gunman shouted, thinking as anyone might that they were going to leave him behind to face murder charges by himself.

But this was not the driver's intention, either. The street was a one-way with two lanes, and the gunman had stepped well into the far lane—to get into the passenger seat beside the driver, presumably—an important tactical mistake, but one anybody could make on his first murder job. The driver swerved at the last millisecond—it wasn't *his* first job—and rammed the gunman, the massive grill bouncing the guy twenty feet, to a point roughly even with my place along the side-walk. The driver then slowed down, and the SUV jumped and tilted as it rolled over the gunman with its right-side wheels. It never occurred to the gunman—another neophyte's mistake—to fire his gun at the driver. I actually heard it clatter to the ground, though it was not for some days until I realized what the clattering sound in my nightmares was. The SUV roared away.

Then a second vehicle, a low sedan, drove carefully, lovingly, consci-entiously, languidly over the gunman for a real quality smearing effect since, as we say at AllPoint, what's worth doing for a potful of money is worth doing right. Dirty work finished, the second car sped away, and the Reverend was all set for a good long run, with no threat of unpleasant revelations.

25

Of the aftermath, I hope you'll forgive my de-scribing only the most pertinent points.

The funeral was as sad an affair as you can imagine, though a real tribute to Mary Ann. Some two hundred peo-ple attended, including Mike Davis, Dixon Phelps, the *Infanta* of Spain carrying a message of condolence from the king, several top theater critics, and the mayor of New York and her husband, who had seen *Revelaciones*. The Reverend did not come, which was appropriate, since it was his people, through the good offices of Messrs. Besby and White, who had arranged Mary Ann's murder, ignorant of her magnanimity, of her cherished joy in life that allowed her to excuse the scum around her. I emphasized this quality in the eulogy I gave, and I was glad to see that it made Frank, who did attend, squirm plenty.

The investigation, however, concluded that Roland Smith—who was also the Boston crowbar-swinger—had acted alone, out of reli-gious fervor. He was a former drug pusher, still on parole, and a born-again radical Christian. Pictures of several pop singers and Mary Ann with their faces slashed, which I thought was a clever touch—were found in his apartment.

The police ultimately refused to believe that the cars I had seen running over Smith were anything other than simple hit-and-runs. For good measure, the second car had stopped down the street at the corner, someone lowered a window despite the pouring rain, and for the benefit of witnesses, the female passenger shouted at the male driver, "But ya ran *over* duh guy, Chawlie! Ya gotta go back!" Neither did the police give any importance to my description of the Reverend's airy confidence in my last conversation with him, which to me clearly indicated that he knew Mary Ann would be dead by the time the *Times* reporter came around. And of course, for me to go to the media and connect the Reverend and his TV producer with the murderer would sound absurd.

The soggy investigation puzzled me at first, and later outraged me, as no further indictments were made and the case was closed. I called Special Agent Fred Wapping and put the clinch on him to find out what the hell was going on. Two weeks later, he called from a phone booth and said to meet him at a Starbucks not far from my office.

"Pressure from above," he murmured over his coffee, watching a cloudburst scour Chicago's streets. His partner kept watch from their car parked outside and across the street. Our meeting was definitely off the record.

"From above," I repeated. "God? Or your Bureau?"

"Washington. Scared senators who don't need the publicity. And the president, probably; he needs Jaalkov. A lot of scared interests want Jaalkov to stay right where he is, shaming congressmen for any drift leftwards. I guess word came down to NY Homicide within hours of the murder: cut it off with the religious nut and close the file."

"Jesus! And you can't—"

He shook his head, embarrassed. "Too big, too deep, too dark." A breath. "The smart word is, Roland Smith was set up with it back in Boston and kept for a rainy day. He was a paroled drug pusher."

I waited. "That's significant?"

"Sure. Drug parolees face long sentences if they get violated back to prison; that makes them especially vulnerable to police pressure. Putting the pieces together, I'd say Besby and White got hold of some conservative G-man and asked him to do the Lord's work. Guy goes to the pusher and puts the scam to him: 'Go through with this, and you're home free. Otherwise—uh-oh, what's this that fell out of your pocket?' So the guy plays. He got into the religious group barely a week before the Boston crowbar thing."

I thought this over. "All this for Mary Ann?"

"As I hear it, the religious interests were embarrassed by your girl-friend's rising star. They were willing to let things ride at first, but the *Davis* thing tipped it against her. They were afraid of more revelations. Reporters were even showing up in Arkansas asking questions, I hear."

So much for that.

One last, and most important, item about the funeral.

As I said, Frank was there—alone, with only one-day's growth of beard, dressed in his TV suit, a crooked tie, his chain, and his peasant suspicion. He insisted on sitting in front, since he was "the father," and the mayor and her husband had to move aside for him. Then, just be-fore the service started, a middle-aged black woman, accompanied by a lanky, cinnamon-skinned son of about fourteen, limped in and said something to the usher. This was Santiago, and his big face lit up, the only smile I saw that day. He made a few excuses to the people up front, and seated them across the aisle from Frank. She nodded to him, and he did a double-take, then glared at her with the purest hatred. And the last mystery of Mary Ann's life was finally explained

"Yeah, I knew my Mary Ann was gonna be a strong one, that girl. She and I lived in that damn barn for two-and-a-half years—two-and-a-half *long* years, I gotta tell ya. The Lord threw at that baby every gawddam d'sease and infection and scratch and scrape known to man, and she fought 'em back. She had the mumps, and all I had to fight 'em with was a cold bath and some salt to stir into it. Didn't matter one doggone bit. In three days she was runnin' around the barnyard again."

Henrietta Breem had the same clean forehead as Mary Ann, the same sure shoulders and well-built neck. Mary Ann's good teeth and thin nose were Frank's, but her thin upper lip and full lower lip were her mother's. After the service, I introduced myself to her and her son, and invited them to a late lunch. It was clear from their reactions to the menu—and the cheap midnight return flight to Memphis—that their income was quite low. It took me some work to convince them that I could afford whatever they wanted to eat. Even then, when son Tucker ordered a steak, Miss Breem snapped at him that a king-sized hamburger would be just fine.

The restaurant was quiet and discreet—the kind of place Edgerton Salk might go to discuss with his security company what kind of measures he wanted taken against Mary Ann. Between the entrée and dessert, I told them everything I could about Mary Ann's life. Tucker was in ninth grade, a high-school basketball star. "This boy, he jumps like three rabbits," said Henrietta proudly. "Studies, too—'cause I told him if he *don't* study he can find himself a room at the Y." Tucker was particularly interested in Mary Ann's dancing, like the ability to raise either leg sideways to vertical.

Then I asked for Henrietta's story.

The orphanage, where she had lived all her youth, more-or-less kicked her out at the age of sixteen. Wandering around Blue Ball, Arkansas, she fell into a job working in the Jaalkov house, this when Frank's mother's health began to decline seriously. Henrietta was glad of the job, which included food and a corner of the barn to sleep in, but it was soon apparent that she was more slave than employee. She was never paid or given more than work clothes. And she was never allowed off the farm, which was quite isolated on a country road miles from any town. Mrs. Jaalkov was apparently as racist as the rest of the family. Nobody called Henrietta by her name; she was just "the nigger."

After five or six months of this, she was trying to figure out a means of escape when Frank, younger than she was, raped her on a dare from his brothers—and several times after that. The resulting "nigger" baby—though Mary Ann's skin lightened somewhat after infancy— was a source of family shame. "They'd 'a' been just as glad if she'd 'a' died," Henrietta said. If anyone, including Mary Ann, asked, she was the Reverend's daughter. But nobody asked because, apart from a sister of the Reverend's, nobody ever came to the farm.

With the years, Henrietta began to argue that the girl had to start getting medical checkups and shots, and the Reverend and his boys were having none of that. Henrietta insisted, and the Jaalkov men decided that Henrietta was getting to be a bore. And there was only one thing to do with boring niggers.

Frank, Ted and Ham took Henrietta out to the woods, where they gave her a ten-minute head start and loosed their hunting dogs on her. To make a horrific story short, she beat back the dogs with rocks, and after three days of wandering with a broken ankle that never healed properly, hobbled onto a county highway where a kind soul found her and took her as far as a hospital emergency room.

"I tried to get the sheriff or somebody to go out and get Mary Ann, but they went an' asked me if we was married, and when I said no, they just kind of figured I was the wrong kinda woman anyway." The other problem was that she couldn't give an address, and only generally knew the location of the farm—thus her story held little water. Also, she was no longer in Scott County, and that apparently complicated things. Friendless, penniless, she wound up at a truck stop, where she traded sex for money. By the time she got up some savings and reached West Memphis, she was pregnant again. There she stayed, determined to do right by her child this time.

It was not until the media frenzy after the *Davis* show that Henrietta heard of Mary Ann Jaalkov. She began to ask around, and had gotten as far as to obtain the name and phone number of the Sergio Adán Dance Company when the news appeared that Mary Ann had died. The recorded message on Adán's telephone informed Henrietta of the funeral.

I showed them a bit of New York, and after dinner we went to Mary Ann's apartment—the taxi ride fascinated Tucker—where tearful Alba and I gave them whatever we could of Mary Ann's: theater memorabilia mainly, some video footage of *Revelaciones*, and a complimentary video copy of the *Davis* interview. Me, I never kept anything of hers; I prefer the memories. I also arranged to be in touch regarding the proceeds of Mary Ann's estate—several tens of thousands of dollars in a bank account, which would be a boon to them.

At eleven P.M. I left Henrietta and Tucker at JFK Airport Security. Both shook my hand, quite formal and serious. Once through the metal detectors, though, Tucker sat his mother on the first chair they came to and kept his arm tight around her shoulders. I turned away and managed to get outside before breaking down—so hard I retched.

I could only think of how thrilled Mary Ann would have been to know that she had a brother as well.

I had work to do the next day and didn't stop for many months. Among my first duties was to make up with Chintsy. They paid in full, lawyers and late fees included. We dropped the lawsuit, though not the criminal charges against Edgerton Salk. A Chintsy press release called him a "rogue element, already under the called-on-the-carpet scrutiny of our Board of Directors, and deeply at variance with company policy." Ah, there's nothing like PR Department rhetoric.

Soon enough, I found myself in Sao Paulo again, and rather than taking Marisa to bed, I took her to a restaurant. I asked her—Marisa speaks a sort of crab-walk English—if she was serious about something she had told me earlier: she wanted to open a shop of headbands and purses and belts and bijouterie and sundry fashion complements; Brazilian women go nuts over them. Yes, trick by trick, she said, she had been saving up, and already had a small bundle.

So I called AllPoint, declared myself on vacation (to everyone's relief, apparently), and spent two weeks going around the city with Marisa and getting her set up. We got her an express business license ("express" because I paid an extra six hundred *reales* under the table for it) and rented a small sidewalk-level shop near a busy intersection that she had had her eye on; bought merchandise, and spent nine days painting and cutting and drilling and putting up shelves and hanging out a bright plastic sign—"Marisa's" (the English name has extra cachet in Brazil). I stayed long enough to see the first customer walk in on a Wednesday morning and buy a couple of jangly steel bracelets. When she left, Marisa thanked me, tears in her eyes, and probably for form's sake offered gratitude of a more substantive nature. I replied that seeing her pretty face in her own shop was more thanks than she knew.

I've done similar, if smaller, favors for a few old bed friends in other countries since then. And I've given up my whoring ways.

I said that I never kept anything of Mary Ann's, but that isn't quite true. I do keep one thing, and it sits on my bookshelf and greets me whenever I come back from my marches across the long spaces of this energy-hungry Earth.

Some months after her death, I went to Kyoto, Japan, for a week-long IAEA conference. The first night I was laying on my hotel bed, deaf and dumb with jet lag, when the memory of Mary Ann's lock of hair popped into my head. At one leap I was at my briefcase. There it was: deep in a side pocket and surrounded by ten others sat the CD envelope I'd put it in. With a feral roar of joy, I snatched it out.

The next morning—conference be damned—one of the hotel staff took me to a fine picture-framer in the old part of the city (such is Japanese hospitality). I explained to Mr. Hamamasu—through his son—that the lock had belonged to my deceased fiancée, a dancer. His son pulled up Mary Ann on some Japanese-language Wikipedia and showed him. Mr. Hamamasu, short and spectacled, a sort of Japanese Sergio Adán, nodded a long time at the screen and even longer at the lock of hair. He said he would try to have the lock framed by the end of week, when the conference ended.

He couldn't, however, and I received a message at the hotel that he would send me the frame by FedEx as soon as he'd finished.

Two months passed.

The frame, the size of a sheet of paper, arrived at my apartment on an indifferent Saturday afternoon. The note with it, written in perfect and miniscule capitals, said that Mr. Hamamasu apologized for the delay and that he'd had to make many "practices" of the design before starting. For his personal collection, he had taken a photo of the final product—another apology—and added that there was no charge for the work.

Which did true honor to the memory of Mary Ann. He had taken her lock apart strand by strand and on pearl-gray silk arranged the hairs in swirling patterns that I can only describe as a starry Van Gogh sky, but made up of gushing sparks of red, blond, yellow, orange, black, brown, white, purple—absolutely stunning. It's amazing how many colors make up a head of red hair.

And how it takes a real artist to make you *see*. My own work—to keep dryers turning and TVs squawking—is by comparison but a plough-horse's contribution to human progress.

Mr. Hamamasu's work has been a great companion over the years. Whenever I'm feeling down, I take it off the shelf and give the glass a good polishing, dust the frame. And I have a fine laugh remembering Mary Ann say that one of these days she had to do something for good ol' Hal.

THE END

ACKNOWLEDGEMENTS:

To properly render matters nuclear and dyslexic and artistic, I needed help, and some kind people stepped up with their knowledge. José Manuel Viguera told me about nuclear-plant construction, both the business and technical sides. Patricia Peral filled me in on dyslexia. And to deepen my understanding of flamenco dance, of which I'm a big fan, I took the subway to the old center of Madrid and climbed steep stairs to Amor de Dios dance studio, which trains generations of professional dancers above a raucous open market, surely the best place for a dance studio where people bang their heels on the floor as fast as a drummer plays a roll. There, teachers and students, the latter group exhausted from a 90-minute workout, answered my questions about their training and about the different styles of flamenco. My thanks to everybody.